"*India's Summer* is a furious, fast-paced, fun romp through the excesses of life in the Hollywood fast lane, with some thought-provoking wisdom interspersed throughout."
– Jane Green, *New York Times* bestselling author

"A book has an energy field all of its own and *India's Summer* has a really great one."
– Ekhart Tolle, spiritual leader
and *New York Times* bestselling author

"*India's Summer* offers a timeless tale of women supporting one another – delivered in a way that makes it feel fresh, alive, and utterly of the moment."
– Arianna Huffington

"India's fascinating character is what makes *India's Summer* a compelling read. She is trying to make a big shift in her life, in her career, in the choices she's making. She's funny, clever and vulnerable and you are rooting for her every step of the way."
– Goldie Hawn

"*India's Summer* avoids the familiar clichés of LA and yet captures the character of the city so well."
– Orlando Bloom

"I love how India learns to trust her inner voice and begins to let her light shine."
– Miranda Kerr, Victoria's Secret "Angel"
and author of *Treasure Yourself*

"I loved this book. India made me smile."
– Kim Eng, Presence of Movement Workshop Leader

India's Summer

India's Summer

Thérèse

**fiction
studio
books**

The Fiction Studio
P.O. Box 4613
Stamford, CT 06907

Copyright © 2012 by Thérèse
Jacket design by Barbara Aronica-Buck
Cover photo © 2011 by Jeff Eamer

Print ISBN-13: 978-1-936558-34-6
E-book ISBN-13: 978-1-936558-35-3

Visit our website at www.fictionstudiobooks.com

For information, address The Fiction Studio.

First Fiction Studio Printing: January 2012

Printed in the United States of America

For May and Fred
with love

Act the way you'd like to be
and soon you'll be the way you act.
— Leonard Cohen

FACEBOOK STATUS – If you can't do it in high heels, I'm not interested.

The crowd was howling her name.

"In-di-a!"

"In-di-a!"

She was vaguely aware of an arm. Yes, it was definitely an arm. She could feel it steadying her, pushing her toward the searing heat. Then came the pounding beat of a medieval drum. She took a deep breath, a very deep breath. There was this weird tingling between her legs. And she was dizzy. Oh my God! The adrenaline. Like swallowing a Motorhead cocktail.

I can't do this. I can't do this, she thought.

Yes you can! YES! YES! shouted another inner voice. Focus … Focus.

What is it you really want? Think.

So she thought: tall, fit, rich, funny, a cross between Orlando Bloom and Hugh Jackman…

"Don't look down! Don't look down!"

Then she heard another voice. "What's your name?"

"India."

"Are you ready?"

"Yes!" she yelled.

"Louder, I can't hear you."

"YES!" she screamed.

She was burning up. She was on fire.

Suddenly, as her feet were plunged in a bucket of ice-cold water, she was clinging to a volunteer like a koala on a gum tree. She had made it. And one by one, every member of her team charged across the bed of burning hot coals into the arms of other volunteers. And within minutes, it was over. Weeks and weeks of planning, and it was over.

For one brief moment she stood there: the very image of everything she wanted to be – a valedictorian, a woman in control of her destiny; her olive skin glowing, her dark eyes shining with intensity, her chestnut hair piled high on her head. Then, overwhelmed with emotion, India started leaping up and down, sobbing, hugging all the kids around her, and waving triumphantly at the cameras.

"We did it! We did it," she cried, rivulets of mascara streaking her cheeks, sweat pouring down her long arms. "Amazing, unbelievable, and I am never, I repeat, never, doing that again!"

FACEBOOK STATUS – Say YES.

"Completely out of the question." This was the wildly enthusi-astic response from Dr. White, the head teacher, spluttering over his cup of tea, when she had proposed the idea of a charity fire walk. India taught drama at a grade school in London. Every year, the school held a fundraiser for the local children's hospital, a fete that to her felt more like a day release for prisoners. There were a couple of cake stalls run by the nearby church, a raffle, some hot dogs, and a smattering of bored parents trailing around with strollers.

But India had recently experienced an epiphany. She would take this year's fundraiser to a whole new level. Destiny had come upon her in a flash while she was watching a TV special – *Breakthrough with Tony Robbins*. His message had hit her like a rallying call, like Moses on the mountain. Yes, she would be a leader not a follower, a be-liever not a doubter, a force and a voice for good. Yes, like Tony, she would inspire people to walk on fire. New wards would be opened and India would cut the ribbon, maybe even paint a few murals. Of course, the entire thing was easier said than done, even after the head teacher reluctantly agreed to attend.

"Okay, if you're determined to go through with this, I want liability releases from all the parents. I want it off school time and off school premises," he'd ordered.

The next major obstacle was to convince the students.

India's practical class demonstration didn't move them at all.

"See? Not even a blister! Ta-da!" she'd preened, swiping her finger several times through the tip of a burning candle. The next day she showed them films of a woman with prosthetic legs climbing a mountain, and a cross-channel swimmer with only one arm winning a competition. Still nothing. Then she took a different approach and tried the spiritual angle.

"Imagine being purified like a Buddhist monk!" she said. "Imagine being fortified, forged through fire like an Inca!" Blank stares.

It was not until she brought in Pete, a trainer from London's own (and impressively Tony Robbins–endorsed) Institute of Firewalking, that they sat up and paid attention. It was probably the silver bolt through his tongue, the safety pin in his eyebrow and the metal hook through his nostrils that sold them, or perhaps, the tattoo of flames on his biceps. The guy had street cred.

"The firewalk, as you know from Miss Butler, is all about conquering fear," Pete announced in the first (and only free) motivational session. "Once you've conquered your fear and walked across those coals, you know you can do anything."

Thirty minutes later, six volunteers had signed up, and peer pressure did the rest. With a mere two weeks to go before the intensive training actually began, India managed to book the grounds of a local hotel, clear the insurance and reassure the parents, check the legalities, write the press releases, even organize a photo call with the local fire brigade.

"Are you going first tomorrow, miss?" one of the students asked nervously. He was hovering by the door after what India quietly hoped was her last ever class on Macbeth.

India froze. Going first? I'm the producer. I'm … well … the cheerleader. I'm the après-ski girl, with the emphasis firmly on the après. I'm not into extreme sports.

"Of course I am," she heard herself say out loud.

After a long sleepless night punctuated by an unsettling erotic dream involving one of her students dressed as a fireman, India was forced to surrender and accept her fate.

"Obviously, I'm going first," she told herself. "YES! I am a leader not a follower, a believer not a doubter. YES! I am a force for good…"

≈≈≈≈≈≈≈≈

Closing her eyes and holding hands with a student next to her, she had waited.

"Think of a time when you were ecstatically happy, powerful, in control of your life."

India scrambled around in her head for an image.

"A time when you felt at peace, in flow," Pete continued.

She was still struggling.

The conference room at the Holiday Inn was dead silent. He gave them a few minutes.

"Hold that image, open your eyes, and when I put up my hand, yell 'YES!' as loud as you can."

India's "Yes" lacked a certain conviction.

"Now think hard," he went on. "What do you want to achieve this year? Because the only thing holding you back from achieving what you want is FEAR! Now think carefully. Think big! One year

15

from now, where will you be? You can achieve your dreams. What do you want? Make a clear mental picture for yourself."

What do I want? India wondered. Right now I just want this all over with … this is insane … okay … focus … focus. What? What? Think…

As she and the kids formed a crocodile line chanting "YES! YES!" in unison through the halls of the hotel, India felt strangely disconnected. It bothered her that she wasn't able to join in the exercises wholeheartedly; that she was holding something back.

FACEBOOK STATUS – Where's my tribe?

"See ya, Miss Butler," shouted one of the students.

"Bye, miss," yelled another.

Maneuvering her way through the groups of kids who were slamming locker doors, India checked her watch. The traffic on the way home would be heavy, but she would still have time to get ready for the next day. Her flight to Los Angeles left at 11 a.m. It was the TV interview on the Morning Show with the head teacher, Dr. White that had finally pushed her over the edge. This was shortly after the fire-walk, when all the positive reviews from the press had started rolling in, and the hospital had received a huge donation from a wealthy businessman.

"Congratulations, Dr. White. What a wonderful achievement," enthused the TV host. "How did you come up with such an amazing idea?"

"Thank you so much," he had said, visibly relaxing and peering directly into the camera. "We all have to take risks in life, don't we?" Then, in an unusually posh accent, he warmed to his theme. "I have long held the belief that young people need to be challenged. They need to learn about helping others."

"Bollocks!" India had muttered at the television screen. "I have long held the belief that you are a jerk."

As she sat in her MINI at a traffic light, she remembered how she had waited in vain for some sort of acknowledgment, for a reference to the wonderfully dedicated teacher who had done such an amazing job. For seventeen years she'd been working at the same school. Where on earth had the time gone? Countless Monday assemblies, seventeen Easter Parades, endless Midsummer Night's Dreams... Sure, her natural enthusiasm and energy and the fact that she demanded a lot from the kids made her popular with them. The colleagues, however, were another story. Take last Christmas when she'd suggested hiring a martini bar for the staff party.

"Alcohol," Miss Roberts, the vice principal, had snorted. "Whatever next?"

A good time perhaps? India thought, but said nothing.

No. This was not her tribe, and worse, she was about to turn forty!

"A milestone birthday," she'd complained to her friend Sarah over a glass of Fat Bastard at her local pub the night before.

"Forty's the new thirty, haven't you heard?" Sarah offered.

"You're only thirty-four," India snapped. "Let's see if you're laughing in another six years!"

"Well," Sarah sighed. "Not all of us have legs up to our armpits and a bone structure to die for."

"Thank you. I can take any amount of that," India said, flattered. "And at least I'm not gray yet," she added, examining the ends of her long dark hair.

It was five o'clock when she turned into her narrow street and ran up the stone steps to her tiny apartment in Queen's Park. Even though it was too far away from Camden Town to be trendy and her street was a mess of seedy Victorian houses that had long lost their grandeur, India loved her place. She had scoured flea markets and junkyards for one-of-a-kind pieces and devoted entire weekends to painting the walls in perfect Farrow & Ball shades of gray and cord. She'd installed the wooden shutters and silk drapes herself to create just the right light. "Benign neglect." That was what the French called it, a look and a feel that was all about ease; where you didn't get neurotic about how you arranged your throw pillows.

Uncorking a bottle of chilled Sancerre, India collapsed on a couch and listened to her phone messages. Her sister, Annabelle, sounded totally stressed.

"I can't wait for you to get here," she said. "We'll send the car. I'm at a shoot in Pasadena and Joss and the girls are already at the house in Malibu. But Maria will be here and I'll be back late evening…"

Annabelle was India's older sister. Older by only two minutes, India thought, but what a head start, because, clearly, in those two minutes, she had worked out exactly what she wanted to do with her life. She was truly passionate about acting. When she was a kid, Annabelle would watch and rewatch movies for days. Bugsy Malone, India recalled with a smile.

India just wasn't driven in the same way. She didn't take private voice lessons, write her own shows, or win a coveted scholarship to the Royal Academy of Dramatic Arts when she was eighteen. She wasn't a household name in England after starring in several award-winning BBC series. And she certainly hadn't married a rock star like Joss. India sighed.

What had triggered her sister's extraordinary drive? she wondered, knocking back her wine. Maybe it was their parents' separation when the girls were teenagers. It was such a cliché: Husband has affair with wife's best friend. "Aunty Dora's run off with Dad," was how it felt to India. She'd watched her mother turn from the vivacious life and soul of every party to a withdrawn depressive. India would come home from school to a house filled with cigarette smoke and the sight of her mother coiled up in the fetal position on the bed.

Annabelle's form of escape, avoiding the house and throwing herself into more and more acting classes, seemed to have worked out better than India's, whose own response had been to throw herself into a world of her imagination. India was the one making dinner and taking care of her mother on those endless winter nights when the house was deadly quiet. She buried herself in books, finding connection in Anna Karenina, Bonjour Tristesse, and works by Lévêque de Vilmorin, hoping that one day her own life might mimic a romance novel.

But at least I'm proud of her — I'm not at all jealous, India told herself. Well ... that's if you don't count her closet. Yes, I plan on spending many happy hours in Annie's closet, she thought, picturing the circular rack that went round at the touch of a button and the light that clicked on when you opened a drawer, and the beautiful hand-painted gold wallpaper and dozens of shoe racks. Most of the shoes had hardly been worn and the names had such a lovely ring to them: Louboutin, Prada, Lanvin. With a sudden rush of excitement India leapt off the couch and ran down the small hallway to her bedroom. I need to get a move on, she thought. La-la Land! Here I come!

India's Summer

Packing for LA was almost as daunting a prospect as walking on broken glass (a follow-up event Pete had suggested and that India had politely declined). What am I going to travel in? She thought, looking at the mountain of clothes on her bed. She'd been planning "rock-star casual" all week (à la Kate Moss in Marie Claire) but right now it was not coming together. "Sod it!" she cursed, flinging her All Saints biker boots across the room. "I'm going on a plane, not a Harley Davidson."

As she folded a couple of white tees, she thought of all the years she had spent trying to develop a "signature" style. A way of dressing that would carry her effortlessly through life; a life in which people would assume she was, well, French.

How India longed to be French. Just the faintest whiff of lavender or baked bread always sent her back to that high school trip to Provence. The confidence, that certain je ne sais quoi... For a while, she'd assumed it must have something to do with baskets. She'd never seen so many; swinging from bicycles, hanging from ceilings, balanced on window ledges. They used them for everything, from decorating doorways and carrying bread or laundry to ferrying babies. On several trips to Paris she'd focused more on clothes and noticed another obsession, this time with scarves, which curiously enough, were often tied around those baskets as well as on necks, heads, purses, bicycles and babies. This marked the beginning of India's extensive scarf collection, which, in the absence of that elusive je ne sais quoi, remained unworn. She also abandoned all attempts to speak the language, after a humiliating experience in a Paris brasserie, where the waiters had met her order with condescending amusement.

She poured herself another glass of wine, then removed a couple of turtleneck sweaters from her suitcase, and the worn leather jacket from her carry-on bag.

After failing to become French, India had decided on becoming quintessentially English. This was when she graduated from high school and moved to the countryside, to a college in Stratford-on-Avon. Forget romantic visions of making love under old oak trees and meandering through fields of cowslips and buttercups in fine white cotton dresses. The reality turned out to be a lot more prosaic. The men she met were mostly farmers and, without exception, the girls all wore green sludge jackets, riding boots, and jodhpurs on weekends, pleated skirts, flat shoes, and pearls during the week. "I refuse to be cloned," she'd decided, giving up the ghost and transferring her teaching course to London, to the joys of a nearby Starbucks and Nine West, her favorite shoe store at the time.

The trill of her cell phone roused India from what was fast becoming a depressing trip down memory lane. She flung herself on her bag and rooted around till she reached the bottom and pulled it out.

"Hello, hello?" she said, breathlessly.

"Been shagging again?" Sarah laughed.

"I wish," India said, and settled down on the bed to chat with her best friend. Sarah was a nurse who lived in the hopes of meeting an Italian aristocrat, being whisked off to Tuscany, and drinking Chianti. So far, the closest she'd come was a blind date with a policeman in an Islington trattoria.

"Here, know what I read in a magazine today?"

"No idea!"

"It said that men are their most honest at the exact moment before ejaculation. For real, that's what it said."

"Who's done the research?" India laughed. "More important-ly – what kind of magazines are you reading these days?"

Sarah laughed. "Marie Claire, as it happens. Get a copy for the plane."

"Will do."

"Are you all packed?"

"Not exactly." India surveyed the chaos around her. "I haven't a clue what I'm going to be doing when I get there. And I didn't check the baggage allowance."

For the next twenty minutes, they talked about her plans, or lack of plans, in Los Angeles.

"Annie and Joss love having me around – well, for the first few weeks at any rate. But visiting isn't the same as moving in, is it?" India said, attempting to button up a cardigan with one hand.

"I suppose even with their great contacts, you're going have to work out what you want to do if you want to stay on," Sarah agreed.

"That's the problem. I'm good at teaching. I had such a pas-sion for it. But if I have to fill in one more standard assessment form… It's soul destroying. If I'd wanted to be a bookkeeper…" She trailed off. "I've got to get out of there, Sarah. At this rate I'll end up some twisted old spinster like Miss Roberts."

"You could get another cat."

"And grow a beard I suppose."

"Just think of it as a vacation for now," Sarah said, laughing. "Try and relax. You're tired; enjoy yourself."

India sighed. "What am I going to do without you?"

"Date Bradley Cooper? Soak up the sun? Shop on Rodeo Drive?" Sarah offered.

"Sarah. I love you."

"Love you too. Send a postcard. Skype me. Or 'whatever,' as they say over there!"

"Will do. Bye."

How Sarah manages to stay so upbeat after giving injections and checking prostates all day is a mystery to me, India thought, clicking the off button and opening her wardrobe.

What would Audrey wear? she wondered. After a few minutes she pulled out her Agnes B. wraparound black dress and held it to her shoulders in the Cheval mirror. "I shall wear my hair up!" she decided. "Très chic."

FACEBOOK STATUS – I'm stuck in a holding pattern.

"Ladies and gentlemen, I apologize for the delay, and thank you for your patience. There seems to be more air traffic than usual. We will be making our descent just as soon as we have clearance."

India fidgeted nervously and tried not to look out at the wing. Were those flaps supposed to be opening and closing like that? She'd never been fond of flying. And her seat had been in an upright position for thirty minutes. She was dying to get up and stretch. Thanks to Joss's air miles, India was flying business class. The copious amounts of decent, free champagne, not to mention the fine Sauvignon, had soothed her nerves for a while, but now she had a slight headache.

She looked again at the "leaving" presents Sarah had given her, at the tiny pink leather Smythson notepad inscribed in gold lettering C'est la Vie and its bright blue companion, Profound Thoughts.

"No guesses which one I'll fill up first," India had joked, touched by the thoughtfulness of the gifts.

Sarah knew India so well, how she was always planning on writing a book and constantly scribbling down notes; observations, one-liners. She tucked the notepads back into her handbag, and, as the plane circled inland, she tightened her seatbelt again. They were so low she could see the lines of freeways, the mathematically precise grid of the streets, and the road signs. Clutching the armrest, she closed her eyes as the Airbus bumped down on the runway and braked sharply. Please, please, let this be a whole new beginning, India pleaded silently. I am so ready to start over again.

An hour later, she was edging her way toward the head of the line at Immigration Control, where a decidedly unwelcoming official greeted her with a nod, and took her passport.

"Press your thumbs there," he said, indicating a plastic screen.

Finger printing? India wondered, awkwardly pressing each thumb as instructed.

"Look into the camera now," he ordered, tapping endlessly on his computer keyboard.

"Do I smile?" she asked, getting even more nervous. More tapping.

Maybe there's an alcohol limit for getting into America, she thought, half serious now.

"What is the purpose of your visit to the United States?" he continued humorlessly.

Okay, India registered. This is not the time to bring up Bradley.

"I'm here to visit my sister." She smiled.

There was a pause. His face remained expressionless, then her passport and visa were thumped, and India stepped into the "Land of the Free."

It seemed that lots of other people had had the bright idea of tying a ribbon around their suitcases. Eventually, she dragged her Samsonite off the conveyor belt and headed toward the line for customs.

"Are you bringing any livestock into the country, ma'am?" a heavily armed official asked.

"Not today," she said, smiling, wondering how one could possibly smuggle a chicken onto a plane and why.

"I do have some English chocolate though," she said cheerfully. "I'll give you some if you promise to ignore the chicken."

"Ma'am, in the United States it is a felony to attempt to bribe an officer," he said sharply, before ticking her customs form and letting her pass through.

Whatever happened to "Have a nice day," she wondered. It's not like I was trying to bring in lard from the Ukraine.

Scanning the crowd, her face lit up the moment she recognized Annie's driver, Robert.

"Wonderful to see you, Miss Butler," he said, reaching for her luggage. "Welcome back!"

The air outside the terminal was dry and dusty. Trailing closely behind Robert as he crossed the frantically busy street, India looked forward to settling into the soft leather seat of the air-conditioned Town Car.

This is the life, she thought, as Robert deftly switched lanes and the car raced away from the International Terminal onto the sprawling lanes of the freeway. Cocooned in the luxuriously cool, dark car, India amused herself, looking at the blur of garish billboards. Number of people dead from smoking this year (Enough?) ... Financial problems? Bankruptcy could be the solution. (Fun solution?)

Taking advantage of a brief traffic jam near the exit, India brushed her hair and touched up her makeup. Then, there they were, driving past the ornate iron awnings that spelt out the magic words, "Bel Air." This was where Annabelle and Joss had their main home and where they spent most of the school year. Picture perfect, India thought, gazing out at a hacienda-style estate lined with dozens of lemon trees, an old mock-Tudor mansion, and what appeared to be a replica of Buckingham Palace, complete with porticos, stone lions, and a spectacular Trevi fountain.

Annie's house was a surreal mix of French and Spanish Colonial styles, beautifully proportioned and elegant, with a pitched tiled roof and a long, gated driveway lined with olive trees. The car pulled up at the carved wooden door where Maria stood, waiting to greet her. A small, dark-haired Mexican in her early fifties, Maria had worked for the family for twelve years and was especially fond of India. Unlike many houseguests, India was considerate and even washed her own underwear.

Leaping out of the car, India embraced her.

"Cómo estás?" Maria said, returning the embrace warmly. "Te ves muy bien."

Taking India's hand luggage, Maria started walking across the impossibly green lawn toward the annex. India loved coming back to the guest suite. The ceilings were as high as cathedrals and the tall bay windows overlooked a small, secluded patio surrounded by a fragrant lavender hedge. Thanking Robert profusely, and unsure about tipping, she hesitated for a moment before catching up with Maria and slipping through the door into her own private paradise.

Nothing had changed. The pale green silk-lined walls were bare but for the strikingly colorful de Kooning hanging on the wall by the shuttered windows. Taking in the priceless, jewel-toned oriental rugs scattered across the polished floor, India smiled. Hardly "benign neglect," she thought. More "benign opulence." Fiddling with the remote control, she was delighted to see the gigantic wide-screen HDTV slide up discreetly from its cabinet.

Then she looked longingly at the California king-size bed with its pristine linen sheets, down pillows, and white Frette coverlet.

But it was Annie's own thoughtful and very personal touches that always meant the most to India: the handmade vellum notepaper, India's favorite Moulton Brown soap in the bathroom, and the card on the bedside table with a note: "Maria's cooked your supper. Please don't wait up for me. I just can't WAIT to see you in the morning. Love you, xxx."

India had yet to master the art of relaxing while staff looked after her and was feeling extremely awkward as Maria laid out a stack of thick Turkish bath towels. To distract herself she started sorting through her English "souvenirs," the little gifts she'd brought from London: Jo Malone candles from Bond Street (but really from the duty-free) for Annie, candy for the kids, and an outrageously expensive Pop art Paul Smith tie for Joss, who liked to wear them when he had dinner with the designer.

The guy's impressive, he said to her once. "Never fails to recognize the exact year and season of every tie. "

After Maria left her alone, she took a quick shower, went over to the house, ate a delicious risotto, drank two glasses of Kermit Lynch Sancerre, and headed groggily back to bed for a good night's sleep.

Thérèse

PROFOUND THOUGHTS NOTE – Wahoo!

The glorious California sun had barely risen over the horizon when India sprang out of bed. It was 5 a.m.

Too early to wake Annie up, she thought, dashing over and opening the wide doors of the walk-in closet. A few sorry-looking linen shifts and two shirts hung there limply, as if forgotten by a departed guest. The rest of her clothes were still strewn across the floor.

Shit, those creases are supposed to fall out overnight, she thought. I should have brought that Ghost dress… Never mind. At least I remembered my new bikini.

A slow, luxurious swim in the infinity pool soon recharged her spirits. Reluctant to get her hair wet, she concentrated on keeping her head above water. What a metaphor for my life, she thought as she did a few more laps. Then she toweled off and ran toward the kitchen. Annie looked up the second the door opened and rushed across the room. Throwing her arms around India, she locked her in a bear hug.

"Look at you." Annabelle grinned, stepping back and taking both of her hands. "Here you are… I've been counting the days."

"I've been counting the months!" India laughed. "I can't believe I'm finally here. I'm really here!" She paused. "You look so beautiful, Annie. Your hair got lighter and your skin's amazing. You haven't even got tiny frown lines, and your forehead's so smooth. Teaching's giving me wrinkles. I'm obsessed. See this frown line here?" she said, running a finger between her eyebrows.

"Thank you," Annie said, turning around to fix the lid of the gurgling coffeemaker. "Good flight?" she asked over her shoulder.

"Great. The seat went almost flat and the food was good, too." She grinned. "I could get used to that."

Annie smiled. "Are you ready for breakfast? I think I know the answer. We have the house all to ourselves. Joss thought we'd appreciate the time to catch up."

"He's so thoughtful. Yes, I'm starving. Have you still got that waffle machine?"

"Ready to go," Annie said, dragging it out of a drawer. "Orange juice in there" – she nodded toward the refrigerator – "and there's a fruit plate ready too."

"It's like I've never been away," India said, opening the heavy steel doors to the fridge. She pulled out a jug, placed it on the kitchen table, and then dashed over and gave her sister another hug.

"I want all the news. How did the girls get on in Hawaii? Do they still hang out with the Nicholsons? Is Bella still freaking out over meeting Jason Mraz? Will I recognize them? Did they get the backstage passes for Miley Cyrus?" India was remembering how shocked she had been seeing them go off to school with their (monogrammed) Louis Vuitton backpacks and Juicy Couture pants, or the time their friend's dad had ordered in tons of real snow so they could all enjoy a white Christmas. That was the year he also flew them in his the Gulfstream jet to a bar mitzvah in Vegas. At the time, India was not sure if she was disgusted or jealous.

"Yes, yes, and yes." Annabelle laughed, setting out a couple of plates. "But not in that order. They're still cute as hell but Bella is starting to get attitude already; can't think who she takes after!"

"And Joss? Are things good?" India probed.

"Yes, we're good. Really good," Annie said with a smile. "He just came off tour and he's loving the Malibu place. It's very laid-back. He's set up another recording studio there. Says he feels more creative by the ocean."

"I can't wait," India said, "and it's a beach party, right?"

"Just a few friends. Joss has it all organized – special charcoal for the barbecue, meat from Spago's kitchen. He's in his element, hanging out."

"So what shall I wear?" India asked.

"Don't even think of worrying what to wear," Annie told her. "Malibu's very casual. It's come as you are. So now fill me in. Tell me, how's Sarah? Is she still trying out the dating agency? How's the job? Any men on the horizon?"

The hours flew by. Annabelle and India hardly left the kitchen all day.

PROFOUND THOUGHTS NOTE – California Casual?

Late next morning they packed up overnight bags and drove out to Malibu. Looking forward to a relaxed afternoon with Annie's friends and her nieces, India planned to swim at the beach, too.

"It's almost like being in the country," Annie had told her.

They drove down Sunset Boulevard past the suburban estates of Pacific Palisades and onto the Pacific Coast Highway. After a few miles, Annie turned the SUV expertly up the incline of a steep hill that led them a few miles into the canyon. Then she slowed down on a tiny dirt road, avoiding the lines of precariously parked cars. The sprawling ranch property was set way back in acres of land. While they waited for the electronic gates to open, India noticed a large sign underneath the surveillance cameras. "Private Party: No Tweets or Video, Please."

"That's funny, Annie." She laughed. "Do we get a full body search? Hope so, it's been a while."

"We try to keep this place a secret," Annie said, laughing. "Well, we're a bit late. Let's freshen up quickly." She climbed down from the car and led India up a back stairway.

India splashed her face and straightened her hair in a bathroom. She had opted for a white linen shirt, black capri pants, and flat leather moccasins. This was working beautifully, or so she thought, until Annie reappeared in a heavily jeweled Tory Burch smock, meticulously ripped blue jeans, and high, gold, strappy Jimmy Choo sandals.

"Come on, darling. Joss and the girls are bursting to see you," Annie said, grabbing her hand and leading India down the stairs and into the garden.

A woman passed by in a long sequined evening dress, also wearing emerald earrings and a choker of enormous black pearls. Obviously this "California Casual" look doesn't come cheap, India thought, and began speculating on the total cost, starting with the woman's highlighted hair, her makeup, manicure, pedicure, shoes, handbag, and jewelry. She'd reached a rough estimate of $5,500 and was about to start on Annie, when she was interrupted by a shout from Joss. He raced across the garden and lifted her up off the ground for a hug as she threw her arms around him.

"My favorite, favorite sister-in-law," he said, planting a kiss on her cheek.

"Your only sister-in law," India replied. "Now unhand me or people will start tweeting about us."

"Ah. Yes. The sign. Last time we had a party it was all over TMZ as it was happening! You can't be too careful in this town, believe me."

"Ha!" India replied. A woman in a low-cut, skintight minidress and eight-inch platform heels teetered by. India whispered: "That's some outfit for a barbecue! Annie said this was going to be really casual for just a few friends."

"Yes. This would be Annie's idea of a few friends, all right." He laughed, eyeing the crowds near the pool. "And you're a breath of fresh air, India. Now come on; let me get you a drink."

Shortly after, she was standing alone, sipping a mimosa, and feeling that weird sense of disconnection she'd had in the session with Pete just before the firewalk. What did she want? What had she ever wanted? She watched Joss hoisting one of the kids onto his wide shoulders and admired the strength in his back as he went toward the haze of charcoal smoke. Incredible to think his band is outselling Zeppelin, she mused. It's different for guys. He just gets better looking every time I see him.

"India! Give us a hug, you gorgeous thing!" shouted a total stranger, a man in tan shorts and an open-collared plaid shirt.

She took a step back as he tried to put his arms around her. "I'm Ben. And I just know you must be Annie's sister."

"You do?" she replied, smiling tentatively. "Have we met?"

"No," he said, gently leading her toward a trestle table that was set up in the shade beneath a wooden trellis covered in wisteria. "But don't worry, I don't bite."

"Me either," she said.

"I'm relieved. Now please take a seat and say hello to Max. Oh, and the ugly one is Adam."

India nearly dropped her glass when she saw "the ugly one." Sarah would die, she thought. And she'd also know the name of every movie he's been in. Oh. My. God. The arms! They were the sexiest arms she'd ever set eyes on. And Max? She'd heard about him, too. He had been one of Hollywood's funniest, most successful comedians, until the drugs killed his career.

"Hey," Adam said, standing up, slowly, to shake her hand and holding eye contact for what seemed an exquisitely torturous amount of time. "How are you?"

"Fine. I … I'm doing fine, a little bit tired today, but doing okay. I woke up earlier than usual though… I'm good…" she said. Shut up now, she thought, it's a form of greeting, not the Spanish Inquisition.

"Glad to hear it," he said, letting go of her hand and sliding over on the bench. "Sit right here, next to me."

India sat down so quickly, her drink spilled.

"Sorry. It must be jet lag," she said, wiping the table with her hand.

"No problem. Where've you come from? Long flight?"

India felt positively light-headed. Her heart was pounding. It certainly wasn't the jet lag or the mimosa. It was his dark, wavy hair, the absurdly broad shoulders, those intelligent, piercingly blue eyes. And forget the thigh muscles…

She started to answer him. "London … just…"

"So India," Max interrupted, touching her elbow. "Ben here is trying to convince us he met Cynthia in another life. He's been seeing a hypnotist and just finished a past life regression. What do you make of that?"

Adam caught her surprised look and they shared what she was sure was a complicit exchange. "Sorry, who's Cynthia?" she asked.

Max lifted his chin. "Over there. The blonde."

India recognized her immediately. She was a very tiny actress, famous for her insanely large bosoms. "I see," she said, not see-ing at all.

But Max was way ahead of her. "My theory about Ben is he's just regressing, period."

Everybody, including Adam, laughed. "Yeah, well, thanks, that's funny, man!" Ben said. "We've all been here before, right? I mean, you're still a Neanderthal!"

Adam glanced in India's direction. "Why dismiss the possi-bility?" he said. "I'm open-minded. Sometimes you do have an instant connection with people. You feel like you've known them before."

He's definitely looking at me, India thought. But was he talking about her, about that instant connection? Feeling increasingly flustered and brainless, she just sat there.

"Well, if I come back," Ben said, "I hope it's not with a bunch of losers like you."

Max focused his attention on India. "You look kinda like Annie, but I thought she said you were twins."

"We are, but we're not identical, we're fraternal; Annie got Mum's blonde hair and blue eyes. I look more like our dad," India said, glancing across the lawn to Annabelle, who was helping some kids get out of their water wings. God, she's thin, she thought, taking in her sister's profile.

Max looked curious for a moment and started to say something.

Please let him shut up now… India thought. Do not come out with some tired one-liner – "two for the price of one … twice the fun" – believe me, I've heard them all.

He must have read her mind because he changed the subject quickly. "So what do you do? Joss mentioned you're some kind of teacher. That's cool. What do you teach?"

India took a large sip of her mimosa. "I'm a sort of teacher," she said, mysteriously. Or so she hoped. She wasn't about to get into stories about grade-school teaching. Adam was studying her out of the corner of his eye, waiting for a more detailed answer. If only she could start the whole scene all over again. This time around she'd be ten years younger wearing a sarong, with an all-over tan and big boobs. She'd be carrying a basket with a scarf twined around the handle, and have a French accent.

"Let's just say I'm on vacation for now," she managed.

But Max wasn't even listening. He was following a girl, more like a child, India thought, as she climbed out of the swimming pool in a flesh-colored string bikini so tiny, India couldn't see it even when she squinted. Leaning over to shake the water out of her waist-length, streaked blonde hair, she then sauntered over to a lounge chair where she began to apply, in what seemed like agonizingly slow motion, a squirt of sunscreen to her long legs. I hope she stops when she gets to the top, India thought, knocking back the rest of her drink.

"Barely legal," Max sighed. "Where the hell do they all come from, anyway? Sometimes I think there must be a factory out near Anaheim or something. It's weird."

India noticed that the girl's performance hadn't been entirely lost on Adam. But she was also relieved and delighted to note that he looked bored. Then, he grinned at her again.

Joss had now joined the group. "Your glass is empty, Indie. Want another?"

"Thanks, but I think I'd better get something to eat. I'm not used to all this sun," she said quickly. She was dying for another drink, several in fact, but one more smile or glance from Adam and she figured she might just faint. Joss started to lead the way.

"Great to meet you," India said to no one in particular, standing up, attempting to leave and realizing the strap of her purse was caught on the back of her chair. Tugging at it with a smile, she gave it one last yank and stumbled off, acutely aware that her linen pants had grown two sizes while she'd been sitting down.

India picked her way through yet another wave of Annie's hundred or so "just a few friends" who were greeting one another with screams of delight. "So great to see you!" "I've missed you like crazy." "How ARE you?" It amazed her. In England, you could have been kidnapped and held hostage in a cave for a couple of years and you wouldn't expect this kind of reception.

Wandering into the kitchen, she aimed for the food table. The room was the size of a tennis court at Wimbledon. Everywhere she looked there were women toting trays, fixing hors d'oeuvres, washing dishes, chattering away in Spanish. Two kids in oversize tee shirts were pouring thick chocolate syrup onto strawberries so obscenely large, India assumed they must be mutant. She had just helped herself to a healthy slab of lasagna when Annabelle appeared and signaled her to come over. Reluctantly leaving her plate behind (not a good look meeting people with a mouth full of food) she stepped across the hand-fired clay tile floor to join her.

"Meet my sister, India," Annabelle announced proudly. "India is staying in LA for the summer after we leave for the house in the Hamptons, so I want her to get to know you all. India, darling, this is my friend Georgia."

"Lovely to meet you," India said, smiling. "What a beautiful necklace."

"Thank you so much," Georgia replied, playing with the sparkling semiprecious stones wrapped around her neck. The necklace seemed to float against her skin. "A friend of mine makes them. She has a little store at Fred Segal. I'll give you her name."

"And this is Tess," Annabelle continued as she turned toward the rest of the group.

An Amazonian blonde squeezed by. "Hi," she said in a husky, low voice. "Excuse me, won't you? I've just seen my director and I need to have a quick word with him."

"Of course," India said, moving aside and noticing the woman's fluorescent white teeth. "Nice to meet you."

"Reality television has a lot to answer for," Tess said under her breath. There was a pause while they watched her make her exit, and then the introductions continued.

"India, I'm Toni. We met a few summers ago. If you're going to be here on your own for a while, I'd LOVE to do some hiking with you. Are you into power yoga? I have this amazing, I mean totally amazing guy who comes over to the house twice a week for private sessions. All my friends are in love with him. Why are all the good-looking ones gay?" She sighed wistfully.

India was enjoying Toni's energy. "I'd like that," she said. "I'd like that very much."

"Great, I'll ask Annie for your number and call you. By the way, your moccasins are so cute. I'm sooo into beading."

"Thank you; they're very old," India said, looking down at her feet.

"A bit like myself," Toni said, lifting up her head. "Had my neck done just two weeks ago; you'd never know, would you? No downtime, either."

India nodded her approval. All this instant intimacy was a bit alarming. You could be at a party all day in London and the most you could hope for by way of intimacy was someone pointing out you had something stuck between your teeth.

"There you are, darling." Annie was back at her side. "Quick, my friend Summer's doing some readings in the other room. Why don't you come in and listen? Some women have so much faith in her readings they don't even decide what to wear without consulting her first."

"It's true," said Cynthia, who had popped back into the group. "The woman is almost scary, she's so good."

"See, India? I told you. And hey, maybe we'll find out your days of being single are about to be over..."

India gave a halfhearted, irritated smile. "You mean maybe my stars are finally in alignment?"

"Don't be cynical, darling."

"Well, I'd appreciate it if you were just a tad more discreet about my spinsterhood, Annie. Please!"

The three of them tiptoed into a chapel-like room where a circle of women were sitting on rugs and cushions, surrounded by lit candles. The walls were lined with bookshelves under a vaulted mahogany ceiling.

"Blessings," said a girl India knew instantly must be Summer, as she was holding a woman's upturned hand in her own, tracing the lines around her thumb. She could have been sent by central casting, India thought, taking in the woman's short floaty caftan, the ton of bangles, the bandanna tied around her head, and the snake tattoo that inched its way up her thigh.

"Trules," Summer whispered, "I can see that you're a very giving person. Your energy is strong, but there's been quite a drain on it recently. You must learn to hold something back for yourself or you will having nothing left to give."

Trules nodded with rapt attention.

"When I do these group readings, I like to take affirmations from others. The energy can help. Do I have your permission to ask your friends if they agree with me?"

"Yes, yes," Trules said. The woman next to her wiped away a tear. "I think that Trules is one of the kindest, most generous, loving, and giving women we know."

There were nods of agreement around the room.

Summer continued in reverential tones. "Trules, you must learn to honor yourself and your own needs first. My gift to you today is this reminder that you are an extremely special person and should be kinder to yourself. I'm also going to give you an affirmation that I would like you to repeat as often as you can."

"Yes, Summer," she murmured, "I will."

Summer gave her a very special smile. "Say this after me: 'I honor and love Trules.'"

"I honor and love Trules," the girl repeated, softly. "I honor and love Trules."

India was squirming on her cushion. The stench of incense was making her queasy. Surely these full-grown women weren't swallowing this sort of bullshit whole?

Then Summer touched Annie lightly on the shoulder and pulled her aside. They squatted on two large velvet cushions and Summer laid out some cards in front of her. The two of them chatted for a while, then stood up and hugged each other.

"Ladies, it's been such a pleasure today," Summer said, turning to the rest of the group. "Thank you so much for being here. And please, feel free to take one of my cards and some leaflets. I'd be happy to offer discount rates for groups of five or more," she said, backing out of the door with her hands crossed over her chest.

It was unbelievable, India thought. The blatant self-promotion. How much did it cost Summer to "give away" a mantra? A blessing? Talk about a business with no overhead... And what about all that stuff about past-life regression and power yoga? She gave herself a mental kick. Relax. You're on vacation. Annie's so glad you're here.

"I'm so happy you're here!" said Annabelle, reading her mind. "You have no idea."

"It's great to be back, Annie. I mean it," India said, winding her arm through her sister's. "I've missed you."

"It's been the most manic year of my life," Annie replied, leaning in closely against her arm. "I shouldn't complain. So many women in this town hit thirty and it's over but here I am with almost more than I can handle."

"I want to hear all about that, Annie. But in the meantime, I have a few questions for you."

As the two of them walked slowly across the lawn, the sound of their laughter turned heads. India was pumping her sister about Adam. "I want all the details," she whispered. "And I mean ALL the details."

"Later," Annie said, looking across the garden. "Joss is calling us over. Let's go watch the kids at the pool. Oh, and by the way, I'm having a little dinner party for you on Thursday night. Some other people I think you'll enjoy meeting. After that, nothing's planned. We're wide open."

As they walked hand in hand toward the pool, India noticed that Adam and his friends had disappeared.

Thérèse

PROFOUND THOUGHTS NOTE – Two glasses good, four glasses bad.

Walking barefoot across the Aubusson carpet, Annabelle reached the French windows and looked around. The long eighteenth-century single-plank mahogany table was glowing from the light of the tiny votive candles that were scattered among sprigs of orange blossoms set in crystal glasses. She swapped a couple of place cards and straightened a gold-edged napkin. How she treasured these precious moments alone before she made her entrance and "the show" began. Giving a great dinner party was similar to giving a great performance. Malibu was perfect for casual picnics and barbecues, but here, in Bel Air, Annabelle could entertain in grand European style. The house reminded her of all the happy times with Joss in Florence while they were courting.

The heat of the day had passed, leaving a faint perfume of jasmine in the air. Her favorite Rothko, an engagement gift from Joss, chosen with the help of a decorative arts adviser at Sotheby's, seemed to vibrate in the golden light. Touching her face, Annabelle did a short turn in front of the floor-length Directoire mirror and sighed. "I do look pretty good," she thought. "Just wish I wasn't so tired. Now, where's India got to?"

India was in Annabelle's walk-in closet trying to wriggle into a Givenchy dress. She'd caught a glimpse of a couple of guests arriving and dashed upstairs in the hopes of finding something more glamorous to wear. After twenty minutes it was finally dawning on her that Annabelle was now a full-size smaller than she used to be. "Shit," she muttered. "Put something on. Anything."

Squeezing her toes into a tight pair of black patent Louboutin stilettos, she smoothed down her slip and stepped gingerly back into her own Agnes B. black linen wrap dress. Spritzing herself, lavishly, with Guerlain Mitsouko perfume, she shook out her hair and checked her makeup. "Now or never," she thought, taking a deep breath as she headed, cautiously, down the winding staircase toward the drawing room. Her toes were already killing her.

"India, I was worried you might have fallen asleep." It was Joss. He was standing with his back to a Jackson Pollock and chatting with a tall, strikingly beautiful woman. India immediately recognized her from the cover of many glossy magazines.

"Heidi, have you met Annabelle's sister, India?" he said as the two women shook hands.

"No, I don't think I have." She smiled.

The waiter was standing at rigid attention, so entranced with Heidi he couldn't move. India picked up a glass of wine from his tray.

"You look alike," Heidi volunteered, nodding in Annabelle's direction. "Are you an actress too?"

India's reply was cut short by a deafening shriek.

"Heidi, it's you. How ARE you?"

Heidi swung around so swiftly she almost knocked the glass out of India's hand.

"Julia!" she screamed, at least ten decibels higher than India thought necessary. She watched as the two women hugged then stood back and admired each other.

"You look amazing!"

"You too. I can't believe I haven't seen you in weeks."

Weeks? You'd think they were separated at birth, India thought.

Heads turned as Annabelle made her entrance. She was dressed in a skin thin azure Pucci dress and flat, silver embroidered thong sandals. She was wearing a necklace of shimmering chocolate diamonds strung like pearls. Her French-braided hair was held up with a single pin splattered with crystals. "Come on in, everyone." She shouted. "Let's move into the dining room."

"Lizzie and Stan just called and canceled," she whispered to India. "So I've put you between Stephen and Matt. You'll like them."

India smiled, hiding her disappointment. Lizzie was the closest Annie had come to a long-standing friendship. She'd been looking forward to a real tête-à-tête; a chance to catch up on all the news. And what about Adam? Her heart fluttered at the prospect of seeing him. I really hope he's going to be here, she thought, settling into the plush, silk-covered chair and nodding hello to the men on either side of her.

"A toast!" said Joss, raising his glass. "To my favorite sister-in-law, who is here from London. I just want to say how happy I am to have not just one but two incredibly gorgeous women around me. Here's to India!"

The shouts of "India, India," reminded her of that moment just before the fire-walk. Delighted, she smiled graciously.

As three movie-star-handsome young waiters in starched white shirts began serving minuscule portions of wild arugula dusted with shaved Parmesan, India made polite conversation with the man on her left. His wife was sitting across from him and kept looking over, which India suspected was cramping his style, because all he talked about were his allergies.

"I can't even drink vintage wine," he said, placing his hand over the empty goblet as a waiter tipped the decanter toward it.

"That must be awful for you," India commiserated, holding up her own glass for more. "I hope they're not contagious ... The allergies, I mean."

The man looked at her blankly as they struggled through a hideous silence.

"Listen, everyone." Annie was tapping the side of her glass. "I want to take a brief moment here to introduce you to a friend, a man I've admired for years. Simon, where are you?" she said, glancing around the table.

"Here, Annabelle," a short, bald man piped up from the other end of the table.

"I'm sure you've all read Simon's books, and in case you haven't bought the new one, which, by the way, is his best ever, I've left a pile of signed copies in the hallway."

India recalled catching sight of Simon on Fox that morning as she was attempting to reset Annie's treadmill. That was a few seconds before it flung her to the far end of the room.

Simon stood up. "I want to thank Annabelle, Joss, and India for inviting me to share this lovely evening. My travels across this great country of ours over the past few weeks have truly humbled me. The response to my work has been even greater than I hoped for. It is, I believe, a testament to the zeitgeist of the moment."

India snapped the end off a spear of chilled asparagus and her knife flew under the table. A fresh one appeared as if by magic. She smiled up at the waiter and reluctantly turned her attention back to the monologue.

"As you probably know," he continued, "I've been working in quantum physics, searching for a way in which we might all create our own realities. Unlocking Your Soul's Meaning marks an important step in that spiritual growth." He paused, then added: "I do believe that when we suspend our conscious minds, we tune in to a part of ourselves that is sacred."

And I do believe we might be building up for another sales pitch, India thought, easing off one shoe beneath the table.

A couple of the men were staring at their laps. My God. They couldn't be texting at a dinner party, could they? India thought.

"This is how we become one with that invisible energy that connects us to our true selves. Anyone who has ever meditated knows this," Simon continued. "My experience with the Sadai monks in Jaipur confirmed my theories and taught me that we should look at the soul, not just as a metaphor, but as something that plays a pivotal part in our inner self and yet still remains outside of ourselves. They believe that the soul vibrates. We just have to sit still long enough to hear it."

Speaking of which ... India was having a harder and harder time sitting still too. She was also wondering if there would be anything left to actually read in the book by the time Simon finished his pitch. Oh. And yes, the men were definitely texting. Maybe she should run over and get her phone. Sarah would enjoy this.

"I'm currently teaching this type of meditation at my institute. I call it 'vibrating soul consciousness.' It's one of the most popular new courses at my Center for Mind, Body, and Spirit." He paused for what seemed an interminable amount of time. "And all of you are more than welcome to visit as guests. Thank you."

Joss looked up abruptly from his lap. "How fascinating, Simon. Thank you for sharing. I saw your great clip from Oprah, too. She seemed pretty impressed when you made that link to the idea of the reptilian brain."

Simon nodded. "Yes, Oprah's open to new ideas. I'm working on a pilot with her for the new network."

India's head was spinning. Was it the wine or the conversation? She was having a hard time keeping up. Reptiles? Where did lizards fit into all this?

Joss was now talking to Matt. "I think with the state of the world right now, we really have to decide if we're going to act on our basest, greediest instincts or not. I mean, I hear it in music all the time. No way we can really deal with this shit if we're not connected at a deeper level, you know?"

Through a haze of alcohol now, India was failing to see any connections. She felt like a child stuck in the backseat of a car during a long road trip, who keeps asking, "When will we get there? When will we get there?" She'd heard more profound discussions among her twelfth graders. And where was Adam? Did he just decide not to come?

As the chat skittered around various other subjects, India devoted herself to calculating the net worth of the room. Between the guy who'd developed and produced the hottest syndicated show in NBC's history, and the biggest-grossing movie star of all time ($20 mil for his last picture, she'd read somewhere), she figured the two of them could settle the world debt. A couple of others at the table (including Joss) could take care of malaria, AIDS, and malnutrition. Then, just as she was calculating the cost of the jewelry worn by the woman in the red satin dress, everyone shifted in their chairs and stood up.

India peeked at her watch. Ten o'clock. The party couldn't possibly be over, could it? In London parties had barely started at ten o'clock. Men didn't even unbutton their top buttons until at least eleven thirty, and where was the port, the brandy, the cheese? She nipped into the restroom and emerged a mere five minutes later to a room that looked as if it had been evacuated during a bomb scare. There were no dying candles, or crumpled napkins, only Maria smiling wearily.

"You would like these orange blossoms for your room?" she offered, handing India two bouquets in crystal glasses.

"Gracias, Maria." She smiled.

India cautiously followed the blue lights around the terrace and pool toward her suite, and fell asleep watching one of Adam's early movies, an indie on the Sundance Channel.

"Will you check in on the girls, sweetheart?" Annabelle said, turning her head to Joss, who was coming up the stairs fast behind her.

"Sure," he answered, giving her bottom a squeeze as she reached the landing.

"Don't be too long." She opened the wide double doors to their master bedroom. Once inside their deliciously carpeted suite, she flung off her shoes and started to unzip her dress. "Damn things," she muttered, as the fastener to her diamond necklace caught in her hair clip. Struggling awkwardly as she walked into the oasis of her private bathroom, she leaned one arm against the Italian marble washstand and fiddled with the tiny clasp in her magnifying mirror.

Free of them at last, she rubbed the back of her neck with relief and then, with a mounting sense of panic, across her throat—across something that felt like a lump. She pushed up close to the mirror again and swallowed hard. She could see it clearly. "Oh my God," she whispered, steadying herself on the vanity chair, frozen with shock. A million thoughts were crashing through her brain and one word circled round her head. Tumor ... tumor... I have a tumor... Annabelle sat down and put her head in her hands.

Thérèse

PROFOUND THOUGHTS NOTE – Emperor's New Clothes

Annabelle was already flipping pancakes when India walked into the kitchen, clutching her head.

"It's the hangover from hell," she whispered while opening the fridge door and grabbing a carton of orange juice. The girls, Cindy and Bella, were sprawled out on the floor in nightgowns, rolling a ball back and forth to Clooney, their black Lab. The dog was barking.

"Shhh! Kids, can't you play more quietly? I'm in pain," India said with a weak smile.

"It's the heat and dry air," Annabelle said, forcing several thick slices of bread into the toaster. "LA's a desert; you need to drink more water."

"And less red wine?" India said, taking an Advil from her dressing gown pocket. "Is that what you're implying?"

"Darling, I'm not preaching," Annabelle replied, placing the plates of pancakes in front of her girls. "Wash your hands, kids," she said. "So what did you think of Simon?" Annie asked, grabbing a chair next to her sister.

India just raised her eyebrows.

"Over here, Aunt India. Look over here," Cindy shouted, aiming Annie's pink iPhone camera at her face.

"Hey, come on kids, give me a break. I'm in my pajamas," she said, trying desperately not to sound as irritated as she felt. Murderous is more like it, she thought, turning back to Annabelle.

"I think Simon talks a load of bollocks. I think he's full of shit!"

"I didn't quite hear that," Annie said, testily. "Would you mind repeating it?"

"Look, you'd think intelligent people would be too smart to believe all that crap about vibrating souls. Anyone could invent some fucking self-help program. And haven't you all had enough of self-help out here? Especially when it doesn't help anyone – you're all still seeing shrinks. And don't tell me you're interested in third-world issues – your idea of hardship is flying first class commercial, and I can't remember the last time you had to do that. I feel like I've had a forty-eight-hour immersion in bullshit. No wonder you all need Prozac."

India was hitting her stride when Clooney trotted over and began licking her feet. She pushed him away forcibly and glared at Cindy, then turned back again to Annabelle.

"And the talk about past lives – that was the best. Past wives, more like it. What was his name? Adam Brooks? He ... and why didn't you invite him, by the way? You knew I was interested in him even though he's probably got the attention span of a gnat like the rest of them. At least he's cute. I tried to talk to a few people last night, like a proper conversation, like somebody please get my joke, somebody drop the veneer, somebody – anybody – ask a question and then listen to the answer for two seconds. It's like everyone's got ADHD. I can't be that frigging boring (don't answer that)! Matt even waved his hand in front of my face to shut me up, when Kenny Goldman joined in, in defense of Ben Stiller, across the table."

Busying herself near the sink, Annabelle stood ramrod straight. "Don't hold back, please…"

India was on a roll. "Trules was in some kind of stupid trance like she was meeting Gandhi. And who the hell calls herself Summer? What does she sell when it's winter?"

"That's enough!" Annabelle snapped. "I don't want to hear another word about Summer or Trules. They're my friends. As for the rest of your lecture, yes, it's California. La-la Land. But we know real when we see it. Simon and his vibrating soul have a PhD in psychology and a medical degree as well. He's on Oprah regularly."

"Precisely. I rest my case!" India snapped back.

The two sisters just stared at each other.

"Over here, Aunt India! Smile!" Bella shouted again through a mouthful of toast.

India stuck her tongue at the phone as Annabelle whipped away the plates. "You're in this kitchen to eat your breakfast, girls, not shoot photographs. Don't you know how tired Mommy is of people taking photos? And you, India… What is your problem, exactly? We make you feel at home in our house. We throw dinners to entertain you. We work bloody hard to get everything we have. Maybe I should give you the name of a good plastic surgeon. So he could operate on that enormous chip on your shoulder."

Suddenly aware of the fact that her two daughters were gazing at the both of them with their mouths open, Annabelle lowered her voice. "To be continued," she said, turning on her heel and leaving the room.

India felt utterly deflated. She'd been tactless, graceless. Maybe it was jet lag; that eight-hour time difference finally hitting her. Maybe it was culture shock or PMS. Maybe she was just a jealous bitch.

Attempting to distract the girls from the scene they'd just witnessed, India chatted to them about their plans to join their father at the marina, and then quietly left the room to shower.

When Annabelle reappeared, India was pretending to skim through a magazine, curled up on a chaise on the kitchen patio.

"More coffee, darling?" her sister shouted.

"Yes, please!" India replied, relieved that the tension between them had eased. Listening to the sound of the coffee grinder as Annabelle made a fresh pot, India debated about whether to share her real feelings with her sister. *If only she could slip into my skin, the way she does with all those characters on-screen,* she thought, *maybe she'd understand.* There was no excuse for such a cruel outburst and certainly not in front of the children. But Annabelle knew nothing about how demoralizing teaching had become; the endless paperwork, all the testing-standard forms and how difficult it was; to be nearly forty and still unattached, to live from hand to mouth on a salary that made even the idea of buying a pair of Louboutins laughable...

Her thoughts were interrupted by a quick kiss on her forehead as her sister passed her a mug of coffee. "The house will be empty in a minute and we'll have it all to ourselves. You can't imagine what luxury this is for me, sitting in my own garden. I haven't even been in the pool once this whole year."

"That's somehow so wrong," India replied, blowing on the hot coffee. "It's right outside your kitchen door. I'd be in there every single day. You're so lucky."

"Remember, I told you how manic this year has been. Well, I meant it. No matter how successful you are in this town, there's always someone coming up behind you." Running her fingers up her neck, Annabelle looked utterly lost. "Nobody sees the pressure or knows the price we pay. And there never seems to be enough time to take it easy."

"Be careful what you ask for?" India said.

"Exactly, darling. Exactly right."

"I did have a lovely time last night, Annie. Honestly. The food was fantastic. I guess it's culture shock or something."

"Yes, well, I kind of understand. I do. It's just that Simon helps put everything into perspective for me. He keeps my priorities straight and connects me with who I really am. And Summer has a gift. You have no idea the things she sees… "

"I get it, Annabelle. I do. And I'm sorry. It's must be foot-in-mouth disease." She smiled weakly. "Not thinking before I speak."

"Not to worry. Tell me about the teaching. How's it going?"

India took her time answering. "I feel like I'm living in Groundhog Day! I'm longing to do something different. I just don't have a clue what it might be. Then there's the guy thing. I mean, you were right about Pete. It was great sex but he was far too young. I was getting out of bed an hour earlier just to fix my face. It was crazy."

"What happened to Mark?"

"Mark? His idea of a great time was four pints at the pub and a burger on the walk home."

"Walk?" Annie laughed.

"There really hasn't been anyone since Dr. Duplicitous!"

"The gynecologist, right?"

India sighed. "Yes. He was married, Annie, and somehow just 'forgot' to tell me – and I have a biological clock ticking away here. You know that."

Annie touched her shoulder, understandingly. "I don't miss dating, that's for sure," she said. "And I adore Joss. But it's lonely for me, too, you know. He's on the road all the time or I'm up at 5 a.m. and on my way to a shoot. And don't think I don't worry about other women. Well, they're not women. They're girls. I've no reason not to trust Joss. But absence doesn't always make the heart grow fonder – his first wife would tell you all about that. You get into this cycle and it's really hard to break. That's all. But yes, I am lucky. So lucky. And you," Annie added, reaching over to caress her sister's face, "are gorgeous. Adam even said so!"

"Adam? As in Adam BROOKS?"

"I did ask him to the dinner. But he was shooting till eleven o'clock last night."

India sat bolt upright.

"He was? He did? You did just say 'gorgeous' as in GOR-GEOUS, right?"

"Yes ... 'your gorgeous sister.'" Annabelle laughed. "Yes. So what would you like to do today?"

"Annie. Let's go out together. Let's have lunch somewhere lovely ... start again. I'm so sorry."

Refocusing with a smile, Annie seemed more energetic. "I'd suggest the The Ivy, but last time, they gave me a table up front and it ruined the whole meal. God! How I loathe that pack of paparazzi!"

She paused for a second. "But there is this great Argentinean place in West Hollywood. It's sort of off the beaten track. Joss loves it. Shall I have Tess call and book it? How 'bout one o'clock? I might even be able to fit in a swim in my own pool."

"Brilliant, Annie. You have a swim and I'll soak up the sun for a bit."

"Oh! And I nearly forgot," Annabelle said over her shoulder. "There's an art show tomorrow night at the Raw Warehouse. Mr. Brainwash – he's a graffiti artist, a friend of Banksy's. You might enjoy it. I'll fill you in over lunch."

C'EST LA VIE NOTE – Nobody in the Polo Lounge plays polo.

Annie had said the words "warehouse" and "graffiti," so India had dressed appropriately: in a pair of old cargo pants and a Mr. Rogers–like cardigan. One look at the hip scene around her and she wanted to vaporize. So this is "rock star casual," she thought, checking out the parade of characters: the bleached denim, the bed-head hair, the Afghan coats (in this heat?).

"Annie, this is incredible. I've never seen anything like it." She gasped as they were ushered into a dark, cavernous space by two bald and heavily muscled armed security guards, and "Mr. Brainwash" himself came up and kissed Annie smack on the lips.

"Enchanté," he shouted to India over the din of electronic disco.

"Moi aussi," she shouted back, proudly, at this short, disheveled looking Frenchman. He had his foot in a cast, which, far from slowing him down, only seemed to make him more wired and hyped up.

"I fall off the ladder," he said, grinning, lifting up his cast before zipping off with Annie in tow.

India just stood there looking around, grateful for the darkness. Thank God no one knows me! she thought. Glancing over at a knot of people clustering around a giant silver rocket, she recognized the Olsen twins deep in conversation with Sharon Osbourne. What could they possibly have to say to each other? she wondered.

Suddenly India's mouth went dry. She felt her throat tighten. It was him. It was Adam Brooks leaning up, lazily, against a white pillar, arms folded across his chest. Turning her back to him, she tried to recover her equilibrium. Where the hell was Annie? And why, oh why, did he have to show up on a night when she was dressed like this? Maybe he hasn't seen me, she prayed, swinging around toward the nearest wall, where she bumped into an image of a gun-toting Elvis.

"Hey! India! Are you avoiding me?"

"Adam," she squeaked, "of course not. I'm delighted to see you."

"So what do you think of 'Mr. Brainwash?' They say he's a genius, you know."

"Yes, but I'm struggling a bit with some of it," she said, pointing to Elvis. "What's with the gun? What does it mean?"

"Forget the meaning," Adam yelled across the din. "Meaning is meaningless in the case of 'Mr. Brainwash.'"

India's chest was pounding. The physical presence of this man made her feel totally giddy. As they wandered through what seemed acres of space, India berated herself. Get a grip, girl. You're almost forty years old. Yes, he's good looking. OK, better than good looking. But it's the intensity you really like. Half an hour later, as they toured the vast spaces, she was still waiting for him to shake her hand and vanish into the beckoning arms of some impatient starlet – maybe that Cynthia girl was about to appear any moment.

India stopped at an installation. "What's that?" she said.

"That," replied Adam with a straight face, "is a junkyard police car covered in graffiti on a plinth."

"In London, if we see a police car covered in graffiti, we tend not to put it on a plinth!" India laughed. Annabelle appeared beside her. She looked exhausted.

"Hi, Adam," she said with a smile. "I don't know about you and India but I have got to get out of here. Are you ready?"

India nodded, hands over her ears. "I'm starving," she shouted. "Can we go eat somewhere?"

"A brilliant suggestion," Annabelle replied. "Adam? Maybe you'd like to join us?"

India pretended that she hadn't heard the question and scanned the room while a voice inside her screamed, Please say yes! Please say yes!

Like an answered prayer, his eyes locked on hers and he nodded. "Great idea! Where?"

Annabelle thought for a moment. "How 'bout the Polo Lounge? It's usually quiet at this hour."

"Give me a minute," Adam said, pulling out his phone and pressing speed dial. "You want a table inside or out?"

"We're easy," Annie mouthed, grabbing India's arm and steering her through the crowds toward the back entrance, where Robert would be waiting with the car.

"Freedom, at last!" Annie sighed, pulling out her seat belt after telling Robert their destination.

India lowered her voice. "Do me a favor," she said as the car took a long turn and glided up past the line of palm trees and banana plants toward the Beverly Hills Hotel. "Don't talk about what I do for a living."

"Your secret's safe with me, darling, but I don't quite get it. I mean, it's not like you're a lap dancer or a stripper. What's the problem with teaching?"

"It's not the teaching. It's just that I want to seem a bit more mysterious, more seductive, I suppose."

"Well, we could always talk about me all night. There's a subject I never tire of," Annie joked as they headed up the red-carpeted stairs.

"Can we go to the loo?" India asked. "I mean restroom."

"Sure, I'll lead the way."

This is so opulent it's surreal, India thought, following Annabelle through the peachy pink circular lobby with its heavy Italian chandeliers, gilded balconies, and velvet settees. As the door swung open India saw two young women puckering their lips and playing with their hair in front of long gilded mirrors. They were both wearing baby-doll dresses and seven-inch Lady Gaga–style shoes.

Shit! she thought, catching her own reflection and pulling her cardigan more to one side over her shoulder. If I had something sexy on underneath – I don't know, maybe a French basque – I could take this off. But as I don't, I'm just going to have to channel Diane Keaton instead.

She took a deep breath. It's all about confidence… she reminded herself. Say YES!

Annie retouched her lipstick and then, as if sensing her discomfort, gave India an impulsive hug.

"Relax, darling. He likes you. He wouldn't be here if he didn't. Let's go."

Sweeping past the now star-struck girls in their baby dolls, Annabelle drifted across the marble lobby and through the mahogany swing doors into the bar of the restaurant.

"Annabelle! How's it going?" said a tiny middle-aged guy in a striped shirt, leaping to his feet and fiddling with his earpiece. "Great to see you."

"You, too, Jeff. It's been too long," she said, leaning down to air kiss each cheek.

Hovering behind her, India took a deep breath as Adam shook Jeff's hand. As the manager escorted them toward a booth at the back of the room, Adam gently touched her waist. "I'm glad I came," he said. India just looked at him, mutely, and smiled.

Only tribal peace talks in Iraq seemed more complicated to India than Annabelle ordering food in a restaurant.

"Does the soup have cream in it?" Annie asked. "Are there onions in the jus?" "And what about the salmon? Is it wild or farmed?"

It'd be simpler to cook it yourself, India thought. You'd have a hard time ordering like that at the Cat and Lion pub.

Annabelle took a while and then gazed up at the waiter. "I'll have the halibut. Baked. No butter. No dressing, please."

"Make that two," India chimed in. "Though I'd like lots of dressing with mine, please."

"So what did you think of the show, Annie? Did you buy anything?" Adam asked, after ordering the filet mignon minus the jus and with green beans instead of carrots.

"I had them put a couple of pieces aside for Joss to look at tomorrow. He's the expert, not me," she said, unfolding a snow-white napkin and placing it on her snow-white pants.

We can't possibly be related, India thought, looking down at her creased cargos.

"I bet the stuff would look great out in Malibu," Adam added. "It really is an amazing house, Annie."

"Thanks. I love it, too. Especially for parties."

"So India," Adam said, breaking into a bread roll and leaning across for the butter, "is it true you live in London?"

"It's true," she said.

"And is it still true that if you're tired of London, you're tired of life?"

"I hope not," India replied, "because, honestly, I am a bit tired of it."

"Well, the city's one of my absolute favorites. I have a friend, a director, who has a fantastic apartment in Green Park. And last year, he asked me to play the lead in a new West End production. I was all set to move and then the financing fell…" Adam paused, annoyed, and reached down into his pocket to silence his cell phone. "I am so sorry," he said, checking out the number. "I hate when this happens. But I think I have to take it."

"No problem," Annie said. "It's LA, right?"

"Yeah," he said, shrugging. "I'll make it quick."

India watched as he strolled through the French doors onto the patio. "It's probably his wife." She sighed.

"He doesn't have a wife anymore, darling, I told you. Relax." Annie smiled.

"My nerves are shot to pieces," India confided.

"Well … I'm feeling skittish myself. I'm so grateful you're here … more than you know," Annie replied, adjusting the linen scarf around her neck. Just as she seemed close to revealing what was really on her mind, Annabelle was ambushed from behind by two hands over her eyes and a whispered "Guess who, darling." The accent was a pure Southern drawl.

"Loretta," Annie said with a wide smile, leaping up from her seat. "You look amazing. What are you doing here? Please, sit down and say hello to my sister, India."

64

"Pleasure to meet you, India," the woman said as Adam arrived back at the table.

"Hi Loretta!" Adam grinned. "You haven't been anywhere near Brazil by any chance have you?"

Loretta gave a deep-throated laugh. "You always cut to the chase, don't you, Adam? It's a good thing I have a sense of humor. Because as it happens, yes. A little R&R, you know?"

India had absolutely no idea what they were talking about.

"Well, it suits you." Adam winked. "The R&R, I mean."

Soon after, the food arrived, and Loretta and Annie plunged deep into conversation. India turned to Adam. "What on Earth?" she said.

"Dr. Perez?" Adam replied. "The plastic surgeon? Surely, you've heard of him?"

"No," India said.

"Which is one of the reasons I want your number. You have no idea how refreshing it is to meet a woman who's never heard of Perez. It proves there's still hope for the planet."

"I get to score points for being out of touch or for not having a face-lift?" she asked, avoiding eye contact and focusing on her plate. (Omygod he wants my number! He wants my number!)

"Both," Adam said, touching her hand. "Like the lady said, I cut straight to the chase." He pulled out his cell. "Damn thing just died," he said, putting it away again. "Can you write it down?"

India fumbled around in her purse for a pencil and ripped out a page from her leather notepad.

"Profound Thoughts?" Adam said, peeking at the cover. "Is that for real?"

"It's a present from my friend in London. There's not a lot in it!" She laughed, finally unearthing a pen from the depths of her purse and scribbling down her number.

Tucking it into his pocket, Adam signaled a passing waiter for the check as Loretta hugged Annie goodbye.

"Who was that woman?" India asked while the trio waited under the awning for a valet to bring Adam's car around.

Annie lowered her voice. "That, my darling, was no woman. I guess you haven't been to Vegas in a long time. Best drag act in town."

India's jaw dropped in astonishment. "You mean…?"

Adam nodded. "Exactly. What happens in Brazil, stays in Brazil."

Annie fell asleep on the drive home while India gazed out the window, daydreaming. Can you daydream in the dead of night? she wondered as Robert pulled past the Bel Air gates and delivered them to the front door.

"Go straight to bed," India said, steering Annie out of the car, into the house and toward the stairs. "I'll take care of the lights and alarm. Don't worry."

"Thanks, darling. I'm too tired for words," Annie said, kissing her and walking, slowly, up the stairs.

Just as India was trying to figure out which button to push without setting off the sirens, her phone rang. Racing across the hall to the table, she grabbed it from her purse.

"So I hope I'm not calling too soon," said the gravelly voice on the other end. "How 'bout I pick you up at ten for breakfast at Urth on Melrose. They make a killer latte."

"Perfect," India replied. "Great!"

"Cool. Have a good sleep and see you then," he said.

"You, too," she replied, in what she fervently hoped was a sultry tone.

India walked across the lawn as if in a trance. Did I sound too available? she asked herself. Should I have said I was busy? Did

I really say "perfect"? Maybe I said "great." Yes, I definitely said "great" … I should have said "cool"…

Once inside, India brushed her teeth, then, without taking her usual shower, she put on her nightdress and sank into the freshly ironed sheets. What to wear? It would have to be casual, but what was "coffee casual"? She was going to get it right this time, blow him away with her casualness. Her meandering thoughts trailed off into a gentle fog as she snuggled down to sleep.

PROFOUND THOUGHTS NOTE – Ohmygod.

"Coffee's made, darling," Annabelle shouted. "OK, Clooney," she snapped, grabbing the panting dog by the collar and attaching the leash. "Bloody dog walker didn't show today. I'll be about an hour. OK, Clooney. Let's go."

India stepped out of the way carefully, remembering Annie had told her the other night that the dog was taking tranquilizers because he'd nipped one of the kids. She'd been stunned to hear they'd hired a professional dog therapist who was taking notes on Clooney's moods.

The dog's got a shrink! she'd thought. That gives whole new meaning to the expression "barking mad."

Blowing on her coffee as she sat at the kitchen desk, India loaded Google onto the wide-screen Mac and typed in "Adam Brooks."

"Shit!" she muttered, wiping hot coffee off Annie's glasses case and turning back to the screen.

"Oh my God!" There was a photo of Adam striding out of the ocean like some sea god, toting a surfboard, his six-pack glistening in the sun, his wetsuit clinging to his thighs. Skimming through the info on his career, she read: "Born in 1965, film actor, best known for his portrayal of…" She moved ahead to "Personal Life."

"Briefly married in 1993 to Chloe Depardu, the French TV presenter… FRENCH TV presenter?" she muttered. "This is bad … really bad."

Yanking her phone out of her dressing-gown pocket, she speed-dialed Sarah.

"It's me again. Okay, I'm online and I just found out Adam was married to some basket-carrying, scarf-tying French TV presenter. If she couldn't hold on to him, what chance have I got?"

"Breathe," Sarah said calmly. "Breathe."

"Sarah, nobody loses out to a French woman. It's just one of those rules."

"Maybe she left him? Did you think of that?"

"That's even worse. He's probably still trying to get over her and listening to some Carla Bruni CD as we speak."

"Hang on, India. I'm googling. Aha! Scroll down the page. See? It was EIGHT years ago. That's practically the Paleolithic Age in Hollywood. I bet he doesn't even remember what she looks like…"

"Oh my God! Check out her boobs," India muttered. "He'll remember those for sure. Shit. It's almost ten o'clock and I'm not even dressed."

"Go for it, girl." Sarah laughed as they both clicked off.

India raced upstairs to Annabelle's closet. Five minutes later, she heard the roar of a car in the driveway. Pouring herself into a pair of skintight jeans (with some stretch, thank God), she grabbed a sleeveless white shirt and peeked out the window to the driveway, where Adam sat in a gunmetal gray Porsche convertible. Yanking her hair into a clip, she dashed downstairs and scribbled Annie a note. Stopping for a moment in front of the hall mirror, she caught sight of Adam's full-blown image still on the computer screen. She opened the front door and slowly, ever so slowly, closed it tightly behind her.

"I heard you arrive," she said, casually. "Thought I'd save you coming in."

"Hey!" He grinned as she headed for the left side of the car. "Are you planning to drive?"

"Oops," she muttered, running around to the passenger side. "I'm still not used to how you all drive on the wrong side of the road."

Bending her knees, she slipped as graciously as possible into the low tilted seat.

"Carmen, okay?" Adam smiled, fiddling with the sound system.

"Perfect," she said, nodding. "I love Italian music."

As they drove down Bellagio and onto Sunset, India soaked up the scenery: So many palm trees, she thought. So why no coconuts? The thrill of being so near him was giving her palpitations. As Adam turned onto Melrose past a row of antiquarian bookstores and interior design boutiques, she smiled.

"What's funny?" he asked, pulling into a space beneath the white veranda of Urth Caffé.

"Urth," she said, pointing to the sign, "I imagined it was spelt 'e-a-r-t-h.'"

"Ha! 'Earth,' right! Never even noticed." He led her up the stairs, the waitress gazing at him adoringly as she escorted them to a quiet table above a tree-lined side street.

"So," Adam ventured, before his voice was drowned out by a pack of bikers swinging round the corner revving their engines and India was left trying to read his lips.

"I forgot," Adam said, apologetically. "It's Saturday. Let's get out of here."

Steering her back down the stairs, he shouted in her ear. "How much time've you got?"

"All the time in the world," she shouted back. "I'm on vacation."

"Cool," he said as they backed out of the parking space. "I'll take the scenic route in that case ... Brooks Tours at your service!"

"Thank you, Mr. Brooks."

"You're welcome." He grinned.

"Just look at that sky and that ocean," India said with a gasp as the car swung down the California Incline. The panorama of crumbling bluffs and endlessly blue ocean almost took her breath away. As they sped along the Pacific Coast Highway she watched the surfers climb up against the white foam of crashing waves before riding them in. She freeze-framed the moment. On the crest of a wave, she thought, contentedly, That's how I feel right now.

Adam's voice and a sudden stop brought her back to Earth.

"Okay. Latte good for you?" he said, climbing out of the car at Malibu Creek and heading toward the Marmalade Café. Minutes later, he reappeared with two cardboard trays and a squashy white paper bag. "Careful, it's hot," he warned her. "We're almost there."

≈≈≈≈≈≈≈≈

India discreetly clutched the side of her seat as Adam accelerated and the car clung to the curve as tightly as wet silk on skin. There was nothing below them but air and ocean.

"The hillside's still covered since the mudslides," he said, slowing down as they came out of the curve and hit a straightaway.

"I thought it never rained in California," India said, desperately combing through her hair with her fingers.

"Yep. It rains," he said. "It pours, and you don't want to be on this road when it does," he added, pointing to a pile of flowers heaped on the roadside. Downshifting as they drove into the Malibu colony, he pulled up sharply into a garage. India followed him up a flight of wooden steps through a tiny, shiny steel kitchen and into a magnificently simple, sun-filled living room, where he yanked open the glass doors and bowed.

"Breakfast will be served momentarily." he grinned. "Pull up a seat."

Collapsing onto a huge blue-and-white-striped cushion, India dangled her long legs over the balcony. Far off in the distance, she saw a couple of low-flying helicopters outlined against the mountains, and closer by, some kids in wet suits dragging boogie boards across the sand. She watched them wading out through the shallow edge of the water before throwing themselves onto their stomachs as they reached the waves.

Adam was rolling back his shirt sleeves when he flopped down next to her.

"Is this where you live?" India asked, surprised that her voice had not come out as a high squeak. She sounded quite normal for someone losing power over her limbs; Adam was now undoing the top two buttons of his shirt.

Just keep looking at the ocean... she told herself, you'll be fine.

"Yeah," Adam said, "How lucky can you get, right? Wish I could be here more often, that's all."

India was grateful that he seemed to be oblivious to the somewhat unhinged state of his guest. Adam took a bite of blueberry muffin and sipped his latte. Following his lead, India did the same. She could see the edge of a sleigh bed in a bedroom off to her right.

"Do you surf?" she asked, swallowing hard. He was very close to her now.

"Used to jet ski," he replied, gazing out at the sea. "Surfing's a young man's game. How 'bout you?"

"Ah yes! Those summer nights…" she said, hoping this implied fire pits and toasting marshmallows with tanned pubescent boys. "The Internet," she said, laughing, "I surf the Internet."

"And what do you do when you're not surfing the Internet? Max asked you that at Joss' party. But you never really answered."

Flattered that he'd remembered, but flustered, India groped for words.

"Well, it's sort of hard to explain, really," she started as he leaned forward and looked at her with eyes that were bluer than the already incredibly blue sky. "I help people develop their confidence and understand what they can do to change their lives."

Adam propped himself up on his elbows and stretched out his legs. "Like a life coach, you mean?"

"Not exactly. More like a facilitator. I use these techniques I learned from Stanislavski." Where did that come from? she wondered. "Do you know his work?"

"Not as well as I should, but I've taken a few American method classes. What kind of techniques do you use?"

"Ah … good question," she said. "Stanislavski took some of the disciplines of yoga and applied them to training actors. He was light-years ahead of his time, you know, mixing psychology with yoga. I've adapted them for non-actors … that's all."

"Sorry. What do you mean?"

I have no idea what I mean, India thought. But Adam's interest, his curiosity, felt as stimulating as a dip in the North Sea. Brushing some crumbs off her lap, she took a deep breath.

"Well, take tai chi, for example. It's an Eastern tradition, right?" (Shit, I think it might be a drink...) But people in the West have adopted it too. It works. Maybe not in exactly the same way as in the East, but it's effective nonetheless."

"Do you teach yoga?"

"No. I rely on the drama techniques I learned at university."

Adam nodded. "And do people really manage to shift their thinking? Make changes?"

"Some of them do," she said, standing up and stretching in what she hoped was a very centered, limber move reflecting years of posture training.

"How many people do you usually workshop?" Adam asked, rising, she noticed, in a single fluid motion from his own sitting position on the cushion.

"I workshop thirty at a time. Any more than that and I lose my focus."

(I workshop? I WHAT? God, I've come over all American. I just used a noun as a verb. Any second now I'll be saying things like "clusterfuck" and "whatever.")

Keeping her shoulders back and her toes out and wishing she wasn't quite so self-conscious, she strolled inside toward the fireplace.

"And what about you? Did you always want to act? Even as a kid?"

"It was an accident. That's the truth. I just stumbled into it. I know people expect you to say it was a long, hard struggle, years of waiting tables and endless auditions. But it wasn't. Not for me."

"And is this your family?" India asked, holding up a framed photograph.

"Yes. That's my dad. He's a playwright. And my mom, she was an artist, a wonderful painter."

"Was?" India asked quietly.

"Mm … yes. She died a couple of years ago. That's one of her paintings above the mantel there," he added, pointing to a hauntingly beautiful watercolor above the fireplace.

"Reminds me of a Rodin," India replied, gently. "Le Jardin des Supplices. The figure has the same auburn hair."

"It was a self-portrait. Mom was extremely talented." He smiled. "I was her only pride and joy."

"You were an only child?"

"Yeah. But I wasn't lonely. Our house was always lively, full of artists and actors. I used to think it was normal to sit in all night on conversations about Edward Albee or Salinger or Brecht."

India tried to block out thoughts of her own childhood; the door slamming the night their father left, Annie's suitcase in the hall soon after, promises to be back at the weekends, weekends that never happened, weeks that turned into months. How she had put her own plans on hold, unable to wrench herself away from her mother. Thinking back now, she felt that same knot in her stomach and tightness in her throat.

"That sounds wonderful," she said, putting down the photograph. "To have all those interesting people around you growing up, all that encouragement."

"I know, believe me. I know. It's why I don't trust myself sometimes. Like becoming an 'overnight success,' you know?"

"I can't imagine what that must be like," she replied.

"It's weird," Adam said. "Makes me feel like I didn't earn it. My shrink tells me I should get over it. But guilt is in my DNA. Maybe I should try one of your workshops."

"Ha! Right." India smiled weakly as he handed her a glass of Pellegrino.

"If you get what you want too easily, too quickly, you lose your drive. I mean, if there's no struggle, the energy just sort of dissipates... What was it Shakespeare said? 'Give me a surfeit...' Hell, what's the line?"

"'The appetite may sicken and so die?'" India offered.

"Precisely," he said.

"We call that middle-aged angst," she said. "It's when not having a problem becomes the problem."

"I like how you fill in my blanks. I'm not used to it."

"Believe me, it's a long time since I've had blanks to fill in," she said, smiling at him.

"How about a walk? Nothing like a walk in Malibu to clear an existential head."

She nodded.

"The thing is, I don't want to make formulaic movies for the rest of my life," he said, hauling some wooden steps down from the deck till they touched the sand. "The last one was just..."

"I'm afraid I didn't actually see the last one," India confessed. "I don't go to the movies much in London."

"Probably because you have a life. People in London have more to do than make movies or go see them. Here in LA, it's like Woody Allen said, 'The only cultural advantage to LA is turning right on a red light.'"

He grabbed her hand to steady her as she landed next to him with a bump on the hot sand, and they walked together to the water's edge.

≈≈≈≈≈≈≈≈

Clooney was slobbering noisily at his water bowl as Annabelle read India's note. She poured two cups of Maria's freshly ground fair-trade Chilean coffee, and walked barefoot across the lawn to Joss' den. Tiptoeing through the wooden doorway, she found him curled up on the couch, reading. She liked this room, maybe because it was all Joss. He'd bought the beautiful antique Native American carpets himself and dragged them home after a gig in Santa Fe. The old oak coffee table had been bought at the auction of one of his silent screen idols. "The poor woman died broke and forgotten," he'd said that afternoon. Sometimes, when he was away on tour, Annabelle would come in, close the door, and just stand there, gazing at the pictures of him; the walls were lined, floor to ceiling, with photographs – Joss with arms around Mick Jagger, another one of him laughing with Rod and Stevie. Dozens of golden discs and graphic cartoons covered the hallway that led into a small, state-of-the-art recording studio. She was as happy as he was in here, always had been.

"Hey, you," she said, walking over and kissing him on top of his head. "Thought you might like some coffee."

"Ah! You're a mind reader, Annie," he said, jumping up like a teenager to give her a hug.

She leaned into him and snuggled. "What time are you and Kenny taking the girls?"

"Depends what time I get out of here, doesn't it?" he whispered, running one hand, slowly, down her back. Moving over to the door, he locked it and gently untied the belt of her robe. She smiled and let it slip to the floor.

≈≈≈≈≈≈≈

Annie was delighted that Lizzie had said yes to a last-minute lunch date at Il Cielo, her favorite Italian spot, but as she sat back in the car, she fought the impulse to touch the lump in her throat. Why hadn't she called the doctor? Because she was terrified, that's why. Because a few more hours in denial wouldn't kill her, she decided. As the car slowed down outside the restaurant in Beverly Hills, she fumbled around in her bag for her lipstick.

"Thanks, Robert," she said as the car came to a gentle stop and the door lock clicked open. "Why don't you take some time off for your own lunch? Lizzie can drop me off."

"Are you absolutely sure?" Robert replied. "You know I don't mind waiting."

"Of course I'm sure," she said, glancing back over her shoulder. "Enjoy the afternoon."

A young waiter was standing under the arched entranceway.

"You are Miss Butler-Elliot?" he said, awestruck.

"So they tell me," she replied, lightly.

He stood motionless, nailed to the floor, gaping. Annabelle was accustomed to putting other people at ease. It was part of her job.

"I'm here for lunch?" she suggested.

"Oh yes, such an honor, my privilege," he said, in a heavy Venetian dialect. Opening one arm wide, as if to take a bow, he directed her to a circular table tucked discreetly amid leafy vines, where he scraped back a wrought-iron chair and gave an Elizabethan flourish to her napkin.

Annie appreciated the secluded spot. But the possibility of privacy had been spectacularly blown away by his theatrics. Still, she was gracious.

"Lovely," she said, looking him straight in the eye. "Perfect."

It wasn't long before Lizzie appeared, waving frantically from beneath the pagodas, and ran over as if jet propelled. Annie grinned as they kissed. "Three kids and you look about sixteen years old. I don't know how you do it!" Annie exclaimed.

It was almost true. Lizzie was the epitome of sleek chic. Her long streaked hair was blown straight, her skin buffed, and her emerald green eyes were accentuated with just the faintest hint of violet shadow. She wore an exquisite topaz necklace around her bronzed neck, and an elegant peach silk blouse and white jeans.

"Ha!" her friend whispered. "Thanks. I feel like shit! Rhonda didn't sleep a wink last night and the boys had me up at five. The housekeeper called in sick and I had to drive, round-trip, for a playdate all the way to the Palisades."

"My God! Why didn't you tell me? I would have come to you or we could have met up tomorrow. I remember showing up on the set after two hours' sleep. It's murder."

Scanning the menu, Lizzie sighed. "Are you kidding? I couldn't wait to get out of the house. Don't ask me how I could feel claustrophobic in fifteen thousand square feet of space, but I do."

The waiter was back. "Miss Butler, let me tell you about the specials we are having today."

"We're not terribly hungry," Annie said, cutting him off, politely. "Could we just order two of your arugula salads, please, with dressing on the side? And oh! Lizzie? A half bottle of Gavi?"

"Great idea," Lizzie agreed. "Maybe even a full bottle. And Pellegrino."

"Excellent choice," the waiter noted, nodding as he backed up. Lizzie touched her friend's cheek. "So where's India?" she asked.

"A coffee date with Adam Brooks."

"Wow! That was fast work. How long's she been here?"

"A week. I'm really glad to see her, but she's having some trouble settling in. I think she's had a rough year. But how's Tom and the flu?"

"He's much better but he gave it to Rhonda. We seem to share everything in our family ... including husbands."

Lizzie was suddenly close to tears. "She's eighteen, for Christ's sake..."

Annie looked at her. momentarily confused, and then concerned.

"I'm talking about the nanny. Eighteen, and my husband was screwing her."

"Oh God, I know, Lizzie. I am so sorry. Do you feel like talking about it?"

Waiting, patiently, until the waiter had uncorked and poured their first glass of wine, Lizzie wiped her eyes with the edge of a linen napkin. "Look, it's not like I thought I married the Dalai Lama, you know? But the nanny? Puhleeze."

"I don't suppose I can ask why you're putting up with it?"

"Of course you can ask. I've been asking myself the same question lately. I told my shrink yesterday I might finally be finding the courage to walk away. Stan has joint custody of his older kids and they're making my life a living hell."

Annie listened quietly as Lizzie shared the weight of her sadness.

"Henry treats me like staff, refuses to pick up after himself and loves provoking Tom and Jack. And I detest his friends. They're just awful."

"Are they around every weekend?"

"And then some," her friend replied, picking her way through her salad. "And don't get me started on Sophie. She's spoiled rotten."

Annie didn't much like the teenage stepdaughter either.

"It's strange," Lizzie said, almost wistfully. "I remember how I admired your strength. That time when you stood your ground with Joss."

"Yeah, well. It was years ago, before the kids. It hurt but I knew that woman was just a groupie. I mean, she was never a real threat."

"But you left, Annie. And he came back to you on your own terms. No way he'd risk losing you again. We all know that. My problem is I'm scared stiff."

"We're all scared, sometimes," Annie said, putting her hand over Lizzie's. "Anyone who says they're not is lying. Or has nothing to lose."

"Whatever. I still admire you."

"Thanks, Lizzie. There are so few people I genuinely trust. And you're one of them. So what now?"

"What now? How 'bout this?" she said, lifting her wrist and pointing to her Cartier Panthere bracelet. "My consolation prize."

"At least he has good taste," Annie said, laughing.

"Right. There is that. But c'mon. You haven't told me anything about you."

It wasn't the time for Annabelle to mention her own terrors.

"I'm exhausted. I mean, more exhausted than I've ever been. And I have two years to catch up on with India. We Skype, but it's not the same as being together." Annabelle looked away, thinking back to the scene in the kitchen, India's outburst.

"You're lucky to be so close to your sister. My brother's off with that firm in Saudi and we've never been close, anyway. He's ten years older than me. But bring India over for lunch. Promise? I love her sense of humor."

"Yes I will. She'd like that."

The waiter was hovering like a low-flying chopper over their table.

"Oh my God, look at the time, Lizzie. Can you give me a lift home? I gave Robert the afternoon off."

"Love to," Lizzie said, standing up and hugging her friend. "You're a rock, you know that?"

"I'm here for you," Lizzie said, taking her arm as they walked toward the valet.

≈≈≈≈≈≈≈≈

"Let's cut to the chase…," Adam said, tearing off a hunk of bread and dipping it in olive oil. "I was married once. The whole she-bang, Notre Dame Cathedral, honeymoon in St. Bart's. It didn't work out."

"Yes, Annie told me the other night," India answered before she could stop herself.

Adam grinned. "Of course she did. So what else did Annie tell you? Does she approve of me hitting on her sister?"

(He's hitting on me! Omygod!) "Well, she damned you with faint praise, but she didn't say anything too damaging," she teased. "So tell me what I'm looking at right now," she said, leaning forward to take in the stunning panorama from the rooftop restaurant.

"Well, that's Santa Monica Bay over there," Adam replied, using his thumb like a hitchhiker to indicate the direction. "And Point Dume's the other way."

"Sounds ominous. What's Point Doom?"

"It's a beach and it's spelled with a u not an o."

"Right, like Urth Café." She laughed. "Spelled with a u not an ea. God, it's breathtaking," she added. "I can't imagine what it must be like to live here. It's been such miserable weather in London."

Adam rested his arms behind his head. "Maybe you could franchise your workshops over here."

"I'm not exactly running a conglomerate, you know." She laughed.

"I'm just saying there's opportunity here. California can always use another workshop!"

"I'm listening. But I'd rather hear more about you and what happened when the marriage was over."

"I worked a lot, partied a lot, the usual stuff. But it's your turn now. I want to hear all about you – the personal stuff."

Holding her hand up to block the sun, more to deflect the question, she realized, India shifted her chair into the shade.

"I'm British, remember? We don't 'do' personal stuff. However, I will tell you that I've never been married and I'm free as a bird. Well, at the moment, anyway." As in, "miserably unattached for some time," she thought.

"That's good news," Adam said, rising from his seat. "Let's swap."

Touched by his gallantry, India changed places. The two girls at the next table were staring at him. One had turned around and was pretending to adjust the strap of her shoe, while the other was checking him out with her makeup mirror.

"Thank you. I didn't plan on being at the beach," she said, "or I'd have worn something more covered." Possibly a straw hat, a polka-dot shirt, white-framed sunglasses and a touch of red lipstick...? "So tell me. What do you do when you're not working?"

Adam sighed. "Last couple of years, I've been obsessed with the fitness thing. Typical, I guess. I run most mornings and I've hired this killer personal trainer. She's got me into yoga and meditation and even some behavioral psychology."

"I've heard of that. Hasn't it got something to do with hypnotism?"

"Yeah. I used it to stop smoking."

"I tried hypnosis to stop drinking," India said, noticing that the girl behind them was still "adjusting her shoe." "The hypnotist reprogrammed my subconscious to stop after the second glass of wine. Unfortunately, by the time I had the second glass, my subconscious was drunk, too."

"I'll drink to that." Adam laughed, raising his glass. "And I sure hope you're hungry."

"I'm always hungry," India said as a huge platter of sizzling king prawns and lobster appeared like magic between them. "And why is everything in America so much BIGGER than everywhere else?" she added. "I mean, how do you swallow something that big?" she said, spearing one of the giant prawns.

"I'll just pretend I didn't hear a double entendre there," he said.

India fluttered her eyelashes. "Mr. Brooks I have absolutely no idea to what you are referring!"

"And so moving on…" He grinned. "Let's get back to this franchise of yours. I have a lot of friends, you know. I'm connected. I could help."

Wrenching a vibrating cell phone from his front pocket, he rolled his eyes. "Hold onto that thought. Okay. I'll be right back, I promise."

Glancing at a young girl sauntering by in a pair of shorts and Ugg boots, India dipped a chunk of lobster into hot pepper sauce. Her heart was racing at the idea of taking Adam up on his offer. But where do I even begin to run workshops for women who wear fur-lined suede boots and shorts in ninety degrees of heat?

She gazed out across the expanse of ocean. Adam was unsettling her. It wasn't just that he turned her on, it was much more than that; he was breaking down her carefully constructed barriers. She wanted to be in his arms. She wanted her head on his shoulder. She would feel safe there. She realized she'd not felt safe in a long time.

He was back.

"Sorry, India. My agent," he said, sliding back into his chair. "He keeps sending stuff over for me to look at and setting up meetings. But nothing grabs me... It's always the same shit, same character."

Sensing his frustration, India sipped her wine. "Why don't you tell him you're tired of it, that you need a change?"

"Don't I wish," Adam replied, stabbing at his salad. "You need a lot of leverage in this town to pull off a trick like that, believe me."

India was flummoxed. "But you're Adam Brooks."

Adam nearly choked on his prawn. "Right. Remind me to remind him of that the next time I turn down a script."

"Well, Annie says that there's always someone coming up behind you; someone younger I suppose she meant, but isn't it different for men?"

"In some ways, but again it's about what scripts get to you. India, you've managed to make the whole conversation about me again. How 'bout dessert? Or tea? Are the English still into tea?"

"Yes, but only if it's made in a teapot," she said, laughing. "No dessert. I'm fine. This has been a wonderful lunch. And I listen to you because I like to listen to you. Your life interests me."

"So I guess listening to you will be a pleasure postponed, eh?" He grinned and signaled for the check. "I should definitely get you back. And I swore to Max I'd be there for the start of the Lakers game. Plus I think we're being tweeted," he said, gesturing at some girls huddled over their iPhones.

Gloriously at ease after so much sun, talk, good food, and wine, India relaxed into her seat on the ride back. It wasn't until she felt the automatic click of her seat belt that she woke up.

"Hello, Miss India. You're home," Adam said as she sat up, startled, and the entire contents of her purse spilled all over the floor of the car.

"It's the heat," she apologized, scrambling for her keys and … Tampax. Omygod! Tampax, she shrieked to herself. And earplugs from the flight!

"Get some more rest," Adam suggested with a grin as he leaned across to open her door. "And I'll call you tomorrow."

"Thanks, great," she mumbled, then disappeared fast round to the side of the guesthouse, where she stopped and leaned up against the wall. I don't believe I did that. I am never, repeat, NEVER drinking in the daytime again.

Annabelle was sprawled out on the chintz sofa in the kitchen with her eyes closed when India aimed for the fridge.

"Wow! That was some cup of coffee, darling," she said with a yawn.

India kicked off her shoes, gave her sister a kiss, and fell onto the sofa next to her.

"How about some nice ice-cold lemonade?" Annie offered, gesturing to the glacier blue ceramic jug in her hand. India was so thirsty, she was ready to lick the beads of icy condensation right off the side of it.

"Absolutely. I'm so dehydrated, I feel like Lawrence of Arabia when he walked into that bar in Cairo."

"Of course, Peter O'Toole." Annie laughed "We want two glasses of lemonade – lemonade with ice."

"Pitch perfect, as ever." India laughed.

"Go ahead. Drink up," Annabelle ordered, while touching her sister's sunburned nose. "And let me get you some aloe vera so you don't peel."

"I'm sorry I didn't call. I was in Malibu."

"I figured no news must mean good news. From that look on your face, I'd say things are going well?"

India nodded. "Apart from this sunburn... Annie, I feel like I'm dreaming. Do we have plans for tonight?"

Slathering her sister's arm with aloe, Annie shook her head. "I thought we might order in, watch a movie? I'm awfully tired. Would that disappoint you too much?"

"I'd love it. Listen, why don't you lot have a quiet night to yourselves? I'll watch a movie on that huge TV in my room," India said, slipping into her moccasins.

"Sounds like a plan, good. And don't forget. We have Fran's fundraiser tomorrow afternoon. I think you might have a good time. I think you might like these people."

"I'm sure I will, Annie. And I love you. I really do, and once again I'm so sorry for my outburst the other day, and I like Lizzie – a lot."

"I have some great friends, you know. Not everyone in LA is a phony, no matter what you might think on the other side of the pond. Sleep well. I love you too."

India fluttered her toes in the pomegranate-oil-scented bathtub and sighed. Could she really be looking at the possibility of making a major change in her life, of launching workshops? Why had she lied to Adam? What was so embarrassing about being a great teacher? Will I always feel inadequate, that I don't measure up? she wondered.

Unwrapping the tissue from another bar of her favorite French milled soap, India flinched at the memory of her meltdown in the kitchen. She'd hurt Annie by criticizing her friends and poking fun at Summer. But it was Simon Clements and his vibrating soul who'd really pressed her buttons. He'd triggered something deep in her. She'd resented him holding the room captive and getting the adulation. Why? Was it because she felt she had nothing much to show for her own years of hard slog? Yes, that was it. But whose fault was that? What had held her back from looking for promotion, for reaching for more? What?

Stepping gingerly out of the tub, India was in such a hurry that she didn't bother to towel herself dry. She'd check out Simon's website, see for herself what this man, such a hero to people here, had to offer. Skidding across the tiles she grabbed a robe and paced the bedroom a couple of times before sitting down at the Louis XVI secretaire and drumming her fingers on the leather top.

Maybe instead of getting angry, she thought, opening up her laptop, I should do some research, work out how to exploit my own "skill-set" as Tony Robbins calls it. Okay ... www.simonclements.com...

Photographs slid across the screen in a horizontal montage; Simon smiling alongside the President of the United States, shaking hands with the Queen of England, hugging movie stars and sports icons, standing bookended by Playboy bunnies. No question about it. He got around. Sanskrit icons directed her to page after page of product; everything from books, tapes, and video to incense and Himalayan crystals.

Then there it was, flanked by a pair of doves flying across a waterfall to the tinkle of wind chimes and a pan flute: "Vibrating Soul Consciousness and the Law of Attraction."

"You should write down what you want to happen in the present tense so as to trick your subconscious into believing you already have it. You can manifest anything. Visualize it clearly."

She bent back the soft blue leather binding of her "Profound Thoughts" notepad and sighed. Okay. It's worth a try, I suppose; I mean, how else am I going to get on Oprah? Picking up the Mont Blanc fountain pen, she began writing.

"I have Adam Brooks." No. Scratch that, sounds too possessive. Okay. "I am a workshop leader. I am successful. I live in California." Replacing the cap on the pen, she shook her head. I'm cracking up. This is insane. If Sarah could see me now she'd go hysterical. Okay. Visualize.

Settling herself flat on the bed, India closed her eyes. She had absolutely no difficulty visualizing Adam, although, curiously, the images that floated past were mostly of him from behind. He did have an exceptionally cute ass.

Okay, focus… I am looking fabulous. I am thirty-six. Scratch that, she thought drowsily. I am almost….

≈≈≈≈≈≈≈≈

Screeching up a side street in her green Prius, Lizzie cursed. "Fucking traffic! Fucking Stan! I've had it!" Her "deconstructed" Frank Gehry showplace wasn't a home. It was some kind of architect's statement. "Fifteen million and the place looks like it's falling apart," she muttered to herself, pulling into the garage. "Just like the family that lives in it." Her jaw was aching. Peering into the playroom window, she glanced at Teri, the third nanny in as many weeks, who was sitting on a sofa, watching a video with the kids in the playroom.

"Hi, guys!" she shouted with false cheer as she slipped into the kitchen, which despite being the size of an airplane hangar, felt crowded. Nothing. No response. Not from anyone. Sophie was literally inside the gigantic double-door fridge, foraging around for ice cream. The marble counter was covered with crumbs, discarded food wrappers, water glasses, and chips. Cell phones, purses, and clothes lay in heaps all over the floor. Two girls in tiny bikinis whom she'd never even met lounged in front of the TV screen, dipping chips in guacamole and screaming obscenities at America's Top Model.

On the verge of tears, Lizzie touched Sophie on the shoulder. "Hey, how are you?" she said.

"Good," Sophie said between spoonfuls of ice cream, and without turning round.

"Aren't you going to introduce me to your friends?" Lizzie said pointedly.

"Sure," Sophie mumbled. "That's Amy and that's Julie."

"Right, very helpful, thanks," Lizzie replied.

Sophie signaled her friends and turned to leave the room.

"Ah sorry, but would you mind picking up a few things while you're at it?" Lizzie said, pointing to the heap of clothing strewn on the floor.

Sophie kicked a few articles of clothing around in front of her before leaning over to pick up a couple of items.

"See ya," she said, heading toward the stairs and tossing her bleached blonde hair over her shoulder.

Lizzie inhaled deeply. There was something so wrong about this picture. It was her house, and yet she felt powerless in it. Where were the boundaries? How could you demand respect? Where would you start to connect with another female who clearly looked on you as the enemy?

After swallowing two Advils, she decided to ignore the rudeness and focus on what kept her sane: her charity work. She and Fran had scheduled a major fundraiser the next day for the African Children's Choir. Turning off the TV, she picked up the phone. Most of her wealthy friends were delighted to write off big chunks of cash for her causes and, as Stan was one of the most powerful entertainment lawyers in town, they had no problem wooing A-list talent to their galas and house events. The last lunch, featuring Rihanna, had made it into a two-page spread in Vanity Fair.

The Advil hadn't made a dent in her headache. She put down the phone. Just the thought of being social, of meeting and greeting people and smiling next to Stan, made her nauseous. "So much pretending," she fumed. "Putting up this façade of being such a happy family. I can't bear it!"

She'd spent years working with families who practically killed themselves to give their kids a chance to go to college, while Stan's kid, Henry, the arrogant, swaggering little prig, would probably just sail into Harvard. No way her own kids were going to live in this absurdly privileged, isolated world of private jets and vacation villas in Mustique and Anguilla, a world where standing in line at Starbucks was as close as they ever came to hardship.

Sophie was another kind of nightmare. The erratic moods and the belligerence … Lizzie tried not to monitor her too much – her hands were full with the twins. But honestly, did the girl do anything other than take fucking photos of herself with her iPhone, puckering and pouting half naked, and post them all over the planet on Facebook?

Lizzie dragged herself up the stairs to her bedroom. After a quick shower, she changed into a pair of pink velvet Juicy sweatpants, pulled her knees up to her chest on top of the empty Kyoto platform California king-size bed, and sobbed herself to sleep.

PROFOUND THOUGHTS NOTE – Maybe...just maybe.

Annabelle valet parked the Mercedes station wagon and she and India walked through an old stone porch, into a pillared marble entrance hall, and out onto the grounds of Fran's residence.

"Valet parking." India laughed. "Try tossing your keys at someone in London and you'd never see your car again."

"True." Annie smiled.

"Omygod, it's bigger than Kensington Palace," India exclaimed, taking in the tall clipped hedges framing a pathway across miles of manicured green lawn. "It's like the Tuileries in Paris," she added, awestruck at the view of the arc of water from a fountain spraying across the infinity pool.

"I feel like I'm in some kind of BBC minidrama," she whispered to Annie. "I should be carrying a King Charles spaniel or something."

"You look great," Annie whispered.

"Yes, well, when you told me it was an afternoon fundraiser I was thinking more along the lines of those school bake sales at St. Mary's, not this," she said, nodding toward a girl in a black satin gown playing the harp. India was regretting the white cotton summer skirt and Liberty print blouse she had chosen so carefully.

"Thank you," she said, accepting a crystal glass of champagne from a waitress who bore an uncanny resemblance to Penélope Cruz.

India followed Annie through the milling guests, past velvet covered auction tables and valuable paintings, silk embroidered cushions and cashmere throws. As she reached the jasmine-covered arbor, where Lizzie and some friends were clustered around a chintz sofa, she took a long sip of the deliciously fizzy drink.

"WOW! India, you look great!" Lizzie enthused, kissing her on both cheeks. You remember Stan? The hypocritical two-timing bastard I married? she said to herself.

"Nice to see you, India. It's been too long," Stan said without intonation. "And this is the extraordinary Florence," he added, putting his arm, protectively, around the tiny, elderly woman next to him. She was so slight and bony, so frail in her two-piece Chanel suit and quilted bag that India thought she might blow away.

"Florence has just made a hugely generous pledge," Stan gushed. "I don't know how to thank her."

"Oh. Stan, please," the woman said coquettishly. "My little gift goes to such a worthy cause. It's my pleasure, always. And you're such an inspiration, you and Lizzie. Such a beautiful couple. You remind me how much I miss Larry."

"I'm sure it must be hard without him," Lizzie said, digging her fingernails into her palms.

"We were childhood sweethearts," Florence said, her eyes shiny. "He waited until I was eighteen to ask my parents if he could marry me. It's not like that these days, except when I look at the two of you."

Lizzie refused to look at Stan, the charming shit who had somehow managed to wheedle a six-figure check faster than Henry could tie his shoelaces.

Nibbling on her third shrimp, India finished her champagne and accepted another from a Brad Pitt look-alike waiter.

"I'm on vacation." She smiled cheerily.

"So happy for you." He grinned back. "Have a good one."

India was admiring Lizzie's effortless chic; her classic, cream Prada sheath, her taupe patent leather pumps, sophisticated chignon and Tahitian pearl studs. Ten grand for the dress, two grand for the shoes, can't see the purse... And I bet she can run on the treadmill for hours without breaking a sweat.

"So India," Lizzie said, turning with relief to chat with her, "how long are you staying? I'd love to have you over for lunch. Are you free next week?"

"I am totally free, Lizzie. And I'd love it."

The sound of a crackling microphone made any further attempts to talk futile. "Forgive me. I'm in public mode today and I think I hear them calling me," Lizzie said graciously before floating across the lawn to meet Fran at the podium.

As Fran made her introductions, India set her phone to vibrate and desperately tried to visualize a text or call from Adam ... He's calling, he's calling now. Then she settled back in her chair, mesmerized by Fran's eloquence and stunned by the profusion of superlatives at her disposal; the myriad ways she found to compliment Lizzie's compassion, intelligence, and wit.

You'd think she was awarding the Nobel Peace prize, she thought. Dr. White could pick up a few tips from her, that's for sure.

As a group of African children sang and danced their way through "The Circle of Life" from The Lion King, India fought off a feeling of being emotionally manipulated and wandered toward a groaning buffet table. Torn between the lavender grilled prime beef tenderloin with artichokes and the miniature lamb chops with mint sauce and fingerling potatoes, she'd decided to have a bit of both, when her phone buzzed. It wasn't easy, prolonging the pleasure of picking up. It lasted for about ten seconds.

"Hey, it's me, Adam. Where are you?"

"At a lunch with Annie," she said, beaming. "What about you?" she asked, juggling the full plate with the phone.

"Can you talk now? Shall I call you back?" he asked.

"No, no, it's fine."

"Okay," Adam said, fading out for a moment. "Listen, we're throwing a bash for Fred Stein at Chateau Marmont later. I'm over here now, pulling it together. Wanna come? Max could pick you up and I can drop you off... You could have another nice sleep on the way home."

"Very funny." She laughed.

"So you'll come?" he said.

"I'd love to. Tell me, who's Fred Stein?"

"Okay, India. Now I really do know you lead a sheltered life. He's the only other living director whose name can be spoken in the same breath as Spielberg."

"Right," she said. "Well, I look forward to meeting him then."

"Max'll pick you up around seven thirty if that works for you?"

"It works for me. Yes. Sounds cool." Did she just say "cool"? Yes, she said "cool."

"See you then," Adam replied.

India now had zero appetite. Dropping the phone into her bag, she abandoned her plate, and then spotted Annie across the garden. It was three o'clock, and her sister looked weary beyond words. Deftly sidestepping a young woman's attempt to engage her in conversation, India moved swiftly across the lawn.

"Thank God," Annie whispered. "Ready to go?"

"Yes. It's been lovely but I'm dying in this heat."

"Take care and thank you so much for coming," Fran said, shepherding an elderly man and his wife down the pebbled path toward their waiting chauffeur while Annie and Lizzie stood near the door.

"Phew!" Fran smiled, kicking off her high heels before coming back to join them. "Those two should have their own star on the Walk of Fame. They've been together fifty-three years."

"Wonderful, yes, gives you hope for us all," Annie replied, opening her blue ostrich leather wallet and handing her friend a check.

"It's too much," Fran said, catching a brief glimpse of the zeros.

"It's my pleasure, darling. I adored watching those kids dance. You're a saint."

"Not quite, Lizzie," she said as they hugged and she turned to India. "By the way, I hear you're keeping very busy. He's quite elusive, your Mr. Brooks. You must be doing something right."

"I'm trying," India said, laughing.

As Annabelle negotiated their way through a detour off Sunset and onto the UCLA campus, India broke the silence. "You're very thoughtful," she remarked. " Anything I should know about?"

"I've been dying to talk to you, darling," Annabelle said, veering away from the throngs of kids on skateboards and bicycles jumping blindly off the sidewalks and curbs and onto the street. "I really have. But the timing just hasn't been right. And there's so much going on…"

"Watch out!" India shouted as a black four-by-four Lexus shot out in front of them.

"Relax, darling. The kids here start driving when they're fifteen after about two lessons. Talk to me. Tell me about what's going on with Adam," she said, keeping an eye on the Lexus as they stopped at a red light.

"Remember that night at the Polo Lounge when I asked you not to mention my teaching? I wanted to seem mysterious?

"Ah yes." Annabelle said as the light changed and the traffic inched forward. "I remember. The thing is, I've always been so proud of what you do, darling – "

Annabelle stopped midsentence and suddenly sat up straighter. After passing them in such a lethal hurry, the Lexus now seemed to have slowed down. "Okay," she said, "lock your door. Don't panic."

"What is it?" India asked. "Omygod, he's out of the car. He's coming toward us."

"Fuck," Annie muttered, as a guy ran up and took their picture through the windshield. Her hands were trembling as she rested her head on the steering wheel.

There was a deafening blast of horns from behind them.

"Do you want me to drive?" India asked.

Annie lifted her head and laughed. "Yes, right. Then we'd really be in trouble. Sorry, you never know… the minute… Just distract me. Tell me more about Adam. I'm fine."

"You sure?"

"Yep!" Annie said, slowly turning the corner and finally moving back onto Sunset.

"Well, I ended up somehow giving him the impression that I teach adults, not kids, and he suggested I open some workshops here. He even said he'd help."

Annie took her eyes off the road for a moment, and smiled. "But that sounds terrific. Everybody comes to LA to reinvent themselves. You could teach acting or become a voice coach or…"

"You really think so? I'm so tired of seeing the same people and doing the same thing every day. And Annie – we're about to turn forty."

"Not in this town darling. Keep that one under your hat. I intend to stay thirty-six for at least another ten years. Seriously though, I do think it's a marvelous idea. And you'd be so good at it. It's not like you're pretending to be a dentist or a surgeon. That would be bad." She laughed. "You're a teacher. Period. Plus, I would love it if you moved over here. I miss you."

"Yes and you're all the family I've got," India said. "At least you have Joss and the kids. You know, I really did think that Dad might have at least put in an appearance at Mother's funeral."

"Darling, even if he had, there's no guarantee he would have turned up sober, and it was bad enough as it was. Let it go…" She paused.

India broke the awkward silence. "Annie! It means a lot to me that you think it's possible."

As the sign for Bel Air appeared in the distance, Annie glanced in her rearview mirror and signaled to make the turn. "And what about Adam Brooks? He's clearly smitten. He's not playing hard to get, is he?"

"No, he isn't. And I'm pinching myself about it," India confessed. "He's arranged for Max to pick me up later for a birthday party at Chateau Marmont."

"Ah! Yes – dear Freddy. I sent our apologies a few weeks back. Joss can't be dragged out these days, he's so over the scene. You'll have fun though."

Preempting India's next question, Annabelle added, "You can wear anything but the new Jimmy Choos."

"Thank you. I love you," India said as the gates to the house swung open and she jumped out of the car.

"Fantastic!" she shouted, running for the guest room to shower. "I'll talk to you later."

≈≈≈≈≈≈≈≈

Lizzie felt so defeated, so empty, after Fran's luncheon with Stan, that her head throbbed. When she'd seen him flirting shamelessly with yet another hot blonde starlet, she'd done something that was totally against her own rules. She left. She left without even saying goodbye. With the car windows wide open, she drove straight toward the ocean at Santa Monica and parked. Breathing in the sea air and watching the neon lights of the merry-go-round, she tried to put her thoughts and her feelings into some kind of order.

Lizzie had always known that Stan was driven, fiercely ambitious. He'd graduated cum laude from Harvard and wasted no time taking advantage of his contacts, building up a law practice so quickly and successfully, people were still stunned. She also knew that his first wife, Joan, had wasted no time in divorcing him. Especially after discovering his affair with her best friend and the godmother of her children. The divorce settlement became the talk of the town and was on record as the craziest payout in the history of Hollywood philandering.

Looking back now, Lizzie understood that Stan had set about finding himself a new wife the same way he might have bought a racehorse. She had to be young, intelligent, socially dynamic, and rich. Lizzie fit the bill on all counts. A civil rights lawyer with an independent income, she defied her own instincts (not to mention everyone else's) and married him. She bought the trophy house for him as a wedding gift, a house she hated. And she spent years entertaining new clients while Stan sipped his Rémy Martin and showed off his art and fine wine collections, and his staged golfing photos at Pebble Beach with Padraig Harrington. The ones with Tiger Woods had mysteriously disappeared some time ago.

Blowing her nose with a scrunched up tissue, Lizzie finally accepted she had to go home, although the thought of checking into the Montage for a deep tissue massage and room service was tempting. Backing up slowly, Lizzie took one last look at the merry-go-round and headed back up Wilshire Boulevard.

Sneaking upstairs, Lizzie ignored the relentless pound of punk coming from the back end of the house and the sounds of Disney in the kitchen. After closing the doors to her bedroom, she clicked the remote and a Gershwin prelude filled the room. This was her reward, a night off all by herself. Slipping out of her tight linen sheath and kicking off her taupe heels, she began sorting through her closet. It calmed her, this ritual of rearranging the padded hangers and touching the soft cashmere.

When she heard the hammering at the door, she dropped a sweater to the floor and grabbed a bathrobe. "Stop hammering," she yelled, impatiently. "I'm coming."

"It's not my fault! It's not my fault!" the girl shrieked. It was Sophie's friend. She looked terrified. She was shaking.

Lizzie went cold with fear and grabbed the girl by the shoulders. "Calm down. Count to three. And tell me what's happened. Is it Rhonda? The twins? What?"

"We were only messing around. I didn't give her anything, I swear," she slurred.

Lizzie felt lightheaded, nauseous. Racing down the corridor, she flung open the door to the bathroom. Sophie was lying in a pool of vomit, her head tilted at an odd angle on the toilet bowl.

"CALL 911 NOW!" she ordered, then pushed past the girl and ran down to her room in search of her cell. She flung herself into a pair of jeans. Where the fuck was Stan?

The girl was whimpering next to her. "Tell me what she's taken!" Lizzie said. "THINK."

"Nothing," the girl muttered. "Nothing."

"It was something. Tell me. Look at her. Tell me right now. What did she take?"

Lizzie looked around. The bathroom floor was chaos, littered with junk food, dirty clothes, makeup. Then she saw the bottles of vodka and scotch. Not sure whether to move Sophie or leave her where she was, she gently lifted her wrist and felt for a pulse. It was there, weak, but there. Lizzie's friend sat down, rocking back and forth, crying uncontrollably. It was just past midnight. Stan should be home.

"Stan! Stan!" Lizzie shouted, desperate for backup. Would the ambulance never come? Her voice was lost in the wail of sirens. At last he appeared at the door looking shell-shocked. Dazed. Flying downstairs to open the doors, she watched as the emergency crew set up a stretcher. Answering their rapid-fire questions: "Drugs? I don't think … maybe … don't know … vodka, vodka yes. Definitely too much to drink…" She looked at Stan as they wheeled Sophie out of the bathroom and toward the stairs. The man, the father of this child, hadn't said a single word.

Lizzie's voice was pure ice. "She's your daughter. Get Joan out of bed right now! Call her, and take responsibility for something for once in your life."

Stan left the room like a child simply doing what he was told.

"Take off your clothes and get in the shower," Lizzie said to Sophie's friend, firmly. "You'll feel better."

Turning the water on full blast, she took the girl's hand. "What's your name? I have to phone your parents."

"Amy. My name is Amy Stein. I'm sorry. Don't tell my parents," she pleaded, stepping into the shower.

"It's okay," Lizzie reassured her as she waited, then handed her a towel. " Lie down. Get some rest. I'll be back in a minute."

"Where the hell is Henry?" Lizzie wondered. "How could Sophie's brother possibly have slept through this?"

Knocking on his door, she told him what had happened and, miracle of miracles, he was calm. He found Amy's cell phone, called her parents, and tentatively put his arms around his stepmother.

"Tea?" she asked, moved by the boy's affectionate gesture, by his youth. "I'll make us some tea while we wait for the Steins."

C'EST LA VIE NOTE – Hope Chateau Marmont is earthquake proof.

India almost had a heart attack when the fire engine screamed up from behind them and Max pulled his silver Maserati briefly over to the side of the road. Cutting and weaving again through the traffic on Santa Monica toward Sunset, he grinned. "You're a knockout!" he said. "Adam's a lucky guy."

"Thanks." India beamed, yanking Annabelle's Stella McCartney minidress down over her thighs.

If I do come to live in LA it'll be Hollywood, this end of town, she thought, taking in the jumble of cowboy bars and shacks, the tacky sex stores nestling along sleek high-rises. As they swung into the steep incline of the driveway at Chateau Marmont, the soft convertible roof slid closed over their heads and Max braked, sharply.

Someone was banging on the windows. India ducked at the blinding flashes of light and put her hands over her ears as the crowd shouted Max's name.

"Hey, Max? How was rehab?"

"Is that your date?"

"Is your sister here, Max?"

"Max, Max."

"Fuck it. I'm sorry, India. I should have warned you. Just stick close to me and it'll be all right."

India sat frozen in her seat before scrabbling around the floor in search of her Jimmy Choo clutch and faux fur stole. "Is it always like this?" she asked Max.

"Yeah. But I'm used to it, you know," he said as they waited in the car for security to help clear a path. "Actually, I just pretend I'm used it to," he muttered before looking her in the eye. "You ready?"

"Guess so," she said, adjusting Annabelle's chandelier earrings, which she was regretting. Two heavyweight bouncers were pulling a guy off their bumper as Max revved the engine, and they edged toward the valet garage.

India clutched Max's hand. "They've really gone for this château thing," she said with a sigh, trying to negotiate the cobblestone path in Annie's vertiginous Louboutins and following him toward a tiny elevator and down a service passage into a crowded room.

"Don't let go," he said, heading for an outside deck where the city lights twinkled beneath them. She let go the moment she saw Adam loosen his tie and make a beeline for them from the bar.

"You look gorgeous," he yelled in her ear before two perfectly toned arms were thrown around his neck and a girl in a midnight blue satin dress snaked her way around the rest of him.

"Angel," he said, kissing the top of the girl's head and hugging her tightly. India flinched.

How could anyone be that thin and stay vertical? she wondered, as Adam introduced them.

"This is Angel, my personal trainer," he said, turning to wave at the bartender. He missed the girl's steely-eyed glance at India before she flicked her eyelashes and disappeared into the crowd. Max had reappeared at her side, nudging a stunningly handsome man forward. She recognized him but couldn't for the life of her remember his name.

"Michael, say hello to India," Max said, before backing up toward the bar.

Omygod Sarah will DIE, India thought. She has his entire BBC miniseries on DVD.

"Lovely to meet you," Michael said in the softest of Irish brogues. "Let me get you a drink. You look like a girl who likes a vodka martini with an olive. Am I right?"

"Well, actually..." she mumbled, just as Adam inched his way between them, cutting off the possibility of further conversation.

"Sorry, mate, but no. She's a Sancerre Sauvignon blanc all the way."

"Ah, Adam," the Irishman said, "you have excellent taste in women, as well as wine." And giving India a charming smile, he turned away.

India took a quick glance around the room. It was amazing how these famous faces looked without airbrushing. The tattooed eyebrows and lids, the collagen pumped lips, the overstretched skin. Only Sharon Stone was as glamorous as India had imagined. Standing in a transparent shift that shimmered in the light, her legs really did seem to go on forever. "Honey, as far as I'm concerned, leopard print's a neutral," India overheard her say to the woman next to her. But where was Adam?

"Adam's doing the intro," Max said, as the lights went up, and Fred Stein walked into the room and covered his face with his hands as the crowd went crazy, whistling and stamping their feet.

From up onstage Adam grabbed the microphone and gestured toward his friend. "Happy birthday, Fred. Now come right over and have a seat in front. You're not the director tonight. For once, I think you'll agree we clearly have the advantage."

Fred blinked away tears. "No crying yet," Adam added, patting his shoulder. "Not until you see Forty Fucking Fabulous Fotos of Fred."

A screen dropped down from the ceiling and a whoop went up at the photo of a one-year-old Fred in diapers.

"Still full of shit!" someone yelled irreverently, triggering a burst of laughter.

India grabbed a barstool. How wonderful, she said to herself. To be here in this room like this. Not alone or a plus one with Annie, but as a real guest with this wonderful, drop-dead gorgeous man who has just sat down next to me ... and is at this very moment squeezing my hand.

A number of Academy Award–winning actors then proceeded to present spoof Oscars to Fred, before a childhood friend popped out from behind a curtain, his wife pulled him onstage, and Barbra Streisand belted out "The Way We Were."

"Wow!" India shouted as she clapped till her hands hurt. When the reggae band came in and began to set up, Adam, now standing near again, looked at her. The electricity between them was so strong, so palpable, she thought she might fall over.

"Let's get out of here," he said huskily, taking her hand and pulling her through the waves of people milling around in front of them. When the elevator doors closed, he kissed her hard, cradling her head in his hands, his tongue searching her mouth. The elevator pinged and she felt the cold of the mirrored wall at her back as she struggled, weak-kneed, to prize herself away as another couple entered the tiny space. Neither she nor Adam said a word on the way to Adam's West Hollywood apartment. The minute he turned the key in the lock, they stumbled in together and Adam tore off his tie. Unbuttoning his shirt, holding her tightly against his chest, he unzipped her dress. She trembled as he gently kissed her forehead, and unclipped her earrings. Fluttering his lips over her neck and shoulders, he lifted her up and carried her into the bedroom.

≈≈≈≈≈≈≈

India had been in such a deep, heavy sleep that she didn't know where she was when the sound of a phone woke her. Rolling over, she saw Adam scrabble around on the bedside table top and turn on the light.

"Who is this?" he said brusquely, as she stretched and gazed up at the ceiling. She looked at the digits on the alarm clock. It was two - thirty. It was the urgency in Adam's voice that made her suddenly sit up and look at him.

"Of course," he said, hurriedly. "I'll be there right away. Give me twenty minutes."

India touched his arm as he sprang out of bed and rummaged through a drawer. "It's Max. He's been in a bad accident. They looked through his wallet and found me listed as the emergency contact."

"Oh my God! How bad?" India asked, pulling herself to her feet. "I'll come with you. I mean, if you'd like me to."

"I would. I'm scared, India," Adam replied, zipping up his jeans and slipping his head through a tee shirt. "People used to say that Max had nine lives. But those nine lives were over years ago."

Quickly gathering together the trail of clothing she had strewn across the floor only hours before, India zipped up her dress.

"It may not be as bad as it sounds," she said, clutching her shoes as they ran down the stairs. Within minutes, the two of them were speeding down Wilshire Boulevard toward the emergency room in Westwood Village, and Adam filled her in on Max's sad and terrifying history of close calls; the car crashes, the overdoses, the crazy all-nighters, the breakdowns.

"It may have just been an ordinary car crash," she volunteered. "Maybe it's not even his fault."

"Yeah, well, it'll be a first if it isn't. Let's hope."

India understood some of what Adam must be feeling. The drive was reminding her all too vividly of another call in the night and a dash to a hospital where she had found her mother wired to a labyrinth of monitors. She was remembering the hours at her side, the faint rhythm of her breathing and then the low-pitched hollow noise she hoped never to hear again; a gurgling rattle. India had sat alone, holding her mother's icy hand for some time before alerting a nurse and calling Annie long distance to break the news.

"Get your head down," Adam told her, as a horde of paparazzi leapt out with a flurry of flashbulbs. "Fucking assholes."

Screeching into the hospital gates, he parked and leapt from the car. India raced behind him to a night porter who gave them directions, and they ran down a long corridor to an elevator and into a starkly lit waiting room.

"Adam Brooks. You called me. My friend, Max Cohen? He's here?" he asked the night orderly.

"Yes," she said. "I'll tell Dr. Lee you're here. Take a seat," she added, gesturing to a line of plastic chairs that India noticed were attached to each other. Why would you do that? she wondered. Who would want to steal them?

They sat in silence watching the swing doors flapping open and closed as gurneys were pushed through.

"Mr. Brooks?"

Adam let go of India's hand and stood as a woman in a white coat approached them.

"Dr. Lee," she said quickly. "How're you?"

"Good thanks. How're you?" Adam answered.

This American formality struck India as weird. You could be lying in a pool of blood, all your relatives massacred and this would still be the ritual greeting? She knew she was on edge. At times of crisis the voice in her head always seemed to throw up the most inappropriate one-liners. Please let Max be okay. Please...

"What's happened? Is he okay? Can I see him?" Adam said in a rush.

"Your friend's been very lucky." The doctor smiled reassuringly. "We're pretty sure he just had a mild concussion, although we can't rule out internal bleeding completely. We'll need to do a scan and a toxicology report. We haven't been able to contact anyone in his family yet. Can you help us with that?"

"Sure," Adam answered. "I'll call his mother. How'd it happen?"

"I'm afraid I'm not able to tell you," she said. "There was a traffic accident. The LAPD were on the scene fast. They'll file a full report. Please excuse me."

India touched Adam's arm reassuringly. "He's going to be fine. He is," she whispered as a nursing assistant led them to a tiny side room.

"You can use your phone in here," the nurse said.

Adam began thumbing his BlackBerry, scrolling down the numbers.

"We're in for a long night," India said. "I'll see if I can find some coffee."

She was back ten minutes later with two Cokes.

"It seemed a safer bet," she said, handing him the icy can. "Any news yet?"

"His mother, Alanna, is on her way. She's a drama queen at the best of times, pretty unhinged. She'll probably put in a call to US Weekly before she leaves the house," he said. "I would guess Max's sister Lauren will come too. They're doing a reality show about their so-called 'relationship.' The two of them are like this scary doppelgänger thing."

"You really care about Max don't you? I'm so sorry. I feel so helpless," India said.

Adam squeezed her hand.

"Yes, I love him. We go back a long way. India, I'm sorry you got dragged into this."

"I'm glad I'm here, Adam," she said. "I understand."

"Where's my son? I want to see my son NOW! Did nobody hear me? Where's my son?"

The middle-aged woman tottering on her pink stilettos toward the admissions desk was wearing an inappropriately low-cut sheer blouse and skintight white leggings and reminded India of a blow-up sex doll. Trailing behind was a girl in a sweatshirt and pajama bottoms stabbing at her phone.

"Alanna?" India looked at Adam.

"How did you guess?" He nodded.

"I'm sorry. Could you please keep your voice down?" the receptionist whispered, covering her mouthpiece with her hand, "I'll be with you in just a moment."

"Do you know who I am?" Max's mother yelled.

Putting down the receiver the woman glared at Alanna over the top of her glasses.

"No ma'am, but I sure as hell think you're going to tell me."

"Max Cohen. Where is he?" Alanna demanded.

India had some sympathy for Alanna's hysteria, but was fascinated that Alanna's botoxed face wasn't conveying any of the emotions she was obviously feeling. That's a lot of work, India thought. Her mouth looks like somebody punched it. Which might be the case any second now if she doesn't shut up.

Adam got to his feet and walked over to her.

"Alanna, he's going to be okay," he said. "They're running some tests. He's in the radiology department right now. The doctors will let us know when there's more news. Let's wait in here," he said, guiding her with his arm into the privacy of their little waiting room. Max's sister looked up for a moment and shrugged.

"Whatever," she said, following them.

I suppose, India thought, playing your life out for the cameras is bound to distort your understanding of what's actually real and what's not.

"Hello, I'm India," she said, giving Alanna a sympathetic smile. "Annabelle Butler's sister."

Ignoring her, Alanna turned to Adam. "What's going on? You said there was an accident? What kind of an accident? Like a car accident or what? Were you with him? Was he drinking? Was he stoned?"

India sat quietly. She was exhausted. If only I wasn't wearing this stupid dress and these shoes, she thought. She was cold and her feet were throbbing. Then suddenly the mood shifted. A doctor appeared and, from his expression, she could see the news was good.

Max was out of danger. He had suffered a mild concussion and they would keep him under observation for a few days. Adam grinned at India and she beamed back at him.

"Thank you, Doctor," he said. "That's a great relief. I know he's in good hands."

As they walked slowly toward the exit sign, India let out a yelp and leapt back as the swinging doors flew open and a team of paramedics frantically negotiated a stretcher past her and Adam. The doors flapped closed and open again, leaving a distinguished-looking man and a somewhat bedraggled woman behind. India stood transfixed. Yes, it was definitely Stan. But who was that with him? They were standing stiffly, turned away from each other. What could possibly have happened? Where was Lizzie?

Adam tilted his head in their direction, indicating they should go over. He led them all back into the room they had been so glad to leave only a few short minutes before. Stan answered their unspoken question.

"It's Sophie," he told them. "Lizzie found her passed out in the bathroom. We have no idea how serious this might be."

Joan sat down. She said nothing, twisting her rings around her trembling fingers, her eyes on the floor.

"We'll stay," Adam said, "if it'll help."

"Thanks," Stan said. "I think Joan's in shock."

"I'll get her some water," India said. "Be right back." My God, she thought, this is like a soap opera with real actors playing all the parts.

Sipping tepid water from a plastic glass, Joan let out a wail and started to sob.

"My baby. My little girl."

India put her arm around her.

"Sophie is going to be just fine," she reassured her. "She'll be okay. She will."

Joan managed a weak smile.

"Where've we gone wrong? She's failing school ... she's ... God, is she going to be okay? Where is she?"

India thought fast, she needed to distract her. "What does she enjoy doing?" she said.

"Acting," Joan said, finally looking directly at Stan. "She likes painting too, doesn't she?"

Stan shifted in his chair uncomfortably. "That's not going to get her into Harvard, is it?" he muttered.

God, he's not helping at all, India thought. The poor woman's distraught. "Don't think about any of this right now," she said. "Drink some more water. Take a deep breath."

India held Joan's hand and they sat in silence for a while.

When, two hours later, an intern called Stan to the desk, India watched as Stan nodded and listened and then shook the doctor's hand. Coming back into the room, he was visibly shaken.

"She'd taken cocaine with a potentially lethal amount of vodka."

His voice had no trace of emotion. "They've pumped her stomach and sedated her. They got her in time. There's no brain damage," he added, pressing his fingers hard on the back of his neck and rubbing it. He had a bead of perspiration on his top lip.

"Cocaine? Sophie?" Joan gasped. "I had no idea. Stan, did you?"

"Do you want me to call Lizzie and tell her everything's under control?" India offered.

"Thanks, but I think I'd better speak to her," Stan said stiffly.

"You must be completely wiped. Let me take you straight home," Adam said to India, putting his arm around her protectively.

Thérèse

India nodded and leaned into his shoulder.

They drove out into the early morning sunshine, both blinking from the darkness of the underground car park. As they reached the road barrier, India's neck lashed as Adam screeched to a halt and slammed on the brakes. There must have been two hundred paparazzi, at least. It was like being in the centrifugal force of a swarm of locusts. India was genuinely terrified this time, but Adam was in no mood for it and swung swiftly into reverse. Zooming up the hospital driveway, he pulled over in front of the side exit. India followed him quickly into the marble interior, where he made a couple of calls. Within twenty minutes, she was en route back to Bel Air, hidden away in the safety of a chauffeured, tinted-glass Lincoln Town Car.

There was no sign of Annabelle. She's probably gone for a hike, India thought, yawning as she scribbled a note to let her know she was home and planning on sleeping late.

Adam drove straight out to Malibu. He knew the pack would be camped outside his Hollywood apartment and he needed to get close to the ocean, to feel the sand between his toes. He parked, relieved to see that there was no "guest" reception. Kicking off his shoes, he scrambled down the slope of the hillside and leapt across the sand to the edge of the shallow waves. The sudden jolt of ice-cold water felt good. He walked fast, hurling stones toward the farthest point of the ocean until his mind became calm and a feeling of utter fatigue overwhelmed him.

≈≈≈≈≈≈≈≈

She couldn't put it off any longer. She had to know. Once Joss had left the house with the girls for their tennis lessons, Annabelle put in a call to her doctor's office.

114

"I'll be over the minute I'm done with surgery," he told her.

"Thanks, Rand, I appreciate it," she said.

Her hand was trembling as she clicked off. She'd hardly slept. She lay in bed all night, listening to the rhythm of Joss' breathing and running the worst-case scenarios over and over again in her head. Her hand kept reaching for her throat. Maybe if I wish hard enough, it will go away, she'd thought. It was too much to take in. This was not supposed to happen. Everything was going so well, maybe too well. As her imagination ran riot, she found herself drafting letters of love for the girls to open on their birthdays after she had passed away. She was even picturing planning her own funeral, with Joss and India at her bedside.

No. I cannot possibly be thinking like this. I am not going to die. Get a grip girl, she told herself, but during the endless night it was impossible to control the waves of nausea that kept flooding over her and the constriction in her chest that made it difficult to breathe. She had never felt so utterly alone or vulnerable.

≈≈≈≈≈≈≈

Lizzie climbed out of bed and struggled into a pink cashmere robe. She looked out of the window. Stan emerged from his silver Mercedes looking worn and tired. She waited until she heard him dash upstairs and slam the bathroom door before heading down to the kitchen. He appeared a short while later, buttoning up his shirt as he walked toward the counter.

"There's coffee," Lizzie offered. "Have you eaten? Do you want breakfast?"

"Eggs would be good," he said. "Sophie's gone home with Joan... I had no idea..." He let the thought trail off.

"No. I know," Lizzie answered quietly. "I don't think Amy's mother was too delighted, either. They'd been at Fred's birthday party. Perfect timing, hey?" she added, flicking the whisk and pouring truffle oil into the mixture.

"Shit," he muttered, fastening his tie and checking the clock. "I was supposed to be at Nate 'n Al an hour ago." Fishing around for his BlackBerry, he speed-dialed his office.

"Tell him something urgent came up. See if he can do lunch … get a table at Toscana… Yes, rebook them for three o'clock. Put back the CAA meeting to four thirty…"

Your daughter almost died and it's business as usual, Lizzie thought bitterly, as Stan rattled off more instructions.

"Reschedule Peterson for tomorrow. I'll be there in twenty minutes."

"Sorry," he said, draining the last of the coffee and gesturing to the untouched plate. Then, hesitating for a second, "Let's talk later."

Yanking his briefcase from under the table, he lifted his key fob. He had pressed the remote for his car before even reaching the front door.

PROFOUND THOUGHTS NOTE – Check in with self

India woke to the squawk of blue jays and the irritating whine of a leaf blower. The afternoon sunshine was streaming through the painted wooden shutters as she lay in bed watching the dappled patterns on the walls and replaying scenes from the previous night: the arrival at Chateau Marmont, the emergency room, Adam leaping up for news of Max, and Stan, sitting there helplessly with Joan. How terrifying it must be to think you might lose someone you love, she thought. To sit hour after hour waiting like that for news. It was bad enough for me and I hardly know the guy.

And Adam. She couldn't believe how long it had been since she'd been in a man's arms, since she'd felt so desired. How easy it had been to tune in to him at the hospital, how they had talked in shorthand like old friends, as if they had known each other always.

Speaking of talk… This was another of those times when she missed Sarah. Thank goodness it wasn't too late to call London. When Sarah picked up, India found herself talking so fast she was out of breath. Then she paused for dramatic effect.

"Okay. Are you sitting down? Okay. Guess who offered to get me a drink? Ready for it … Michael Mulholland."

There was a high-pitched scream. India held the phone away from her ear.

"O my God. I hate you. Did you tell him you had a friend?"

India laughed. "I didn't get the chance. Adam was over like a shot when he saw him talking to me."

"Okay, this is all just too much. I am seriously jealous, Indie. Go on … I'm assuming… Am I assuming? Was it amazing?"

"Sarah, we are talking hot. I mean, it was off the Richter scale," she whispered. "I think I used some muscles I've not used in some time. In fact, I think I used some muscles I never knew I had!"

"Okay, India, I get the idea. You can stop right there; show a little pity please. As you know I have not managed to get laid for some considerable time… But I do want daily reports, please, and if you see our friend Michael again, I will not be speaking to you if you don't give him my number and tell him how fabulous I am."

"Promise. I promise, Sarah. Cross my heart."

India took a long, leisurely shower. The water felt prickly against her newly awakened skin. It was as if all her senses were suddenly raw and alive. Drying herself with a thick white towel, she picked out a bikini and an oversize cotton shirt and waltzed off toward the kitchen. Pure contentment, she thought, drinking in the smell of freshly mown grass.

Closing the picket gate behind her, she noticed an unfamiliar car in the driveway. The doors to the main house were closed over, too. When Annabelle caught sight of her through the French windows, she waved for her to come in. India went cold.

It was obvious from Annabelle's expression that something was terribly wrong.

"What is it?" she asked immediately. "Is everyone okay?"

"Yes, everybody's fine." Annabelle said, quickly. "Darling, meet Rand, he's an old family friend and my doctor. Randy, I don't think you've met my sister, India?"

A tall slim man in his late fifties with graying hair and a deep tan stood up to greet her.

"Lovely to meet you," he said warmly, shaking her hand. "I can see the resemblance."

"Good to meet you as well ... shall I leave you two alone?" India asked politely, keen not to intrude on what seemed like a very intense conversation.

"I hadn't planned on worrying you or Joss. I wasn't going to say anything until I had some definite news, but as you're here, darling, sit down for a minute."

India perched on a stool, holding her stomach. It felt as if she'd swallowed a stone.

"What is it, Annie? Tell me."

Annabelle hesitated and looked over at Rand, who picked up her cue._

"I'm going to send Annabelle for a scan later this afternoon. I suspect she has a benign growth on her thyroid gland that can be treated easily, but it's important we check it out to make sure. She's had a shock, but as I've been telling her, the lump doesn't feel solid. In ninety-five percent of cases these growths are noncancerous."

India was listening intently.

"How long will it take to know for certain?" she asked, desperately trying to get a fix on what she was hearing.

"I've put in a call. She's having a UFA later today."

"A what?" India was not thinking straight. Her head was spinning. "UFO?"

Rand smiled.

"UF-A," he emphasized, "an ultrasound fine-needle aspiration. It's a painless procedure and I'll have the lab results back within twenty-four hours."

"What will this involve?" India asked. "I mean if it's…" India avoided the word "malignant." "If it's what you just said, benign?"

"Well, we'll move forward when we have all the information. It's soft to the touch, which is a good sign."

"What do you mean?" Annabelle asked, tentatively.

"I mean, I really wouldn't get too alarmed at this point. Thyroid cysts are very common and treatable."

Rand stayed for another half hour or so, reassuring them patiently and answering question after question.

After he left, India rushed over and hugged her sister.

"How long have you had this? It's going to be okay;. you know that. You heard what he said."

"I found it yesterday," Annabelle lied, stretching her neck up and letting her sister touch her throat, lightly. "But God! I'm glad you're here. Can you imagine how I'd cope if you were five thousand miles away?"

"Don't be ridiculous; I'd have been on the first plane over," India choked out. She clung to her for a moment before reaching over the countertop to grab a paper napkin.

"You always said the thought of me being so far away brought a lump to your throat," she joked, blowing her nose noisily.

Annabelle laughed out loud.

"I'm going to stay as long as you need me, Annie. I can help look after you and Joss and the girls. You are going to be just fine; I know it. But I'm not going anywhere until you're completely well and over this. And I'll come with you for the test, of course. Just let me go and put some clothes on."

"We need to leave in about an hour," Annabelle shouted after her.

India raced across the garden. What the hell was happening here? One minute life was one big party, the next it was unraveling before her eyes. Annie would be all right. She had to be. Flying into the suite, she opened her laptop and began scanning the Internet for information about the thyroid gland.

A little while later, Robert held open the doors of the Town Car and the two of them climbed into the cream leather interior.

"Miss Butler, you seem to have attracted quite a crowd out there today," he told her.

"Sorry, Robert?" Annabelle was too preoccupied to catch his remark.

"There are a lot of photographers out there today, Miss Butler," Robert said as he began smoothly easing down the driveway.

"Really?" Annabelle was genuinely alarmed. Had word already gotten out she was sick? That was impossible. Nobody except India knew, not even Joss.

As the Lincoln approached the electronic gates, the inside of the car went dark and a frenzied mob swarmed around the car, pressing tight up against the tinted gray windows. Robert kept up a steady crawl then picked up speed, forcing them to scatter. As they reached Sunset Boulevard, Annabelle turned to India, who had gone pale.

"Did you hear that? They were shouting your name, India. What's going on? If the media finds out I'm headed for the hospital, there'll be photographs of me picking out a memorial stone by the morning."

"A memorial stone? What do you mean?" India looked at her terrified.

"I mean that they'll trail around after me and whip up some story that I'm dying, or, at the very least, having work done. I'm a name, India. I have to be careful. There are major privacy issues here."

India began to fill her in on the previous night's events, about Sophie and Max. As she spoke, she could see Annabelle was fighting to control her temper. Is she angry with me? she thought. Does she understand the way it all happened, that it was out of my control?

"This is all I need right now," Annabelle snapped. "It couldn't be worse timing. They'll be camped out for days until they get something they can sell, and while they're stalking you, someone will work out where I'm going and…"

Annabelle didn't even get to the end of the sentence. She couldn't face it, the thought of what might happen if Rand was wrong. What if I need chemotherapy? she thought, panicking. What if I'm one of the five percent?

Annabelle stared fixedly ahead of her, fighting back tears. India clutched her sister's hand until the car pulled underneath the parking lot of the black glass medical building, where a nursing assistant led them into a private elevator and then into the imaging department.

≈≈≈≈≈≈≈≈

"You answer it," Annabelle said.

Joss, jaw clenched, and wrenched the handset from the kitchen wall. The pulse in his temple was palpitating. Listening intently, he nodded and mumbled affirmatives.

"Thanks, Rand," he said, smiling reassuringly at Annabelle as he handed her the phone.

India was keeping busy, making Annabelle's favorite pasta: Farfalle Alfredo. "Shit," she muttered as boiling water spilled over the saucepan and scalded her hand. Turning down the heat, she stood perfectly still and held her breath.

"Okay," she heard Annabelle say eventually. "In the morning. Thanks, Rand. Thanks."

Throwing down the tea cloth, India rushed over to the couch and grabbed Annabelle's hand. "So, she said gently, "what did he say?"

"The results are good from what he can see," Annabelle said quietly. "And he sounded very calm," she added, almost as an afterthought. "But I still have to have surgery to remove the lump and be a hundred percent sure it is benign."

India gave Annabelle a hug. "Right," she said. "This is very good news. I think we could all do with a drink." Swallowing hard, she was walking across to the refrigerator in search of wine when her cell phone rang. It was Adam.

"Hey. How are you?" he said. "Did you get some sleep? I tried to reach you yesterday but you didn't pick up."

India glanced down at her screen. There was a string of missed calls.

"I'm so sorry, Adam. But can I call you back? This isn't a great moment."

"Sure," he said, uncertainly. "No problem, I'm here."

Shoving a pile of newspapers to one side of the coffee table, she poured three large glasses of Sancerre.

"So what else did he say?" she asked, conscious that her hands were shaking.

"He wants us to call him in the morning, so he can explain the practicalities."

"He told me it would explain why you've been losing weight, Annie," Joss added.

"Yes, he said it's a common thing, something that often happens after you've had kids … hormones going insane," she murmured.

"You're going to be absolutely fine, Annie," India said. "We'll get through this together. Whatever you need, it's yours. In the meantime, I'll have dinner ready in about twenty minutes. So why don't you two go into the den and we can eat in there by the fire?"

"Good idea. Thanks, Indie. I'm glad the girls are at a sleepover," Joss said, gesturing to the empty beanbags and scattered backpacks. They'll be at summer camp soon, too. Which means I can focus all my attention on you, Annie."

India watched as Joss steered Annabelle out of the room. He's so solid, she thought. He loves her so much.

Back in the kitchen, she drained the pasta and piled it into a giant serving dish, whisking some Dijon mustard into a vinaigrette before tossing the salad and throwing French bread into a basket. Then piling it all onto a large tray, she carried it into the den.

"Here, you must both be starving," she said, setting it down on the salvaged-oak table.

"This looks amazing," Annie said, sitting up. "I'm feeling quite lightheaded now. I've not eaten properly in twenty-four hours."

"Awesome, Indie," Joss said appreciatively. "Where's your plate?"

"I need to make a quick call," she said, topping up their wine-glasses. "You get started,; I'll catch up in a minute."

Leaning up against the countertop, India stretched her neck muscles and then foraged in her purse for her cell. Adam picked up immediately. His tone had changed. He sounded distant and strained.

"I'm sorry, Adam," she said. "Family stuff. I didn't mean to cut you off. How's Max?"

"He's doing okay," he said, the warmth returning to his voice. "Depressed, embarrassed, ashamed, I guess. He was drunk, you know. He nearly killed himself and somebody else."

"Max had been drinking? So the accident WAS his fault?"

"Yeah, and I suppose I should have seen this one coming. All the signs were there," he said. "He's going straight from UCLA to rehab again next week and then – "

"I'm so sorry, Adam," she interrupted. "I really am, and I want to hear the full story, but I'm about to have dinner with Annie and Joss. I do need to talk to you... There's a pack of paparazzi camped outside the gates here shouting my name!"

"Shit," Adam muttered. "Yeah, I've got company too."

"I'm in all evening. Can I call you back in about an hour?"

"Sure. Anytime," he said.

India clicked off and stood looking out at the garden. It was hard to imagine that anything could have taken her mind off Adam Brooks. Fred's party seemed like years ago. The panic about Annabelle had frozen time.

Picking up her plate and glass, she joined Joss and Annabelle.

"God, it's cold," she said, shivering as she perched on a foot-rest close to the fire. "I'd no idea it gets this chilly at night in August."

"We'll have to get you some Uggs," Joss said, tossing her a cashmere throw. "Put this around your feet."

"This is delicious, darling," Annabelle said, resting her fork and flopping back into the downy cushions. "I've been ignoring the warning signs, you know." I've pushed through so many walls of exhaustion, I've forgotten what it feels like to have energy."

Joss nodded. "I noticed, but I thought you just needed a good vacation."

"Yes. Well, I do, but I also think I need to make some changes," she continued.

India smiled. "Well, you're about to get a lovely long break," she said, standing up and lifting a couple of plates. "You two have a lot to talk over. I'm going to give Lizzie a call. I'm sure last night must have been pretty awful for her."

"I'll fill you in," Annabelle said, as Joss looked at her quizzically.

"Have an early night, you two. You look like you need it. It's been a long day. I love you more than words can say."

Annabelle smiled up at her. "I'm so glad you're here," she said. "I love you too."

≈≈≈≈≈≈≈≈

Lizzie was sitting in the pitch dark in her living room. The house seemed to reverberate with the echoes of the fight with Stan, a fight that had left her immobilized with rage.

When he'd had the gall to suggest that she should have been watching Sophie more closely, she'd exploded, screamed at him. Hurled every abuse she could come up with. She'd told him to get out, go fuck the nanny, and while he was at it go fuck himself.

Hoisting herself off the couch, she blew her nose and made her way upstairs. Kissing the top of Rhonda's head, and taking a moment to breathe in her soapy smell, she turned down the bedside light. "Sleep tight," she murmured, closing the door and making her way down the wrought-iron stairway. The phone rang as she got to the kitchen.

"Hi, Lizzie, it's India. I hope this isn't a bad time, I meant to call yesterday," to make sure Sophie was okay."

"Hi, India. Hang on a minute, will you?"

"Sorry about that," she said in hushed tones, closing the door. "How did you know about Sophie?"

"Oh, I'm so sorry Lizzie; I just assumed Stan would have mentioned I was there at the emergency room when they brought Sophie in." India hoped she wasn't intruding.

"You were? Are you okay?" Lizzie asked.

"I'm fine, but a friend of mine was rushed into the ER and I spent some time with Stan and…" she trailed off, hesitant to mention Joan by name.

"I haven't really spoken to Stan much since the other night," Lizzie replied. "He has a big case on and…," Lizzie paused. "Oh, fuck it, India, we aren't exactly having the easiest time right now." Her voice cracked with emotion as she tried to choke back tears.

India was shocked; calm, beautiful, poised Lizzie in absolute bits on the other end of the phone?

"Lizzie, I am so sorry… I didn't mean…"

"India," Lizzie said quietly, pulling herself together quickly. "No, I'm glad you called. It's just that I'm completely done with pretending I'm okay when my life is falling apart. Your sister is one of my closest friends. I don't know you so well, but I feel I can absolutely trust you. I'm the one who should be apologizing."

"Not at all… I'm…"

"It's really kind of you to ask," she said, more calmly now. "Sophie is doing fine. I spoke to her this afternoon. I think this has been a wake-up call for her."

"Sometimes it takes a crisis," India said. "You know, teenagers look like proper grown people, but their brains aren't fully formed and their hormones are going crazy. It's a wonder so many of us survive."

Lizzie laughed weakly. "Yes, I drove my mother insane, but it isn't the same; the drugs that are around nowadays scare the hell out of me. But listen, would you still like to come over for lunch one day this week? I would love to see you and Annie and if it's all the same, I don't feel I can talk right now."

"Of course, Lizzie. We'll call you tomorrow."

"Thank you, India. I'm so sorry."

"It's fine, Lizzie; we all get bad days. I'll see you very soon," India said, putting down her phone before pouring herself a glass of Pellegrino.

The night air was alive with the electric hum of crickets. India looked up at the crescent moon and the North Star. I see that same star from my London apartment, she thought as she walked across the garden to the annex, putting her hand up to her throat. Oh, how she needed to talk to Adam.

"Okay, it's me … finally," she said when he picked up. She'd taken a long hot shower and was snuggled under the quilt. "Tell me about Max. I can't really make sense of all this."

"You can write the script," he said. "He's had serious issues around alcohol since I've known him, but he's been in good shape for at least a year, right up until he split with Pearl."

"Who's Pearl?"

"Okay, India." Adam laughed. "That's hysterical. There's only one Pearl. Have you heard of Madonna by any chance?"

"Name rings a bell…" She laughed. "Okay, THAT Pearl, the singer. Of course, go on."

"He stopped going to AA meetings a while ago. He couldn't buy into the whole God thing. But he knew he had a problem, and last month he checked himself into rehab."

India looked at her glass. The thought of never being able to have another drink depressed her. How awful would that be? she thought. No more Sancerre? What, not ever?

Adam sounded exhausted.

"Go on," she said.

"That was after Pearl walked out on him, ditched him for that Spanish guy, Juan Inglesias, or however you pronounce it, went off on his yacht, shored up in his villa in Majorca… Anyway she was there with that guy at the party the other night. Last thing Max remembers was watching them make out and then knocking back a couple of vodka shots. Blackout. Not good."

"I'm so sorry…" India sighed, not sure what else to say.

"Adam, I'm sorry, I'm completely worn out, but I have to ask you. It's important. How do we keep the paparazzi away from me? I feel like I'm in some bad B movie, like I'm losing touch with reality."

"Welcome to California," Adam said wearily. "I'm sorry. This is a giant fuckup. I shouldn't have let Max pick you up. I forget sometimes. If you went around anticipating this kind of stuff all the time you'd go insane."

"I can see that," India answered. "Look, I'm not blaming you, but I do have to figure out the best way to deal with it. I don't want to pull Annie and Joss into any of this."

India desperately wanted to tell Adam about Annabelle's scare, but she stopped herself. She was too tired to think clearly.

"Let's talk tomorrow," Adam said "You sound exhausted."

"Yes. I'm wiped. But it was good to hear your voice."

"Yes," he said quietly. "It's late ... and I know you're a girl who needs her sleep. I'll call you tomorrow."

≈≈≈≈≈≈≈≈

Joss tossed a bunch of newspapers on the bedside table and gently kissed Annabelle's cheek.

"Wake up, sweetheart. It's past nine."

Annabelle opened her eyes and stretched. "Coming back to bed?" she whispered, turning over to look up at him, blearily.

"Annie, I've left you alone as long as I could. But I went to get you some magazines and there's something in the papers you should see," he said.

Annabelle sat up as Joss fixed the pillow behind her back. Taking the coffee cup from him, she took a sip and put it down the second she saw the cover of Us Weekly.

MAX AND ADAM IN LOVE TRIANGLE? screamed the headline above a picture of India getting out of Max's convertible, her dress barely skimming the tops of her thighs, and another of her in Adam's arms on the beach.

"What the...?"

She threw it down and picked up the Enquirer, which carried a blurry image of Max's mangled car alongside a separate photograph of India barefoot, surrounded by flames.

Annabelle sat bolt upright and began reading out loud.

"Was Max Seeing Double? Annabelle Butler's Twin Sister Caught in Dangerous Love Fest." She carried on: "Max ... recently split from Pearl ... crashed his car in the early hours of the morning.... Distraught Adam Brooks rushes to his friend's bedside... I can't read any more of this crap. Where's India? What's going on? I'm getting up," she said, throwing back the bedcovers. "I'll be down in a minute. Have you spoken to her this morning?"

"Not yet. She's showing Maria how to make scrambled eggs English style." He picked up the papers and the half-full coffee cup. "I had a feeling this might blow up after what you told me last night," he said, shaking his head. "I'm still not sure how they've managed to spin this one."

"Me either." Annabelle pulled a long La Perla cream satin tee shirt over her head. "Give me two minutes to brush my teeth."

India gave Annabelle a cheery grin when she appeared soon after. It's important to keep up morale, she'd decided earlier, arranging fresh-cut peonies from the garden as a centerpiece and setting the table with an array of jams and marmalade.

"Perfect timing," India said, setting down a fruit plate and a jug of soy milk. "How did you sleep?"

"Good darling, I slept surprisingly well. This looks wonderful." Annabelle dragged out a chair and reached across the table for orange juice. "Want some?" she asked Joss.

"Sure," he said, piling his plate with eggs and turkey bacon and waving a piece of toast on his fork. "Well done, Maria."

"Gracias." Maria smiled, balancing a full laundry basket under one arm and opening the utility room door with the other. "Enjoy your breakfast."

India joined them. "That was fun. I think Spanish could be my second language. Much easier than French. Everything just seems to have an o on the end of it ... plastico, bueno, and my new word of the day, cuchillo – bread knife." She beamed.

"Darling, I'm sorry to ruin your moment, but you need to see these," Annabelle said, pushing a few plates aside.

India looked at the magazines, openmouthed. "Omygod! "Omygod. I'm sorry but I…"

"No need for apologies, Indie, we live with this all the time," Joss said, pouring himself more coffee. "But right now my priority is making sure Annie doesn't get hassled. I'll get a fucking injunction to keep them away from the house if I have to. And I'll get CAA on the case too, but I need to know exactly what's going on."

"Of course ... of course...," India affirmed, realizing this was the first time she'd ever seen Joss so angry. She quickly outlined the night, starting with the drive to Chateau Marmont. "I've just remembered something else," Her eyes widened with surprise. "Adam called Max's mother to tell her what had happened. I thought he was kidding when he said she might call US Weekly. Do you think she did? Surely she wouldn't, not right in the middle of that kind of crisis?" She hesitated for a second. "And I told Alanna I was your sister when I introduced myself." "Okay. We need to deal with this before things get any worse. I'll make some calls," Joss stood up and wiped his mouth with his napkin. "That was a great breakfast, Indie. Thanks."

Annabelle stared at the pile of papers spread out in front of them and sighed.

"What's this?" she asked, flicking over the picture of India high-fiving.

"It's me straight after the firewalk," India said proudly. "I called you about it. It was incredible."

Annabelle had a vague flashback to something about fire, but India had been gabbling, not making sense, and Annabelle was only just home from a shoot.

"You did a firewalk? You did? How? Why? Why would you do that?"

"Not only that, but I went first!" India announced, thoroughly thrilled all over again.

Annabelle's jaw dropped.

"I know…" India smiled proudly. "I know."

Then India clapped her hands over her mouth and gasped. "But where would they have got that picture from, Annie? Hang on. I'll call Sarah."

"There's that picture of me at the firewalk in the papers to-day," she blurted to Sarah,

"Good evening to you too." Sarah laughed. "Here I am curled up with the cat on one of my rare nights off, with a nice mug of hot cocoa, watching a rerun of Pride and Prejudice. Have you no pity?"

"Sarah, it's the one you sent me where I'm leaping up and down like a lunatic."

"That wouldn't exactly narrow it down," Sarah quipped. "They must have got it from the Gazette, I suppose. One of your kids, Pete Davies, landed in the hospital last week. His latest thrill was joy riding. He was a very lucky boy, nearly killed himself. The article said something about adrenaline rush and linked it to the firewalk. I didn't want to mention it."

"That's awful. Sarah, Pete had a death wish before I ever taught him. I'm really glad he's okay, though. I'm sitting here with Annabelle trying to fill in some of the blanks. There's a pack of paparazzi camped outside the house and well … look, get back to your program, I'll e-mail you."

"I hope Annabelle's feeling okay. Call me again as soon as you have any news. I'll be thinking about you both. Sorry I can't help more. And India – breathe!"

"Thanks, I will." India put down the phone on top of the papers.

"It's a picture our local paper got hold of," she explained. "Annie, it's obscene how the gutter press go round making things up and twisting things, isn't it?"

"Yep." Annabelle stood up. "It is. And I'm sick of it. I'm going to take a shower and call Rand, find out when I'm going in. I told him I'd need a few days to sort out the kids for camp and get myself together."

"Let me clear the dishes while you do that," India said, scraping off a couple of plates and gathering up the silverware. So is this how I get my five minutes of fame? she thought, glancing down at the papers again. If they're looking for a scarlet woman, they've got the wrong girl. Me a femme fatale? Hardly. A love triangle – I don't think so. God, Annie could do without this right now.

PROFOUND THOUGHTS NOTE – If I'd known I would have had my teeth whitened.

"Set up the swing over there. The rainbow goes in front of the lemon trees. Cover the pool; olive trees over here. Statue, to the right a little more. Why am I working with morons? Move sweetie; you can fix your nails after you're fired."

Standing by the French windows, India took in the scene and stepped out onto the lawn in the white cotton robe Annabelle had told her to wear.

What an entourage, she thought. Hadn't Joss said "just a few photos?"

Roadies were everywhere, dragging giant reflectors and yards of steel lighting racks, erecting lines of canvas canopies. The garden was reminding India of an outpost in Out of Africa (minus the crystal glasses and Meryl Streep).

How long do they plan on staying? she thought, eyeing the foldaway tables of sandwiches, salads, and pastas, the Cokes and Arrowhead water bottles. They've even brought their own barbecue grill.

Andy Goldberg, Annabelle's PR rep, had moved quickly to set up the exclusive with People magazine. He'd set out the ground rules: schmaltzy focus on twin sisters, inconsequential fluff, sound bite on Annabelle working with Adam, India meeting him on vacation. No romantic links, all "just good friends." Scripted. Period.

"India?"

India swung round. A guy in a cutaway Zadig & Voltaire tee and harem pants tucked into biker boots was at her side.

"Enchanté… I am Cameron, your stylist today," he announced.

Cocking his head and placing one heavily tattooed hand on his hip, he swept his eyes over her. "Hmm… You're an eight. But I do like a challenge. Brings out my creative side."

Cheeky bastard, India thought.

Following him into one of the tents, she stood waiting while he thumbed endlessly through racks of clothing.

"Too small, too fitted… What is Karl THINKING this season? Valentino – don't think sooo. Too short, too low… Okay THIS is DIVINE. I can work with this. We can pin the back; you're clearly between sizes." He held up a diaphanous white Rozae Nichols shift.

"Thank you," she said icily, then followed him to a makeshift changing room.

Next, India's toes were painted ballet pink by a young man whose fascination with her feet would have made her decidedly uncomfortable, were it not for the fact that he was wearing the same shade of ballet pink himself. While he fanned her toes, someone named Sebastian blow-dried her hair and then the makeup artist, a girl in a black sheath dress, took over. India noticed she was wearing no makeup except for a bright Chanel-red lipstick. She's clearly going for the Tilda Swinton Award, India thought. The girl scrutinized India for a few seconds.

"I'm aiming for a very soft, natural look. "You have beautiful skin. Close your eyes please."

After what seemed an age, India squinted a bit, wondering what could possibly be taking the girl this long, and realized she was tweezing on false eyelashes, one tiny clump at a time. Three applications of eye shadow, two layers of mascara top and bottom, a sponged-on foundation, blusher, lip liner, lipstick and a dousing of fine powder later, India had begun to writhe in the chair.

"That's it," the girl announced, holding up a hand mirror. "Barely there, a honeydew glow, and they'll correct any flaws when they digitally enhance the photographs."

India was surprised. "Barely there? After all that, I should look like a cross between Coco the Clown and Mae West." She laughed.

India looked across at Annabelle. She looks positively transcendent! she thought as Annabelle walked elegantly toward her in a long pink Alexander McQueen silk dress, chiffon scarf, and Manolo silver thongs.

Annabelle was grateful for the opportunity to premiere this new look. Randy had told her the scar would be thin but it would be a few months before it could be completely disguised. She planned on wearing accent scarves until then.

"Okay, Miss Butler. We're ready for you." The guy at their side hesitated. "Should it be Miss Butlers plural?" He laughed.

"Yes," India said, turning to Annabelle. "If we were men it'd be 'Messrs.' as in 'Messrs. Boodle and Dunthorne' – you remember the jewelry store in London, Annie?"

Annabelle didn't answer. She was already in role, prepping herself for the shoot.

So this is "magazine casual," India thought, balancing precariously on one side of a double swing that was covered in garlands of old-fashioned pink roses and staged in front of a porcelain cherub statue.

"Does anybody seriously believe we hang out in rose-covered arbors of an evening?" she whispered to Annabelle. "Don't answer that." The wind machine blew off a rose and a girl in a faux leopard coat apologized and told them to stay still while she adjusted a petal. A redhead in a short red polka-dot dress and extremely high platform boots proceeded to spray each rose with water.

How do you get those jobs? India wondered.

India and Annabelle were directed into poses: asked to look at each other and laugh, throw their heads back in gay abandon, or put them together for a more intimate shot. Then they were directed to a squashy white linen couch where an anonymous voice from behind a still camera and a heap of trailing wires directed them.

"Heads together, laugh, look over here – lift your chin, India. Great. Good. Okay, lean forward. Lean back. Look up. Toss your hair. Powder please! We're going shiny… Great smile. To the left, up here… Beautiful … yes…"

Make your mind up, India thought irritably. It must be a hundred degrees under this frigging canopy.

"Okay. It's a wrap."

It was over. My God, if only removal men in London worked like that, India thought, as within seconds the set was dismantled and the equipment disappeared into black vans.

Sasha the journalist arrived full of apologies for being late. She's so tiny, she looks like she fell off a charm bracelet, India thought. She's even thinner than Angel, that trainer of Adam's.

Blocking out the thought, India took in Sasha's cream shift dress, which was cut wide at the neck and fell to one side revealing a razor-sharp shoulder blade. She arranged herself opposite them, and then, tucking one long leg behind the other, threw back her waist-length blonde streaked hair. She paused for effect before going through her list of tightly scripted questions, and the sisters gave their answers from crib sheets.

"Thank you both; this has been awesome," Sasha gushed.

Annabelle stood up. "It's been a pleasure," She turned to the young man who had appeared at her side.

"Miss Butler, my friend is such a huge fan of yours ... would you mind?" he said adoringly, holding out a pen.

This subterfuge still amused Annabelle. "Of course." She signed his notepad with a practiced twirl.

Sidestepping crates and boxes to get to the house, India was horrified to see the "rose-arranger" trashing the roses, breaking the stems, and throwing them into a plastic bag. What a waste, she thought. I'd have loved to have had them in my room.

"That was great, darling. You were fantastic," Annabelle said, climbing into the Lincoln next to India a short while later. "You handled it all like a pro."

"I enjoyed it." Understatement of the year, she thought, tugging at a few stray false eyelashes. Now I know what it feels like. It must be incredible to get paid so much to do what Annie does. It didn't feel like work at all.

There was a mob of paparazzi at the end of the driveway. Paparazzi. India thought, Why do they have such an exotic name? They all look so scruffy and ordinary.

India put her head down as Robert steered the car through the gates. "Don't worry; they can't see us through this glass,"

Annabelle reassured her. "And hopefully they'll drop the story once the piece is out."

"I think I'm having an allergic reaction to the makeup," India complained. "My face is stinging. Have I gone all red?"

"It'll settle down, you look fine," Annie soothed, peering at her own face in a tiny compact and then snapping it shut. "Now tell me again what Lizzie said. She was on edge when we had lunch and that was before any of this other crap with Sophie happened. I'm worried about her."

"I wasn't surprised when you told me Stan had been having an affair with their nanny," India said, frantically searching her purse for lip salve, "I wouldn't trust him an inch. He has that creepy way of undressing you with his eyes."

"Yes, and there's been a string of affairs." Annabelle sighed. "Right here, Robert, please… Darling, don't mention anything to Lizzie about me going into hospital. I don't want to worry her; she has enough on her plate already."

≈≈≈≈≈≈≈≈

"You'll either hate Lizzie's place or love it," Annabelle told India when they were a few minutes away from the house. "Stan chose it… Always a mistake to let the man pick, don't you think? Especially a man like Stan? Apparently he had the travertine marble in the garden shipped in from Bagni di Tivoli. It's like a miniature Getty…"

Robert pressed the intercom, waited for the buzzer, and the gates swung open. Neatly avoiding a couple of kids' tricycles in the driveway, he delivered them to the front door where Silvia, a large Hispanic woman in a black dress and white cobbler apron greeted them with a broad smile. Lizzie appeared behind her.

"I'm so happy to see you both." She gave them each a warm hug. She looked fragile but stunning in a pair of tight white jeans and a pale blue tee that barely covered her toned stomach. "We're eating outside. Come on in. What would you two like? Champagne?" She ushered them through the house into an architecturally landscaped garden with tall clipped hedges sectioned off by razor- edged bamboo pathways.

"Perfect," India and Annabelle answered in unison.

Lizzie popped her head inside the kitchen door and Silvia appeared with a shimmering bottle, three tall- stemmed Simon Pearce flutes and hand-sewn cutwork napkins on a large silver tray. Minutes later she brought out an array of toast, beluga caviar, and finely sliced onion with chopped eggs and crème fraîche.

Standing against a backdrop of travertine marble steps spilling over with cascading water, Lizzie expertly eased off the cork and filled their glasses.

"To friendship and women." They clinked their glasses.

"And good health," India toasted, taking a delicate sip of the delicious chilled Cristal.

"So what's been going on?" Lizzie asked. "India, I'm so sorry about the other night." She looked at Annabelle. "I had a complete meltdown on the phone."

"India did tell me things aren't so good. Are you okay, Lizzie? How are you? Do you want to talk right now?" Annabelle probed gently.

"More than anything else in the world," Lizzie answered. "Are you ready to eat?"

"Yes! It's been a busy morning – I'll tell you later." Annabelle said.

"Silvia, por favor," Lizzie signaled with her hand as they sat down. Silvia returned with warm spinach salads and fresh lobster flown in from Maine that morning. She kept the champagne flowing while they ate.

"I can't go on living like this," Lizzie said, after a while and pushing away her plate. "How could I ever trust Stan again?"

Annabelle nodded.

"And the person I really don't understand is that girl … the nanny, our nanny. Aren't there enough men out there for her to get laid without destroying other people's lives? She lived in our home. She took the kids to school. She pretended to be my friend and all the time…," she paused, eyes full of tears. "I just don't have the emotional equipment to understand how she could have done this to us."

"I think there are men's women and women's women," India volunteered. "Some women look on other women as friends, others see nothing but competition. They're needy and desperate. All they can think about is themselves."

"That's so true," Lizzie said. "I hadn't thought of it that way, but you're right. Some women freeze you out the minute there's a man around, like you suddenly went invisible."

Over coffee, Lizzie brightened up a little.

"Girls, this has really helped me clarify things. If I do nothing, it's like giving him permission to do it again. I have to get a sense of control, put some shape into the future and stop reliving the past. Whatever I decide, I've made up my mind, from here on in I'm not going to play the victim."

"Now THAT'S the Lizzie I know." Annabelle smiled, picking her Miu Miu quilted purse from the back of her chair and rooting for her phone to call Robert. "It's four thirty. I could stay here all evening, Lizzie, this has been wonderful, but we'd better go. I have to help the girls pack and be up early in the morning to see them off."

"Thanks so much for inviting me, Lizzie," India said, taking Annie's cue and sliding back her chair. "I don't know what I can do to help, but I'm around, and if there's anything at all..."

"Thank you both," Lizzie responded with a grateful smile. "Group hug?"

They folded their arms around each other.

Lizzie stood at the door for a few moments after the car had left the driveway. Then turning inside, she went across to the vintage Bauhaus mirror and took a long look at her reflection. She straightened her back, picked up her phone and dialed 411.

"City and state, please," chirped the automated voice

"Beverly Hills, California."

"Say the name of the business you want, or say residence."

"The legal firm of Wright Keller and Partners," Lizzie said clearly, then pressed 1 and waited to be connected. Her hands were shaking.

≈≈≈≈≈≈≈≈

"How's it going? What're you up to?" Adam shouted, over some unexpected static. "I feel like I'm under house arrest here."

India checked the time on her phone. It was eleven thirty.

"You woke me up actually." She yawned as the drone of a low-flying helicopter drowned out her voice. They waited a few moments until it circled off.

"Say it again," Adam teased.

"What?"

"Say 'actually.' No, wait. Say 'wawta.' It turns me on."

"Wawta, wawta everywhere and not a drop to drink," India enunciated slowly. "Are you absolutely crazed now?"

"I'm getting there," he said. "Try 'actually' again; that works for me every time."

"Mmm … well, actually I was thinking about the night of Fred's party … the private after-party, actually." She slid her leg against the silkiness of the sheet.

"It's stayed with me too," he said. "I have a few ideas for a sequel."

"I like the sound of that…," she murmured, rolling onto her back. "What exactly did you have in mind?"

"Well … let's start with – "

"Damn," India cursed as Bella hammered on her door. "Auntie India … Wake up … Auntie India, we're going."

"Sorry… The girls are shouting at me. I have to go. Joss is taking them to Laguna, to summer camp. I think they're about to leave … I'll call you later," she said. "But I want to tell you something. It's why I sounded a bit off the other day." She paused. "Annie found a lump; it's on her thyroid. They're pretty sure it's benign but she has to have it removed. She's going in tomorrow."

"I'm sorry to hear that, Indie, I really am. I'll let you go. Let me know if there's anything I can do. I'll call you tomorrow."

"Thanks. I wanted to ask her if it was okay, before I told you. She was fine about it, said you were hardly going to announce it on Twitter!"

Adam laughed. "I hope she's okay. Give her my best."

"I will. I've planned a movie fest. It'll be just Annie and me here all day. After that we're going to swim and soak up some sun before dinner."

"The image of you in a bikini will keep me company all day…," Adam said huskily.

India flopped back against the pillow and sighed. Who knew where this relationship was going? But she certainly intended to find out. The intensity was exhausting. She was emotionally raw and her physical desire for Adam was palpable. She ached at just the sound of his voice…

"Auntie Indie…"

"Okay, okay, I'm coming," India yelled back, wrenching herself out of bed and racing barefoot across the lawn, darting around the sprinklers to get to her nieces.

"Right," India said, as the tail end of the car, hands waving out the windows, disappeared around the corner. Annabelle was fighting back tears. "Evening gowns it is."

"You've got to be kidding!" Annabelle laughed.

"Nope. It's our very own screening. We're starting with Bugsy Malone, and then I've lined up Breakfast at Tiffany's. India grabbed the still-protesting Annabelle by the hand and dragged her upstairs to her closet. "I'm thinking long black Audrey for me and a flapper Bugsy dress for you."

"You're cracking up, darling, I swear." Annabelle was helpless with laughter as she slid into an Alexander McQueen sequined silver dress.

"I need pearls and you need a headband."

"Maria will think I've gone mad," Annabelle said as India tied a velveteen ribbon across her sister's forehead.

"Let's go," India replied, twisting her own hair in a topknot and securing it with a diamante pin before reaching for Annie's hand.

"Please take your seat," she announced with a flourish, indicating one of the plush burgundy armchairs in the Art Deco screening room. "The show is about to begin."

Hours later, Annabelle and India sat enjoying the warmth of late afternoon sunshine under the shade of canvas umbrellas as

Maria grilled vegetables and levered thin-crust pizzas from the Tuscan fire oven.

"Darling, that was exactly what the doctor should have ordered," Annabelle murmured, dreamily, sipping Sancerre. "What a perfect day…"

"Yes, I loved every moment. Took me right back – do you remember before Dad left how often we played dress-up?"

"I do, darling, and did I ever tell you how grateful I was for how you looked after Mother? I know I'm probably being over-dramatic and nothing's going to happen to me tomorrow … but I want you to know how grateful I am. You never resented me for taking off or coming here…"

"Well, let's not get carried away…" India joked, looking at Annie, her eyes shining with love. "Thank you… I wanted you to follow your dream. You always had such a passion for what you do. Holly Golightly could be talking about you, back there, you know; when she asked if the girl was, 'deeply and importantly talented.' It's a great way to put it, Annie. You ARE deeply and importantly talented."

"I've been lucky, that's all," Annabelle said, squeezing her hand.

"I sometimes envy the fact that you always knew what you wanted to do. You were so clear about it."

"True. But you were the one with our dolls and teddy bears lined up giving them spelling tests and singing lessons all the time. You're a born teacher, darling. You're importantly talented too."

Then why do I feel like I'm in the wrong place? India thought. I always wanted to teach. Why isn't it enough for me? Why?

≈≈≈≈≈≈≈≈

Tangled in a confusion of sheets and mixed up dreams, India tossed around in bed all night. She was relieved when sunlight eventually streamed through the shutters. She showered, dressed quickly in a pair of blue jeans and tee, and took off in search of coffee. Joss was already pulling the SUV round to the front of the house.

Annabelle was in the kitchen. Her purse was lying open, everything from it strewn across the table as she hunted frantically under a pile of cushions. She wore a long black halter dress and flat Manolo thongs. With her hair pulled back in a loose knot and without a trace of makeup, Annie hadn't looked so vulnerable or beautiful to India in years.

"Have you seen my phone?" she asked India. "I've looked everywhere. I remember having it at the hospital the other day. I don't think I've seen it since."

"No. Sorry," India said, checking her watch. "I think we should get going. We're already running late. I'll look for it for you when we get back; you won't need it. I have mine."

"Where could it possibly be?" Annabelle said, flinging her makeup bag and wallet into her Fendi fringed tote with trembling hands. "And I can't even have a cup of coffee this morning. I can't think straight."

India stepped over and put both her arms round Annabelle's shoulders. "There's no need to be frightened, Annie. Nothing bad is going to happen, I promise. Remember what Rand told you. He's sure it isn't anything scary. This time tomorrow it will all be over. You'll be just great."

"I know, darling. I know." Annabelle hugged her tightly. "Thank you. I love you."

She took a deep breath. "Okay. I'm going to pretend this is a movie. I'll play the part for all it's worth!" Straightening her back and lifting her chin, she strode toward the door and punched the air.

"Fear nothing!" she cried. "In God's name, forward boldly!"

"Annie, you may want to think this through... Joan of Arc ended up burnt at the stake. How 'bout you channel Scarlett O'Hara?"

"You're right, darling..." Annabelle laughed, turning round as she reached the door. "And after all ... tomorrow is another day..."

Annabelle was delivered to the prep room minutes after they reached St. John's Hospital. India and Joss were left sitting side by side in the carpeted waiting room. The hours dragged by. They took turns going outside for some fresh air, and, at one point, India stepped out to call Adam.

"My nerves are shot to pieces. I don't know what I'd do if anything happened to Annie. She was due out of the theater an hour ago and nobody's told us what's going on."

"Don't worry. You said yourself this is really routine. They always misjudge the time – believe me I know; I played a surgeon on Grey's Anatomy."

India laughed nervously. "That's very encouraging. Thank you, Dr. Brooks. I have to go."

India's mind was a complete blank. She couldn't even find the energy to speak; then a heavy wooden door opened and a doctor came toward them smiling as he took off his surgical mask. Joss sprang up and India rushed to his side.

"She's doing really well," the surgeon said, looking from one to the other, kindly. "I'm sorry we took a little longer than expected, but we removed part of Annabelle's thyroid gland where the nodule had grown."

"What does that mean, exactly, Doctor?" Joss asked, his voice tremulous.

"It means that the lump was contained. It was small. When we do a biopsy we'll be able to make certain that it was a benign tumor. I've seen a lot of these and I'm pretty certain it was."

"So my sister is going to be okay?" India cut in. She needed more reassurance. She wanted to hear words like "clear, successful, noncancerous."

"Yes," he said; then, with more emphasis, added, "She is going to be absolutely fine. In fact, you can go in and see her, though she may not be making a lot of sense. Remember, she's had a very heavy anesthetic."

India and Joss followed an orderly down the corridor to a private room where a nurse was checking Annabelle's pulse.

"Miss Butler, you have company," she said.

Annabelle looked up at them. Her face was ashen and partly hidden by an oxygen mask.

"How do I look?" she mumbled.

"Absolutely beautiful," Joss told her, kissing her forehead gently and taking her hand.

This is the kind of love that's worth hanging out for," India thought, quietly slipping out and leaving them together.

"She's going to sleep now," Joss said, catching up with India along the corridor a little while later. "Let's find the car."

Joss looked thoughtful as he steered the Jeep out of the parking lot, and they started to crawl up the Wilshire Corridor in thick lunch-hour traffic.

"I'll take Annie off for a vacation just as soon as she's fit enough to travel. I'm thinking Hawaii," he said. "She's finally realized she needs to slow down. We both know that'll last all of five minutes, but let's enjoy it while it does."

"You look like you could seriously do with a vacation yourself." India smiled.

"Yes. Well, I think we should avoid the Hamptons right now – too many familiar faces, and Annie needs rest. It can get pretty social out there. I was thinking that we'll be away longer than we planned. So maybe you could stay on … take some of that sabbatical you're always dreaming about."

India beamed at him. "If you're happy having me around for a while I would absolutely love to."

"Great," Joss said, changing lanes and edging through the bottleneck at the freeway. "That's sorted. By the way," he added, "I haven't forgotten you girls have a birthday coming up, either. How cool you'll get to spend it together. We have to do something really special."

"Not too special. We're only owning up to thirty-six, remember."

"I'll make sure it's special," he said, honking his horn as he turned into his driveway. "Don't mess with me today, pal," he muttered as a guy with a camera leapt backward. "Don't even think about it."

India raced across to her room to call Sarah, who picked up immediately.

"She's going to be okay," she told her breathlessly.

"Phew. I've been thinking about you all day. I'm so glad."

India hesitated a moment, knowing how much Sarah was missing their Indian takeouts and trips to the pub.

"Joss asked if I'd like to stay on. I mean … he meant maybe for a few months."

"Well, I'm sure you're not in any rush to get back here for a whole range of reasons," Sarah chirped.

"Yes. You'd be right, a whole range of reasons…"

"I was wondering about that the other day. There's a new auxiliary looking for accommodation here. She's lovely, works long hours but needs more than my sofa to crash on. If you like, I'll let her have your place on a short term lease; that way you won't have to worry about the rent."

"You're a gem. I'm going to call Dr. White in the morning and see if he'll give me a semester's leave. I don't suppose there'll be a problem. They can get a substitute teacher with this kind of notice."

"Yes, he'll be heartbroken."

"Ha!" India laughed.

"By the way, it's now official."

"What is?"

"There are no eligible men left in London," Sarah sighed. "I signed up with that new dating agency. The guy I met this week was completely delusional. How can you be ten years off on your age and six inches off on your height?"

"You crack me up. How tall was he?"

"Think Tom Thumb … or, in LA speak, Tom Cruise. Pocket-size."

Thérèse

C'est La Vie Note – My fifteen minutes.

It was the third morning of visiting St. John's, and India knew the drill.

"Grande nonfat iced mocha, please," she yelled. "And a tall low-fat iced soy latte. Oh, and a blueberry muffin."

The girl took a pen to the side of the paper cup. "Name?"

"India."

"You're India Butler, aren't you?"

India turned. The voice belonged to a woman in an unflattering pantsuit. Do I know you? India thought. Generally I make a point of not knowing people who wear Day-Glo colors unless they happen to be firemen. "Yes. That's me," she said, smiling and handing a twenty-dollar bill across. She grabbed her change and moved to the side counter, where she sensed the woman still looking at her. Meandering her way out of Starbucks through the hospital bookstore, India's eyes were fixed on the headlines on a magazine rack. "Everything's Coming up Roses for Annabelle and India."

Juggling her cardboard tray, she picked up a couple of copies of People, joined another interminable line to pay, then raced to the elevator to get a proper look.

152

"Double page spread!" She grinned, handing Joss the tray and opening the magazine carefully on top of Annabelle's bed-covers. "One for the family album, I'd say."

"Wonderful," Annabelle said with a smile, lying back against the starched pillow and closing her eyes.

"You're tired today, Annie," India whispered. "I'm going to leave you and Joss to have some time together. I'll take a taxi home and see you in the morning. I love you."

Squashed uncomfortably in the back of a worn yellow cab that reeked of stale cigar smoke, India opened her own copy of the magazine.

Do I actually look like that? How much have they airbrushed? she wondered. She really did look a lot like the girl in the picture and that girl was so ... well, dare she think it... beautiful?

Over the next few days, several other complete strangers came up to India and introduced themselves. Even at Starbucks, her mocha was ready within seconds and delivered with a know-ing smile. So this is what it's like to be famous? she wondered. Maybe it's time for a change of image.

When her phone rang, India was in Annabelle's closet ap-praising herself in torn jeans, London Sole flats, a wraparound cashmere shawl, and aviator sunglasses. She tossed aside a base-ball cap. I draw the line at that, she thought. American women must have different shaped heads or something.

"So how's it going?" Sarah asked. "It's pissing with rain here. How's Annie?"

"She's doing great and really cheerful. All the tests came back clear."

"Wonderful. You must be so relieved. By the way, I loved the pictures and the article, but I thought you hated sushi. And when did you two ever go bareback riding together?"

"I do and we didn't." India laughed.

"So what now?"

"Annie's going to Tranquility – it's a medical spa. She'll be there till Sunday … and I'm going to Malibu to spend the night with the beautiful Mr. Brooks."

"Well, you've earned it. And I'm going to Tesco to fill my empty fridge and sleep all day Sunday," Sarah said, laughing. "Enjoy.

≈≈≈≈≈≈≈≈

Adam was standing at the entrance to his duplex when India climbed out of the car. She was wearing Annabelle's black Balenciaga dress and a pair of Chanel ballet flats.

"Perfect timing. You look beautiful," he said, lifting Annabelle's Louis Vuitton overnight bag from the backseat of the car.

"We're having seafood linguini with clams and, before you get too impressed, I had it delivered from Capo." He grinned, leading the way to the sitting room. India followed, resisting the urge to grab his butt as he took the stairs two at a time with his shirttail hanging out of his Levi's.

"Well, I assume you didn't have a decorator do this," she said, clapping her hands with delight at the magical atmosphere; the scattered candles across the mantelpiece, the table set out for two in front of a crackling log fire, and the gentle strain of a Chopin Étude in the background.

"I can't take all the credit. Angel is pretty talented."

I bet she is, India thought. Don't let that spoil the moment. Don't.

"And you are just in time for the sunset. It's going to be spectacular tonight. Step outside and watch while I open the wine."

"You're right," India gasped, a few minutes later, taking the glass from his hand. "I don't think I've ever seen a more gorgeous sunset. There's nothing between here and the ends of the Earth."

They stood together on the deck as the ocean turned first red and then became an expanse of shimmering silver light.

"You're shivering," Adam said, putting his arm around her. "Let's go inside. Hungry?"

"Always." There's that electric shock, she thought, as he guided her toward the fire.

"Great. Dinner will be served momentarily." He bowed.

On Monday morning, India woke up alone back at Annabelle's. She curled into a tight ball and hugged the pillow. I'm in love with a man who can have any woman he wants, she thought. I'm in Tinseltown, and I'm terrified.

She closed her eyes again, reliving the weekend; lying in Adam's arms listening to the sound of the ocean, the yap of the seagulls, walking miles of beach before going back to the duplex and making love again in the haze of the afternoon, snuggling up in front of the fire, eating Chinese noodles, drinking wine. She could still taste him. All her senses were alive.

How could she possibly ever go back to Queens Park? But in the real world, the proper grown-up world, there would come a moment when ... when what? She could not live on this fluffy white cloud indefinitely. She felt out of control, giddy. Get a grip, she told herself. Enjoy it for what it is ... a summer romance.

The trill of her cell phone snapped India out of her reverie.

"Hey, you..." Adam said softly. "I'm lying here in bed and I miss you."

"Me too," she murmured. "I had such a wonderful time."

"Yes. I was thinking, I meant to tell you. I'm going out of town for a week or so."

India snapped wide awake. Where are you going? Who are you going with? Why didn't you say? Stay cool, sound casual, she thought. "Where?" she managed.

"Max is coming out of rehab tomorrow. We're going up to Joshua Tree."

"What's that? You're going to see a tree?"

"It's the desert. We're going hiking on the mountain trails, taking some time out. He can't just come back here to all his shit yet. He has to get his head together. It's like nowhere else … the night sky is awesome."

"Sounds wonderful. I've never been to the desert… Joss and Annie leave for Hawaii in a couple of days," India said quickly. "I plan on…" What? What do I plan on? "I'm planning on doing some writing … some workshopping course work."

"Sounds good. Okay, well, I have to get moving. I have a six-hour drive. I'll call when we're back."

"Yes. I hope Max is in good shape. Give him my best."

"Will do … and India, I think you're very special and I had a great time."

"Me too," she said, clicking off quickly.

That's it, she thought, getting up and heading for the shower. He's going off to the desert with Angel. I shouldn't have stayed the weekend. I must have come on too strong. I was too available. I'll never see him again … no, it's okay … he definitely said I was special and he said he'd call … he did. I'm sure he did. Yes … he said very as in very special.

God, this house feels horribly empty, India thought, cautiously sidestepping Clooney, who was padding up and down by the French windows making a weird whining noise. "Don't come anywhere near me." She was afraid that maybe the dog hadn't had his tranquilizers. "Maria!" she shouted. "Maria…"

Maria appeared at the door. "Bueno. Bueno. Perrito…" she cajoled, rubbing noses with the panting animal.

India shuddered at the idea of all that saliva on Maria's face. I am not in a good mood, she decided. What AM I going to do for all these weeks with everybody away?

By lunchtime, India had half convinced herself that Adam was into Scientology, was bisexual, or both. Why hadn't he mentioned his plans when they were together? After all, he was a movie star and this was LA. "Maybe Angel's going to marry Adam and Max in the desert," she said aloud. "Is gay marriage legal in California? I have to get out of the house. I'm talking to myself… Where did Annie say she left her car keys?"

India drove the mile or so into Bel Air canyon extremely cautiously. Wide open spaces. Just what I need right now, she thought, pressing off the sound system. Stopping on a track off to the side of the road, she took in the splendid panoramic view. A stampede of Apaches could come over that hill any minute… It's really still the Wild West.

Getting out of the car, she began walking up the gravelly hiking path, pausing every now and then to let the occasional jogger pound past her. "Focus," she told herself out loud, gathering momentum and striding faster. "Focus… What is it you REALLY want? Think."

"God ! I'm out of condition!" She gasped, grabbing hold of a boulder as another runner thundered past. What was it Pete had said in the training session, just before the firewalk? What was it he was trying to make them do? He talked a lot about fear. What was she afraid of?

Did she stay in her job because she was afraid of change? Was she afraid that she would never measure up to Annie? Afraid that she would not be enough for someone like Adam? Was that why she picked guys who were safe, even when they were boring as hell? Right now in LA, everyone was telling her how beautiful she was, how valued, how special. But she felt as if she were walking on glass. She knew that there was no going back. Everything had already changed. Falling in love with Adam (and she had to admit it, she had) experiencing that sick sense of what losing Annie would mean... All of it had jolted her. She would have to fight through her fears, stop talking about making changes and actually do it. But what? And when was she going to tell Adam that she had lied about running workshops in London?

India's head was beginning to ache as she struggled for answers. Come on. Visualize! Focus! You're a leader not a follower, a believer not a doubter, remember?

A few minutes after she started the drive back, she screeched to a halt and pulled over to the side of the dirt track. Looking beyond the roofs of the houses to the outline of the hills in front of her, she suddenly felt a rush of excitement. Yes, I can do this, she thought. I know exactly what kind of courses I should offer. There would be no turning back. She was certain. Grabbing her phone, she pressed speed-dial.

Lizzie picked up right away.

"Hi, Lizzie, how're you?"

"Good, thanks. How're you?"

India paused. She was getting the hang of this convention now.

"Lizzie, I've an idea I'd like to run past you as soon as possible ... if I may..."

"Of course," Lizzie said. "I'm just done with my hike. I'm on San Vicente. How 'bout we meet at the Coffee Bean in say, half an hour?"

"Perfect."

"I'll be there in about ten minutes, India, and I'll grab us a table."

≈≈≈≈≈≈≈

"Great to see you, India. How is Annie? How're the kids?" Lizzie asked, air-kissing her then sweeping a pile of LA Times off the table.

"All good, Lizzie," India said, squeezing into the tiny space. "Sorry I'm a bit late – I couldn't find a meter."

"It's okay, I was catching up with the news. So Annie's going to be just fine? That was one hell of a scare," Lizzie said, adjusting her wide-brimmed Nike baseball cap. "It must have been tough on you all. But she's okay… Thankfully, she's okay."

"Yes. I'm still reeling. She has such amazing stamina though, always did. Joss' friend flew them to Waikiki in his V5. I thought it was all a bit soon, but apparently there's a great hospital on the island and she can have all her follow-up appointments there. This way she'll get complete rest and privacy."

"Joss is wonderful. She'll be absolutely fine," Lizzie said. "I loved the piece, by the way, it really captured how close you two are." She paused. "So now, go on. How can I help?"

"Well, before that, tell me how you are… I mean really."

"I'm hanging in there." Lizzie took off her Gucci aviator sunglasses. "Taking my time, getting legal advice. I need to understand my options."

India winced and put down her cup. "Sorry. That's hot." She slurped. "I'll never get the hang of cappuccinos. How do you know where the frothy bit stops?"

Lizzie laughed. "I think that's where this comes in handy," She handed her a white plastic spoon and a paper napkin.

"Thanks. Well... I'm pleased you're okay... Sorry. So I wanted to talk to you about a couple of things. I'm staying on for a while to be with Annie," she said, wiping off her foam mustache.

"That's great. I've often thought it's a pity you two live so far from each other. I know she misses you."

"Lizzie,I hope you don't mind my bringing this up, but I keep thinking about the night at the hospital." She paused long enough to see that Lizzie was up for the conversation and lowered her voice. "I keep seeing Sophie, unconscious on that gurney, and Joan in shock. I keep imagining what you must have gone through when you found her. She could have been brain damaged for the rest of her life. What if you had been too late?"

Lizzie was listening intently. "Go on."

"Well, everything here seems so perfect from the outside, then when you get up a tiny bit closer it's all... Well, it's sort of a mess. I need to understand more, Lizzie. I just assumed these kids were different, that they had it made. Now, of course, I can see they still have their own shit to deal with. But I want to know where they're coming from. I've worked for years with teenagers who have nothing. They don't have cell phones unless they've stolen them, they don't drive, they're angry, and they hate being in school. But I love working with them. I get a real kick out of seeing them do something they didn't know they could do." She blew on her coffee. "I used to think I stayed on the job because I was stuck; because I was afraid of change. Now I know it's because I know it's worthwhile. I relate to the kids. They're so vulnerable underneath all the bravado."

"It's obvious you're a great teacher," Lizzie said.

"How so?"

"India, you have such a spark and such great energy."

"Thank you, that means a lot."

"So … where to start?" Lizzie said, breaking off a tiny piece of croissant. "Okay. What can I tell you? The kids here aren't legal to drink until they're twenty-one but they can carry a gun when they're eighteen."

"And they can drive a car when they're sixteen. What's that about?" India interrupted.

"It's crazy. They don't know how to make a sandwich for themselves but they're on the roads in those Escalade tanks or their BMW or Mercedes. That's the divine right of every sixteen–year-old around here," Lizzie continued.

"It's surreal. I mean, what do you have to look forward to if you get everything so easily? What's that teaching them?" India tore at her chocolate muffin, swiping away the flying crumbs.

"There's no school uniform, so you see all these twelve-year-olds with their Chanel backpacks and Louis Vuitton purses. If it wasn't so sad it would be funny," Lizzie said, dryly. "So how is it different in London?"

"We have our fair share of drug problems, believe me, and kids start to drink young, but I put a lot of that down to a lack of money. The class sizes are huge. Annie's dog gets more individual attention at Doggy Daycare than my schoolkids do. She gets a printout of what Clooney's had for lunch each day, for God's sake."

"India, you have no idea how dysfunctional these families can be," Lizzie answered. "I worked as a civil rights lawyer down-town for a while; only half an hour away from here and yet it's another world; real poverty, teacher shortages, crime rate through the roof. To me, it seems almost like a kind of abuse not to train these privileged kids on this side of town to give back."

"How do you mean?"

"Well, at Sophie's school the 'community service' requirement is a complete sham. They can pass it just by picking up trash on the playing field. There are no real volunteer programs, no weekly social responsibility. So they live in this vacuum where everything's easy. At some level, they're bored." She looked thoughtful for a moment. "Why don't you apply for a job here? We're desperately short of teachers."

"That's just it, Lizzie. I don't want to be in a school or a college. I want to work with people, have a laugh with them, challenge them, but not go home to mark a thousand essays and write reports and fill in endless grading forms."

India paused for a second, then asked her the direct question she had been asking herself.

"Do you think I could somehow run some workshops, courses for parents? They could be sessions where I would give them some practical help with managing their kids. They must be feeling pretty lost themselves to be letting everything get so out of control. I mean you were … Joan is." India blushed. "That came out the wrong way, sorry."

"No, it's fine. A lot of my friends have younger kids, like me, and we're thrown into this world of teens unprepared. I've been coping with Sophie and her clique of cheerleading friends without any guidance for an eternity."

"That must be so hard," India said, shifting her chair to let a woman with a baby in a stroller get by.

"It's really difficult to fight the culture, and yes, I think there's room for something here. I mean, there's all this advice for toddlers; the Supernanny books and her reality show. And what you say is true. You hit the teen stuff without a road map. There's not a whole lot of help out there until there's a crisis." Lizzie sighed.

"I know I haven't got kids of my own, but I do have a lot of experience with teenagers and mothers. I've learned a lot over the years that I could share, but I don't really know how I would get started here in LA."

Lizzie smiled. "Well, Supernanny's English, and she doesn't have kids of her own either, but we all listen to her because she makes a lot of sense. I'm thinking this through on my feet, but how does this sound for a first shot?" She paused. "We create an invitation-only evening at my house, with handwritten invitations, the same way I promote my friends' jewelry lines and books."

India leaned forward on her elbows, listening hard.

"So people come to your house and then what?"

"Well, we'll have wine and canapés and you can do a little presentation about how to survive your kid's teenage years. You'll make it entertaining – how could you not? You always make me laugh and think at the same time."

India smiled and Lizzie continued her train of thought.

"Then you can tell everyone that you're starting a support group… You could also say you're planning on writing a book, a 'survival guide' for parents, and you want their help with it."

"That's a fantastic idea. You're brilliant, Lizzie, and you know, I could write a book on all this. I really could. Like Supernanny – Superteacher. I can't thank you enough."

"Listen, I really love this idea. I'm more than happy to help. Sophie and Henry are not my favorite people right now, but I also know they're not bad human beings. Deep down they're lost and scared … just like me." She paused, then said quietly, "And you know, it did happen on my watch. I should have been paying more attention."

"Don't beat yourself up," India said. "We do the best we can at the time. By the sound of it, this was always going to happen and thankfully it WAS on your watch."

Lizzie smiled. "Let's talk more about this when I've had a chance to think it through. We can make this work. We need you here." She stood. India rose too, and they lifted their Styrofoam cups in a toast. India scooped her leftover chocolate muffin in a napkin and threw it in the trash, while Lizzie picked up India's sweatshirt from where it had fallen under her chair.

"Everything happens for a reason. At least that's what I tell myself lately," Lizzie said, hugging her. "I'll call you later."

PROFOUND THOUGHTS NOTE – Check exchange rate.

India gulped and stared at her bank statement in horror. There's been some dreadful mistake, she thought. Maybe I'm the victim of identity theft.

Swallowing a mouthful of coffee, she pulled the gilt bergère chair closer to the secretaire and scrutinized the figures. The trip to Agent Provocateur (a wise investment that had certainly given her and Adam a great return) had come out at fifteen hundred dollars (plus tax).

The highlights, lowlights, waxes, manicures, pedicures, threading, teeth whitening, dermabrasion facials, and Botox added up to another two thousand terrifying dollars. (All the more horrifying when converted to pounds on her English credit card.)

Clearly the jaunt to Fred Segal had been a grave error, but she would need the yoga pants and cutoff tops (in a variety of colors) for her workshops and the Fendi tote to carry her papers. The La Perla bikinis and Louboutin clutch had seemed imperative at the time.

And then there was the outrageous Smythson bill. India sat back and ran her finger over the gold lettering and the blind-embossed pressed flowers of the hand-engraved invitation card.

What a moment that had been, sitting with Lizzie on the leopard-print chaise, sipping champagne and picking them out. The expense had clearly been worth it; as Lizzie predicted, the acceptances were flooding in. Lizzie had moved at warp speed to set up India's event and now, just ten days later, it was only a matter of hours away. The idea of making a speech to thirty or so of Lizzie's contacts was daunting enough in the abstract, but now it was a terrifying reality.

India scrunched up a bundle of receipts. She had much more important things to be doing right now. She closed her laptop and picked up the Mont Blanc pen.

How to begin? she wondered. "Dearly beloved…" Scratch that. "Friends, Romans, countrymen…" Been done. Okay, get serious. Two hours and several laps around the garden later, India decided she was as prepared as she was ever going to be. Tossing aside her notes, she ran inside, stripped, skipped into the steamy shower, and spent the next twenty minutes singing to loosen up her vocal cords.

"They tried to make me go to rehab, I said no, no, no…"

She toweled off, spritzed herself with Mitsouko, and climbed into an Agent Provocateur satin body and a tiny lace thong. How can they charge so much when there's so little fabric involved? She mused, carefully pulling on a fine mesh stocking, then zipping her ruched silver Nicole Miller dress and wriggling it down until the hem skimmed her knees. Picking up a tiny stack of copper-plate business cards (with hand-painted edging), she put them inside her new sequined clutch and snapped it shut, then squeezed into Annabelle's patent leather Prada four-inch pumps. She did a full turn in the long mirror.

Good, she decided. A look that says "gravitas" and at the same time, "call me sister."

166

India ran outside, surprised to see that Robert was waiting.

"Miss Butler called from Hawaii," he explained, opening the car door for her. "She said she wanted to make sure you didn't get to Beverly Hills via San Francisco."

"Ah … she has a point, Robert. I still can't get the hang of that GPS. Thank you."

When they got to Lizzie's, Robert said, "Miss Butler, when you're ready, just call. I'll be two minutes away. Have a wonderful evening."

"Thank you, Robert. I will." Omygod, India thought, catching a glimpse of waiters weaving between cocktail tables balancing trays of champagne and women milling around in the stone courtyard. Slipping in unnoticed through the side entrance, she stopped to admire the Henry Moore sculpture, the garden, and the geometrically arranged tables draped in white cloths with orchid centerpieces. Lizzie had really gone all out for her. Squeezing behind the line of stewards taking instructions from the chef, India was reminded of being backstage before Annie went on in a show at Covent Garden. And then she realized: Omygod. I AM the show!

Lizzie was waiting by the kitchen door to greet her, looking elegant as ever in an Yves Saint Laurent Le Smoking suit.

"Great. You're in good time, India. I'm going to start getting people into the drawing room. Do you want a few minutes to yourself? You look amazing."

"Thanks, Lizzie. I'd no idea you were going to go to so much trouble. This all looks incredible. I'm so nervous."

"You'll be great. Relax. They'll love you… Through there…" Lizzie said, directing her to the bathroom. "I'll see you in a minute."

Thérèse

India darted in and decided against using the Toto toilet. It had too many options. She didn't want to risk a misplaced water jet and wasn't sure she had time for a full blow-dry. She checked her hair and makeup, went over her opening lines a few more times, then took a very deep breath.

Focus. You can do this. You want this… FOCUS… Are you ready? SAY YES!

≈≈≈≈≈≈≈≈

Lizzie beamed at the group of women assembled around glass-topped tables, sitting on low banquettes, or swinging their legs in the basket-style seats of her high-ceilinged drawing room. "What an amazing turnout. Thank you all so very much for coming, and thanks to Forest Wood School for extending the invitation to so many parents. Please meet my wonderful friend, India Butler."

A healthy smattering of applause greeted India, who stood up and joined Lizzie at the oversize brick fireplace. "India has been an absolute inspiration to me and to my family," Lizzie continued. "I would like to share just a few of the qualities of this remarkable woman, who has brought such a light into my world. India is one of those women you know instantly you can trust. She is an extremely sensitive facilitator with more than eighteen years' experience dealing with teenagers in London. She has worked with countless parents to help steer them through the turbulent years when children can be at their most challenging. Knowing her I have discovered new depths in myself, and I have begun to appreciate my strengths and my resilience."

Lizzie paused to wipe away a tear, and India began rapidly reframing her own opening words. I'm going to have to be more effusive, she decided.

"India is writing an exceptional book that will help guide us through these emotionally turbulent years. I will have the privilege of hosting her first series of workshops here in my studio. I hope that you will all sign up for them tonight. Congratulations for the courage you have shown by being here this evening. We mothers need to 'come out,' admit when we are struggling, and ask for help. We must be supportive of one another. With India's help I know we can do this. Please join me in welcoming my dear friend, India."

Another round of applause and Lizzie gave India a hug.

"Thank you so much, Lizzie," India said, surprised at how emotional she was suddenly feeling. She continued: "Lizzie is taking my dream of working with you all and helping me turn it into a reality. I can't thank you enough, Lizzie."

Lizzie smiled at her and sat down on one of the Eames armchairs.

Five hours later, India called Sarah. "I can't remember a single thing I said!" She laughed. "It's all a blur. But it must have been good, because nearly everybody signed up. Lizzie gave me such a buildup, I thought she must have been talking about someone else."

"I'm sure you were brilliant," Sarah said. "I'm so excited for you. How was dinner?"

"Wonderful. All these women kept coming over to say how much they're looking forward to the workshops. The food was incredible, though I was too excited to eat much. Sarah, I miss you madly, but I'm having a wonderful summer. I love it here. You have got to come out at some point, promise?"

"Try stopping me! Love you. And India – well done, you deserve this."

India knocked a water glass off the bedside table as she scrambled to grab her phone. It was Lizzie.

"Hope I'm not calling too early. I just got the kids off to school. You were great last night. I told you… They all loved you. Twenty-nine women signed up. You've got yourself two classes a week! Congratulations!"

"Lizzie, I cannot thank you enough. It was a wonderful night. I hardly slept. I was so pumped up on adrenaline. It really did go well, didn't it? And you put together such an amazing dinner. I'd no idea it would all be so … well, glamorous … and the food was to die for. Thank you. Thank you."

"You are most welcome." Lizzie laughed. "I just want to give you a heads-up. You can expect a call from Larry Hertz this morning. He's an agent at CAA. He's such a celebrity fucker – he loved the idea of Annabelle Butler's twin sister writing a book."

"Omygod, Lizzie, you're a fast worker."

"Let me know how it goes and if there's anything else I can do."

"I will. I'll call you later. Oh. And Lizzie, I want to give you something for the use of the studio and also I hope you know that any work you might want to do in my courses will always be on the house, always, Lizzie. I mean it."

"Okay, India. I might take you up on that offer. I could certainly use the help. But the studio is just sitting empty. It's yours. No charge. If it all goes well, you can open up in Brentwood Village at some point."

"That's wonderful, Lizzie. Thank you, thank you so much for all you've done to make this possible."

India kept her phone tightly clamped in her dressing gown pocket as she did laps around the room. She was too excited to even think of getting dressed and too distracted to do anything more than make coffee and sit on the kitchen sofa waiting. She bounced up the second her cell buzzed.

"Larry Hertz putting in a call for Miss Butler. Can you hold, please?"

India hung on for what seemed an age and then found it almost impossible to keep up with Larry as he yelled in her ear at machine-gun-fire speed in a thick Brooklyn accent.

"I've put in a call to a few of my contacts to see if they'll bite. I'll need a proposal to do a real pitch. Celebrity endorsements sell. This'll sell. I might be able to get an advance ... can't promise ... publishing business is in the toilet, but with the right hook... It's all about getting an angle."

India wasn't at all sure what he was talking about. He seemed to be using a lot of fly-fishing terms.

Larry got back to her within a few hours. "Okay, they're hooked and I reeled 'em in. I need a fast turnaround on a proposal. Peter Cohen in my office is expecting your call. 310-693-..." India didn't have a pen, and he'd already dropped the line. She took a deep breath and then called the CAA switchboard.

Larry had made writing a book proposal sound easy, but by the time she'd finished talking with Peter, she needed to lie down for half an hour. The guidelines were straightforward but involved all kinds of research. What were the competitive books in the field? The comparable ones? How did she plan to market it? How fast could she get Larry a one-page outline, a summary, an overview, sample chapters, a résumé, a list of signed A-list celebrity endorsements? Could she make sure it was double-spaced, in 12-point Calibri or Times New Roman and draft a cover letter? And a strap line to go with the title?

India's head was racing as she started her research and began googling.

Thérèse

Why is Supernanny wearing hot-teacher glasses? she wondered. Everyone knows nannies don't wear glasses or suits ... what's with that? Well, nobody's persuading me into a cap and gown no matter how many books it'll sell.

≋≋≋≋≋≋≋≋

"Hi, India. Have you got a minute?" Lizzie whispered. "I thought of you just now, and I have to share."

"Absolutely. I've been stuck in front of the computer all morning," India said, closing the shutters in her bedroom. "Go on ... but speak up a bit, there's a lot of background noise."

"I've come into the garden to make sure nobody's listening. Can you hear me okay now? Good. So ... Joanna, one of Sophie's friends, has just left the house. Stan's sending Sophie off to New Leaf for a month, and from the way she and Joanna were clinging onto each other, you'd have thought they were auditioning for a part in Titanic."

"What's New Leaf?" India asked, settling down on one of the walnut Louis XV tapestry armchairs and resting her legs on the matching footstool.

"It's a rehab facility in Malibu. I think Stan's lost it, but that's not why I'm calling." Lizzie lowered her voice. "Okay, so Joanna just turned seventeen, and she arrived in a three hundred and fifty grand, fully- loaded Maybach, a birthday present from her father. And you want to hear the worst of it?"

"What?"

"She was pissed that she didn't have a full license and can't carry passengers yet.."

"You can't be serious," India said.

"I am. I tell you, Jack was more excited about getting his goldfish last week. Apparently Diddy bought a Maybach for his son and so Joanna asked for one too."

"That's outrageous."

"Yes, well, I thought you might like to see what you're dealing with here."

"Omygod. That's serious."

"Yes, well anyway. Look up New Leaf and tell me what you think. Call me later."

As soon as she clicked off, India went back to her laptop and searched for New Leaf. A couple of weeks sleeping in the wild, somewhere like Uganda, would be a better solution, she thought as she stared openmouthed at the five-star facilities with spas, views of the Pacific, and luxurious private rooms with king-size beds. Lizzie's right. Stan's lost all sense of perspective.

≈≈≈≈≈≈≈≈

India worked with such laserlike focus over the next few days that she hardly even missed Adam. It felt as if he'd been gone for months already. Accustomed to unreasonable deadlines and burning the midnight oil, she pulled her résumé together. Then she began decoding the jargon. Supernanny had a "program." That's what teachers call a "curriculum," India realized. I need a six-week program. Okay, brainstorm. Week One, Stress Management. Week Two, Boundaries. Week Three, Creativity ... and I definitely need some "steps." Step One... Focus... Step One ... Step UP and Take Control! Okay. And Step Two ... mmm... Take a Step Back. Sounds like a dance routine, but I kind of like it, she mused. Sinking back in her chair, in a flash of inspiration, she leaned forward again and wrote "Two Easy Exercises Needed."

Which gave her the satisfying acronym "TEEN." She typed it in bold.

Supernanny also had "tools." As in "resource materials" – worksheets, templates, and PowerPoint presentations. No problem there, Supergirl, India thought. I've changed way more slides than you've changed stinky diapers.

She would also need "case studies" for her sample chapters. "Case studies" translated to "progress reports." Omygod! I've done a zillion of those, she thought, although not with adults, so I'm going to need fresh material, and I'd better tape the sessions.

She called Lizzie.

"Hey. Quick question. How do I go about recording my sessions?"

"No problem. I have a 4x Pro. You can download it onto Windows. We have camcorders as well. I wish now I'd had them installed in Sophie's bedroom." She laughed. "And just a thought, India: I'll draw up some disclaimers for you."

"How do you mean?"

"This is personal stuff. So you'll need to cover yourself. California's one of the most litigious places on Earth. You need to own the rights to every story you publish."

"Thanks, Lizzie. I'd no idea."

India flicked through Simon Clements' book. It was crammed with affirmations and inspirational quotes. She'd need some of those too, but that'd have to wait. She'd just had a text from Adam. Her man was back in town.

≈≈≈≈≈≈≈≈

India was sitting out by the pool, about to take a bite of her tuna melt sandwich, when she glimpsed the caller ID. Play it cool, don't be too keen, she thought. He's the one who scooted off on safari.

Putting down her plate, she took a sip of her lemonade and picked up. "Adam, how are you? How was your trip? How's Max?"

"I'm tired, really tired, but good."

"Guess what. I have news – I'm going to be running some workshops in LA starting tomorrow!"

"Fantastic. Fast work. Great. I want to hear all about it … when can I see you?"

India paused. "I'm free this weekend," she said, too quickly she thought. "Well, Saturday, anyway."

"So let's make a plan. Please. I'm going to stay over at this end of town, keep an eye on Max," Adam said quietly.

"Why don't you come over here?" India replied. "I've the whole place to myself. And I could do with your help. I'm writing a book proposal and it turns out I don't write American. It's a foreign language – even the punctuation's different. But sorry. You said you're tired. How come? Was it a long drive?"

"You're in that bubble again Indie … I guess you haven't seen a paper or the TV this morning?"

"No … I can't work out how to use all the remote controls. Maria must think I've had a lobotomy or something. But I've never seen so many options and if I grab the wrong one, the drapes fly open."

"That's funny," Adam said. "Well, I could hardly get Max in and out of the courthouse this morning with all the fucking cameras and TV vans. Alanna and Lauren were there… It was a total shit show."

"Why was he in court? Was it the accident?" India asked, shunting out of the sun and climbing under a canopy.

"Yeah. He was arraigned for DUI. Easy bail. His attorney's pretty sure he'll get off with a fine. He's already been to rehab and nobody died. But he's not in the clear yet. There's always the chance the judge'll get heavy just to prove she's not starstruck. We stopped off at Kate Mantilini for a burger on the way back."

"Joss told me they do great mashed potatoes there."

"They do. I'll pick some up on my way over Saturday," Adam said, "but I'd also like to take you out somewhere special. It's been a while. Let me think. I'll text you, but how 'bout we aim for seven?"

"Perfect. I'll see you then."

India put down her phone, stood up, and took a running dive at the pool. "He's back! Wahoo!" she screamed before performing a magnificent belly flop.

C'est La Vie – Let's get this party started.

India was checking out the sound system when Lizzie stuck her head in.

"All okay?" she asked her. "I've told everyone to park on the road and walk up."

"This is perfect." India beamed, looking around the spacious octagonal room with its maplewood floor and long windows. "I love the Zen Garden. It's beautiful."

"Yes," Lizzie sighed. "Pity, I never use it myself. Good luck! And promise to drop by before you leave to let me know how it went."

"I will. Thanks, Lizzie."

Adjusting the strap of her Turlington tank top and smoothing down her Nuala capri pants, India forced herself to smile before coming out from behind the Shoji screen divider.

"Hello, lovely to see you. It's Georgia, yes?" she said, ushering in a woman who was wearing a deep crimson monogrammed pantsuit and stepping gingerly around a Happy Buddha statue.

"Please sign in. Leave your shoes at the door and help yourself to iced green tea."

India gestured to a black lacquered table set out with a china urn and Harmony motif teacups, and made a pretense of arranging some leaflets. When she had counted in all but one of the women she was expecting, India waited a few minutes and then directed everyone into a circle on the bamboo rug.

"Welcome," she said, with what she hoped was a beatific smile. "Please sit down and let's get to know one another."

India had rehearsed her opening remarks but was having trouble remembering them with fourteen expectant faces turned to her.

"It's lovely to see you all here this morning," she said. "And what a beautiful day. Just look at that California sunshine." She paused. "Now please join me in taking a deep cleansing breath."

A deep sigh echoed in the room.

"Okay. I'd like each of us to take a moment to introduce ourselves to the group. I realize being here might feel awkward at first. So, I'll make it easy… I'm India, I'm from London, and I'm here to share my experience of working with teens." She nodded encouragingly to the tall tan woman with the long streaked blonde hair sitting to her right. Dressed in boot-cut workout pants and a tie-dyed tee, she looked barely older than a teenager herself.

"I'm Amber. Hello everyone," she drawled. "I'm a mother … of two … my son, Harper, is twelve and my daughter, Serenity, is fourteen. They both go to Forest Wood." She stopped for a split second and tucked her hair behind her ear. "What can I tell you? I'm from LA. I'm a certified masseuse. I specialize in reflexology and aromatherapy, I also love kayaking and surfing, any water sport really. I ride a Harley Twin Cam 88 most weekends… There's this awesome bike trail in Malibu where I – "

"Thank you so much, lovely to meet you," India cut in politely. "So … and … you are…," she said, gently, to the woman next to Amber.

"I think we've met," she said. "I'm Summer. I did a reading at Annie and Joss' party… I'm a clairvoyant. I have a daughter. She's twelve. Her name is Charity."

"Yes. I do remember," India said quietly with a smile before inviting the brunette next to her to speak.

"And you are?" she asked.

One after another, the women introduced themselves with the slick professionalism of game-show contestants.

"Some of them stopped just short of giving me their blood type," India told Sarah the next day.

"Okay, everyone," India said, jumping to her feet, realizing she had drastically misjudged the time she'd allocated for introductions. "First off, I would like to show you a short piece of film. Before I do, can anyone guess who said this?" She pointed to a white board.

"Sometimes when I look at my children, I say to myself, ' _____, you should have stayed a virgin.'"

"I think that's me, India," shouted Trules, another woman India remembered from Joss and Annabelle's Memorial Day party.

India laughed. "Okay, I'll tell you. It's Lillian Carter, mother of the thirty-ninth president of the United States." She added, "Just to let you know there may yet be hope. So now, a short film. This, I think, is inspirational. It's a program happening in the UK. What you need to know is that all the young people here were convicted of petty crimes. But instead of going to prison, they were sent on a twelve-week intensive dance program for young offenders."

The screen lit up and the room went silent as the women watched a group of disaffected, monosyllabic teens transform themselves through discipline and teamwork into young men with warmth and connection in their eyes. The clip ended with a dance performance. Immediately after it was over, a woman in a white smock and blue jeans struggled to her feet.

"I'm sorry. I need to share," she said, choking back tears and twisting the pink diamond rock on her finger. "Last week the LAPD turned up at my house at two o'clock in the morning." She paused, swallowed hard, then stammered. "They arrested my son for aggravated burglary... I feel so guilty. How come, how come... I didn't even notice he had a drug problem? How could that happen? We gave him everything."

There were looks of sympathy exchanged among the women as another mother stood up. "My daughter's fifteen and has been in rehab for cocaine addiction twice," she said.

A woman with short black hair dressed in black leather pants and a tank top raised a sculpted arm. "My son Daniel is eighteen. He's getting good grades. He's on the soccer team and he's dating a fifteen-year-old. I've found used condoms in his room. Under-age sex here, well, it's statutory rape if he's caught." She hesitated. "I'm worried sick and he won't talk to me."

India listened hard as more of the group talked about how helpless they felt living with the strangers their kids had become; the lies, the anger, the fear, the years of coping on their own, and how it was affecting their marriages and their other kids.

"Well, I think we've broken the ice here, today," India said to a ripple of relieved laughter. "This has been pretty intense. But talking is the first real step to changing things. Nobody should have to feel isolated. Today has been about sharing, and you've done all the work. Next time we meet, I will have some tools we can use to help us move forward. I'm not a therapist, I'm not a counselor, and it may well be that some of these issues we've touched upon need professional guidance. We'll see. What I hope to give you are some strategies for coping; some tools that will give you support."

India shouted through the spontaneous applause. "Thank you all for coming. I can assure you that everything you have shared here today is in absolute confidence. Nothing we have recorded will be used without your express permission. Have a good week."

≈≈≈≈≈≈≈≈

Adam clicked open the gate to the guesthouse and walked up the path.

"Hi! I'm not quite ready yet," India said, opening the door in her ivory satin Victoria's Secret demi-bra and negligee with the black velvet side ties.

"I'd say you're absolutely ready," he said, closing the door behind him and following her with his eyes as she sashayed toward the bed. Leaning against the wall he began unbuttoning his hand-made white twill shirt. "Don't move," he said. "Stay right there."

An hour later, they were in the car. Adam called the restaurant as they zoomed along Sunset Boulevard. "Adam Brooks. I had an earlier booking … for two … yes … delayed; we're on our way. Thanks." Adam pulled out his earpiece and swerved to let a biker pass. "They've kept the table. Hungry?"

"Yes," India nodded contentedly and rested her hand on his thigh. "I've worked up quite an appetite."

"Me too." He grinned. "You'll love this place. It's got a real New York vibe and the food's amazing. The guy who owns it is about a hundred and eighty but as you English say he's 'as fit as a fiddle.'"

"Oh no, Adam. Paparazzi!" India said, pointing to a cluster of guys with cameras who were standing calmly under a line of coral trees by the entrance.

"Yes, but they're tame here. They have an injunction; nothing without permission within a hundred yards of the restaurant. Just smile and say nothing and they'll leave us alone."

Soon they were ensconced in a black leather corner booth.

"So, tell me about the workshops," Adam said.

India was distracted by Ellen DeGeneres and Portia de Rossi, heads together in the booth next to them. Maybe my nom de plume should have a "de" in it, she thought. India de Butler? No. Maybe not. "This is delicious. What is it?" she asked, swirling her glass and sipping the amber wine.

"Gavi," Adam said, touching his glass to hers. "Finest Italian Cortese grape. Salute."

India took another sip and then filled him in on Lizzie hosting the evening and Larry Hertz pitching her book.

"Adam, I've only been here a few weeks. I can't believe all that has happened in such a short space of time."

"Well, I can't take all the credit, but I did tell you your workshops would fly here, didn't I? I mean what is it they call it? Modeling, that's it. You take something successful and reproduce it somewhere else? I'm amazed you're so surprised. I mean, clearly at your level it was always going to happen."

"I suppose…" India hesitated.

"The book sounds like a brilliant idea. It'll sell internationally. You've already got your English market established and here the celebrity factor will give it leverage." He looked up at the waiter. "Indie, do you know what you want?"

"You pick," she said. "It all looks delicious."

Adam snapped the menu shut. "Okay, then we'll have the porcini mushroom and truffle risotto, the grilled barramundi, and two green salads to start."

"Grazie mille," the dark-haired waiter said with a slight bow.

"So you said you were having translation issues," he said.

"Yes. Well, first off there's spelling… There's a distinct absence of vowels … specifically u, like in flavor, color, neighbor, and then other words are spelt differently, like 'theater' or 'realize,' and you don't use double l's. It's not just that, though; it seems you're all rather fond of short paragraphs, commas, and colons, and you use words and expressions that I'd never dream of using."

"How so? I think you have a pretty extensive vocabulary, and you certainly don't hold back in the bedroom."

"Well … okay." She laughed. "I'll admit there are some universals there!" Sitting up straighter, she looked at him. "Okay, I'll give you a great example – I have to say 'period' instead of 'full stop' and you know what a period is in English right?"

"Not personally, I can assure you," he said. "But I hear what you're saying. It's the languaging that's different."

India burst out laughing. "There you go … you 'hear what I'm saying.' That is NOT English. And there is no such a word as 'languaging.' You can't make 'language' into a gerund." India leaned back as the salad plate was put in front of her. "Joking aside, I'm getting really frustrated with it. I'm used to flinging words on a page and having them stay there, and don't get me started on nouns … we take the lift, you take the elevator."

"I tend to take the stairs."

"Very funny, but I'm not just talking about 'you say tomayto I say tomahto.' It's not pronunciation I'm struggling with – it's nouns, verbs, sentence construction, vernacular terms. This'd be easier to write in French."

"You speak French?"

"Un petit peu…kind of…" India said, glancing down and slicing into a leaf of endive.

"Est-ce que tu veux un autre verre?" Adam asked, gesturing to her empty glass.

"Thanks," she said, nodding. Omygod, his wife … Shit, of course he speaks French. Help.

"Well, I can see how frustrating it must be. But you said the agent's helping right?"

Phew… she thought. "Yes. It's all good, just so much more work than I was expecting."

Taking a forkful of steaming risotto, Adam thought for a moment. "Somebody once said we're two nations divided by a common language. Who was that?"

"George Bernard Shaw, I think … but for once he was wrong. It's a completely different language."

"I love the way you pick up on my references," Adam said. "Though I think it may have been Oscar Wilde."

"What-ev-er." India laughed. "Don't worry, I'll be bilingual in no time."

≈≈≈≈≈≈≈

India was in her element. Perched on a high stool in her low-rise Prana yoga pants and sleeveless tee, she felt totally in control and confident.

"You're dealing with 'millennials,'" she told the group. "There's absolutely no way millennials think the way we do. Okay, I know, it's California." She smiled. "But even if we're not owning up to our age, we are a different generation, mostly Gen Xers. It's another world. We're a long way from the days when you worried about your mom finding your diary or waited for your prints to come back from CVS."

"Absolutely," Lizzie said, nodding.

"That's for sure," A tiny thirtysomething woman with a spray-on tan agreed.

"Just look how the Internet's changed everything," India said. "These kids are their own brand, with their own fan clubs living in cyberspace. They're communicating with each other at the speed of light but hardly communicating with us at all."

A petite redhead in a plaid skirt and butter leather jacket murmured, "So true. My daughter, for instance, wouldn't dream of ever answering her phone when I call. She texts, if I'm lucky."

"They can create their own movies and star in them," India added. "They can disappear into a labyrinth of untraceable connections. So how do we watch them? What can we do?" She paused. "And you know what's the scariest part of all? We pretend that it isn't happening and try to relate to them the same way our parents did with us."

"We all feel so helpless inside and yet we pretend we're doing great," Lizzie's friend, Farrah, volunteered. "We might be falling apart, but you'd never know it from the speeches at the bar mitzvahs or sweet-sixteen parties."

"We have to start with being honest, Farrah, and try to understand what their world is like," India said. "But enough from me. Let's split up into groups and do some work." She hopped off the stool. "Find a partner."

Back at Annie's that evening, India curled up on the couch in her fleecy dressing gown and new chocolate brown Uggs to write up her notes and plan a different communication strategy. In an open discussion later that afternoon, it had become clear that some of these women had been deep into drugs or promiscuous sex themselves as teens. Clearly, they were not going to come out and tell their precious offspring how they popped Ecstasy tabs or shagged around at raves between marriages. She would need a different approach to this part of her course.

She sucked on her pen. Still, she thought, this is heaven. How amazing to be teaching and facilitating without that awful commute, with no bells or assemblies, no mind-numbing lectures from Dr. White, no playground duty on freezing winter afternoons. How wonderful to have Adam. India could not remember a time she had felt happier in her life.

≈≈≈≈≈≈≈≈

India and Adam were sipping Bellinis in the lobby at Shutters.

"I can't get over this place," India said, tucking her feet under a velvet cushion on the luxurious fireside sofa and wrapping her Paul Smith pashmina round her shoulders. "It actually feels English, like the Soho Hotel in London, all the paintings and flower arrangements. It's so cozy."

"It's got more of an East Coast vibe, that's for sure," Adam said. "But listen, it's my turn for news," he added, grabbing a handful of rice crackers.

"Go on," she said. Please don't tell me you and Angel are moving in together. Please.

"I've finally read a script that's working for me. I'm excited."

"That's brilliant!" She exhaled with relief.

"Fred Stein's directing. I'm gonna play a Russian guy who moves to London to find work. He leaves his wife and daughter behind in St. Petersburg. It's contemporary. Apparently, London's full of Russian immigrants right now?"

"Absolutely," India said. "The papers are forever running articles about the Russians and Poles taking 'our' jobs. They seem to forget we marched around the world invading everywhere. It's karma if you ask me."

"Right. Well, London isn't exactly Nirvana as my character finds out. He ends up on the streets for a while … then he meets someone … sounds cheesy, but it's really tightly written. We'll start shooting here and then there'll be a few weeks on location in a village outside St. Petersburg in December. "

"Fantastic," India said, her heart sinking at the idea of him so far away.

"Do you have a fur coat?"

"Sorry?" India spluttered, trying to mask her excitement. Omygod … omygod! He's expecting us to still be together in December. That's almost four months away.

"I repeat. Do you have a fur coat?" He grinned.

"I don't," she said, "but I'm seriously good at the vodka shots. Are you asking me to come visit?"

"Absolutely," he said. "I can't wait to get you naked in the snow. I want to see you in a pair of boots, a pair of black leather thigh high boots…"

"Okay. It's a deal." She laughed. "You know ever since I read Anna Karenina I've wanted to go to Russia. I played the mandolin for a while; maybe I could learn the balalaika."

"We'll also be shooting in London, of course. I'd love to go visit your studios when I'm there. Maybe we could go together. Where are they based?"

"Oh … all over really," she stammered. "I'll see what I can fix up nearer the time."

"Za vashe zdorovye," he said, raising his glass. "To your health."

"Down the hatch!" She laughed. "That's English for 'cheers.'"

≈≈≈≈≈≈≈≈

India pulled out the scalding chicken casserole dish with thick oven gloves and set it down on the range. Checking the browning roasted potatoes, she poured oil over them and went back to the armchair to catch the end of an episode of Supernanny.

Yuck. What's with that red skirt suit? she thought. This is not doing anything to improve the image of the English.

Springing to her feet a few minutes later, she hit the remote as she heard the car roll up in the driveway. Clooney, who had been snoring loudly by the door, looked up lazily.

"Get out from under my feet," India muttered, tripping over him in her rush to get outside. Annabelle was already climbing down from the Range Rover in a pair of pale blue jeans. Her hair was streaked blonde from the sun and the rich coral of her embroidered smock was accentuating her golden tan.

"I've missed you," India yelled as Annabelle slammed the car door behind her. "You look absolutely wonderful."

"Darling, you too. You look so LA in your sweats," Annabelle said, hugging her. "We've had the best time. Hello, and I missed you too, Clooney."

"I think he's due for one of his pills," India said, backing away from the dog as he lunged between them.

Joss swung down from the Range Rover and swept India up in his arms. "So how are you? You survived without us and from what I hear you've been busy." He grinned.

India beamed. "Lots to tell," she said, backing away from the hyperactive dog, who was now sniffing around her groin.

Joss yanked him by the collar. "Sit, Clooney. Sit."

"I've made supper. You two go freshen up and I'll tell you over dinner. Anyone fancy a glass of wine? Rhetorical question I know."

While Joss dragged the heavy cases into the house, India went to the kitchen, opened a freshly chilled bottle of Sancerre, and lit the collection of chubby scented candles she'd arranged in the center of the kitchen table.

"This smells delicious, darling. I'm so ready for home-cooked food," Annabelle said, dragging out her seat. "So tell me about you and Adam. One-liner e-mails weren't doing it for me. I want to hear all about the great romance. I know some of where you've been from the weeklies."

"Yes," India said. "We're having some privacy issues. But they've mostly just been pictures of the two of us walking around Montana, and there was a nice one of us coming out of Marmalade Café. I love that café. It's like Paris.

"You're a good-looking couple," Joss said, forking a potato.

"Yes, well, I'm on the alert these days. They're not catching me with my knickers down again." India laughed.

"Which is not a rule you're applying to Adam Brooks, I assume," he teased.

"Okay. I set that one up nicely for you," she said, blushing. "Well, Mr. Brooks and I have been getting along extremely well and … as they say … moving swiftly on… My workshops are going brilliantly. I've been doing two a week and working on the book proposal in between times."

"Lizzie e-mailed me the other day to say you're incredible," Annabelle said. "She told me you have the most wonderful way of bringing people out and guiding them gently. She said it's heavy stuff but you make it fun."

"That's great to hear. She's wonderful, so generous."

"She's amazed you have so much knowledge and common sense. That was the part I found the most surprising, the common sense." Annabelle laughed as India topped up their wineglasses.

"It's been the best summer," India said, sitting down again. "Though I really have missed you. I absolutely love LA. Everyone's so friendly and helpful. It's been the most incredible time for me and I can't thank you enough."

"Darling, how could I possibly have got through everything without you?" Annabelle said, grabbing her hand.

Joss wiped his mouth with his napkin and leaned back from the table. "That was so good," he said. "Annie and I were just saying how happy we are you're staying. I'm not on the road until January, so you and I will get a chance to work out our schedules and make sure Annie doesn't get overloaded."

Annabelle smiled at him. She seemed more relaxed than India had seen her in years.

"Yes. We'll all be together for Thanksgiving this year for the first time ever. Oh and Halloween. You can do the costumes with the girls – and there's our birthday. I feel like doing a little happy dance. It's so good to be alive!" Annabelle said, raising her glass.

"To us!" They clinked their glasses and raised them in the air.

"To health, wealth, and happiness, in that order," Annabelle declared.

There was silence for a second, and then she added, "I'm not going to take anything on until the New Year, you know. I'm serious, I don't want to look back years from now and think I missed the time with the girls. What was it you called them once, 'the special years?'"

"Yes. It's a special time. Right now they actually want to spend time with you. They won't always," India said, carving up the apple pie and piling slices of it into china dishes.

"Yes. I'm grateful for it all, believe me." Annabelle paused for a second. "Lizzie's started divorce proceedings; I'm sure she told you."

"Yes, she really is remarkable. She's determined not to play the victim. Her heart's broken but she's all about the kids. They'll work it out I'm sure and with a bit of luck she'll meet someone who'll show her some respect," India said, handing her sister a jug of fresh cream.

"Mmm ... it's been ages since I tasted your pastry, darling. You haven't lost your touch."

"Thanks. I've been cooking in between writing. I love this kitchen." India licked apple off the back of her spoon. "One of the things my workshops have made clear is how many of these teens are in the middle of custody battles or dealing with step-mothers young enough to be their big sister. Lizzie's been coming to some of the sessions and I think it's been an eye-opener for her."

"Stan's been a good friend to me, but he's lousy husband material. I'll see him next week; there's a launch at CAA," Joss chipped in.

India could see this was probably a conversation best kept for when she and Annie were alone. She might easily hit a nerve. After all, Joss hadn't exactly spent the sixties in a monastery.

"Stan's a decent guy in lots of ways," he said. "I don't suppose he wants to make things harder for her than they already are."

"Let me tell you about our trip last weekend to Santa Barbara," India said, changing the subject quickly. "We had the best time ever. We stayed in an amazing estate on a private vineyard belonging to you'll never guess who…"

Thérèse

PROFOUND THOUGHTS NOTE – In my element!

"This looks interesting," Trules said, scanning the meditation room and pointing to the poster-size sheets of cardboard and neat clusters of crayons on the floor.

"Yes. We're getting creative this morning. Give me one more minute," India said, trying not to fixate on the inked image of a bleeding sacred heart with embellished crucifix on Trules' exposed shoulder. She fiddled with a Norah Jones CD and adjusted the volume.

"India, now that I have you on your own," Trules whispered, "I have to tell you how much I'm getting out of these workshops. It's not easy to admit it, but bringing up Sam on my own is really tough. I never thought I'd ever trust another woman again after Kenny left. I want you to know these sessions are changing my life. You're the real deal. You're wonderful."

India glowed. "Thank you so much, Trules. That's wonderful to hear … yes, with me what you see is what you get."

"I know that and I wanted you to know how much it means to me."

"Well, thank you. That makes me very happy… Hi!" India said with a smile as Summer poked her head in the doorway.

192

"Come on in. I love those," she said, admiring Summer's shredded blue jeans.

"Thanks. Got them from Barneys. They're J Brand."

"We're working on the law of attraction this morning," India said. "I think I might attract a pair of those to myself."

"Law of attraction? Hey, I'm up for anything. I haven't enjoyed myself this much in years. Who knew having issues could be this much fun?" Summer quipped, bending down to help India spread out sheets of paper as the room began to fill up.

"So ladies, today we are going to stop focusing on your lovely offspring and spend a whole morning on you. We're going to create vision boards," India told them. "You have to work fast. Don't overthink anything. Your subconscious will do it for you once you get into it. Take a couple of magazines and flick through them really quickly. The minute you see a picture of anything that you feel expresses you, just cut it out, rip it out."

"It can be anything at all; a picture of someone doing something you love to do, or something you want to have; anything that feels meaningful to your own life right now. I'll give you half an hour and then tell you what we'll do next. Go!"

They're really getting into this, India thought after a while, watching the fierce concentration on everyone's face. I must do one for myself sometime.

"Now if any of you are wondering what this has to do with parenting, I'll tell you," she said, breaking the silence when the time was up. "Mimi, you can stop ripping paper now."

Mimi, the proud owner of the largest bosom India had yet to see in California, laughed and put down her magazine.

"I believe that if you do something every day to nurture your own spirit then you can handle all the other stuff you have to deal with so much better. Women often put themselves last. We get sucked up into other people's needs and expectations. We forget who we are, who we used to be. This exercise is an incredibly powerful tool for getting back to our own spirit, to our connection with ourselves and to what we want. Let's get on with it."

The three hours flew by as they pasted their images onto the cards, and by the time they were saying their goodbyes, each woman was carrying her poster like a prized work of art.

"Next time we'll talk about what we've learned. Sleep on it. Have a great week, everyone. Thank you all for coming."

As the group began to trickle out, India started clearing up, and checked her phone. There was a short message from Adam. She could hear the strain in his voice.

"Hi, Indie, sorry to miss you. We're downtown for the hearing. Try you later."

≈≈≈≈≈≈≈≈

Closing the glass doors and crossing the garden quickly, India tapped on the kitchen window. Lizzie waved her inside.

"I was hoping to catch you today," Lizzie said, resting the dish towel on the countertop and giving her a hug. "You look more like Annie every time I see you."

India had a glow about her like she always did at the end of a good class. "Thanks," she said, pulling off her bandanna and stuffing Annie's pendulum crystal earrings into her purse. "It's going well. I'm feeling good. How're you?"

"I'm okay. Sorry I missed your session this morning. I'm only just in. Rhonda had to get her typhoid shot. I just dropped her back at school." Lizzie rolled up her sleeves and filled a pan with water. "I've given Silvia a few days off; her sister's just had a baby."

"Can I help?" India asked, lifting up a potato peeler.

"Sure. Thanks. I'm making fish pie."

Lizzie began carving the halibut while India plopped potatoes into salted water and shelled the iced shrimp that were floating in the sink.

"I had a drink with Stan last night," Lizzie said after a few minutes. "He's being civil. It hurts, but you know in some ways things aren't that simple."

"In what ways?" India asked quietly. "What do you mean?"

"Well, I've been doing a hell of a lot of thinking and looking back on how it all went wrong. At first I was blaming Stan for absolutely everything, but then I realized that I've been so wrapped up in the kids. Well, frankly India… I think I may have gotten a bit boring. I was bored rigid myself and going quietly mad. That can't have made me a bundle of laughs to be around."

She started expertly chopping red onion on a marble slab. "I can't say it's an excuse for what he did, but I can see that maybe he felt excluded. I've been very much in charge, like the house and the kids was my job."

"But it is your job," said India, desperately trying to understand and wondering if she would ever get the stench of fish off her fingers again.

"Sorry, I've only just started to work this out myself, so I'm not making sense," Lizzie said, wiping the corner of her eye with a paper towel. "What I mean is, I'm not the kind of woman who can be completely fulfilled just running a house and kids with some projects on the side. I need more. I need my career back."

"I can sort of see what you mean, but I don't think you could ever be boring," India replied, thoughtfully. "Are you and Stan trying to work things out then?"

Lizzie paused for a moment. "I was certain it was over, but listening to some of those women talk in your sessions has made me look at life differently. I'm giving myself permission to imagine that we may be able to resolve some of our issues. Stan's agreed to come to counseling with me and we're setting up new ground rules…" Lizzie sniffed, her eyes full of tears. "It's the onions," she said, turning away from the countertop and blowing her nose. India watched as she ran her hands under the faucet.

"Are you okay, Lizzie?"

"The thing is, I love him, despite all this…" Lizzie faltered. "I thought after the scare with Sophie that it was just business as usual. He seemed so detached, but now I realize he just doesn't know how to talk to me anymore and some of that might be my fault."

She sat down on the Gubi stainless steel chair. "He's been spending time with the kids lately and Henry is a different boy now that his dad's actually giving him some attention. Oh, I don't know, India. It's all so overwhelming."

"Well. I've never been married or had kids, but I do know one thing," India offered, sitting down next to her. "I think a lot of people give up too easily. When I look at Annie and Joss I can see that it's all about seeing it from each other's point of view. It's about loving enough and being able to grow together. I really do believe that. If you still love each other and can learn to trust again, then maybe you do have something that is worth hanging onto. It comes down to honesty. So many things do."

"Yes. Well, we'll see," Lizzie said thoughtfully. "We'll see."

≈≈≈≈≈≈≈≈

"India, I've never been the possessive type, but I haven't heard from you in over a week." Sarah sounded mournful.

"Oh! Sarah, I am so so sorry! Everyone's back, the house is full and I'm crazy busy with the workshops and getting the book proposal finished… But tell me, please, how are things?" India put down her pen and got up to stretch the muscles in her back.

"They've increased my hours at the hospital. I'm knackered," Sarah groaned. "I was hoping you could bring me up to speed on life in La-la Land so I can live through you vicariously. Are you certain Adam's friend isn't looking for a thirty-four-year-old who's not scared of vomit and is prepared to become his sex toy?"

"I told you, Sarah, I am not introducing you to Max … not ever."

"I was kind of hoping they'd lock him up so I could write him long distance and we could get married in jail… I like the idea of knowing a guy's not going anywhere."

"Very funny, Sarah. Seriously though, it was a bit nerve-racking. Adam was so relieved they let Max off."

"I'm sure … only joking. So how's Bella? How's Cindy?"

"Great. They've come back with a whole new appreciation of home after all those weeks of hard beds and municipal food. I think summer camp's a brilliant idea. I don't know why it's never caught on in England. The kids learn so much independence and the parents get a break."

"So what are you up to tonight?"

"Adam's coming over for a swim then we're all going to an Italian restaurant called Vincenti. Sarah, I'm hopelessly besotted. It's not just the great sex… He's, well, he's so intelligent and kind and funny and…" She trailed off.

"Has anyone used the L-word yet?"

"No … we're taking it really slowly, but I did tell you about Russia; I'm sure I did."

"Yes. Near Christmas right?"

"Yes."

"Well, I may have to gate crash that party," Sarah said. "I'm having visions of you playing Lara in Doctor Zhivago. Though there again, happens not. I could end up with a kid called Boris."

"That'd be bad. I agree." India laughed.

"Okay, Indie, gotta go. I'm due in work. I was just checking in. Have a great evening. Love you."

"Love you too," India said, closing her phone and running outside to join Annabelle. She spent the rest of the afternoon reading in the shade and napping until Adam arrived early evening and joined Joss and the girls in the pool for a raucous game of Marco Polo. After quick showers they crammed into one car and drove off in the direction of Brentwood.

During dinner, India looked across the table at her two nieces in their 'mini me' hippie dresses, sitting either side of Joss, who kept making them laugh through mouthfuls of spaghetti. Annie leaned across and wiped Bella's chin and Adam put his arm around India. A feeling of pure contentment washed over her. She looked at each one of them and took a mental photograph. I'm surrounded by the people I love most in the world, she thought, my little family and my wonderfully kind, sexy gorgeous man.

≈≈≈≈≈≈≈≈

India squeezed her book proposal into the padded white envelope. "Fingers crossed," she said, smiling and handing it to the FedEx guy, who looked at her blankly. "You have a wonderful day, ma'am," he said.

India sank down in the kitchen couch and gave a deep sigh. She'd sent the proposal off with the working title Tuning In to

Your Teens. She felt it needed more work, but she had exhausted the process.

Now what? she thought, recalling yesterday's call with the immigration lawyer, a friend of Lizzie's who'd charged her an inordinate amount of money for ten minutes of his time. At that rate she'd be working just to pay his fees.

"I take it you are a nonresident visiting alien," he'd said.

"An alien?"

"I'm assuming you are an alien who has not passed the green card test," he continued.

What was this? Avatar? she thought, outraged. What else was he assuming? What was a green card and how could she have failed a test she hadn't taken? It was all horribly offensive and confusing.

She would need a visa, and would be required to file taxes. Then apparently there were different rules if you were a visiting "consultant" or an "international writer." I have to make this work, she thought. I can't face the idea of going back to London. I belong in LA even if they think I'm an alien.

≈≈≈≈≈≈≈≈

"I fucking HATE you. You've RUINED my life," screamed Trules.

Trules and Mimi were standing at the far side of the studio in front of the rest of the group, who were sitting cross-legged on mats on the floor.

"Tell me, Trules, are you playing the mother or the daughter here?" India asked, then waited a few seconds for a couple of women who were convulsed in the corner to stop laughing. "What we are trying to do … is to remember how it feels to be physically out of control. We learn to deal with our hormones better as we get older."

Trules and Mimi exchanged looks.

"Okay, you remember I said 'better,'" India said. "What I'm getting at is that our hormones get into a relatively, and I stress relatively, more stable rhythm eventually. But a teen's raging hormones are chronically unpredictable and put together with their emotional immaturity you have a time bomb that can go off without warning at any point, as you all well know."

"That's for sure," interjected Amber, who today was sporting pink and green hair extensions.

"So I want you to find another partner now, decide which one of you is playing the teenager, and when I say stop, describe exactly how you're feeling and, most important, tell your 'parent' what they could do to make you feel better. Do this, then I'll let you swap around so you each get a turn."

India watched in amazement as they all went into character.

There's something in the gene pool of Americans. They're just natural performers, she thought.

Stan's ex-wife Joan had joined her Wednesday classes. India was happy that she and Lizzie were getting on okay. Lizzie seemed to be making strained efforts to communicate, and India had deliberately paired them this morning.

Summer was a brilliant actress. India watched as she mimicked her daughter's outbursts and flung the contents of her purse across the room, shrieking and pulling at her hair with tears streaming down her face. It was getting a bit too realistic for India's taste; it was almost as if she were channeling. Maybe she is clairvoyant after all, India thought. Didn't Annie tell me that at her card reading in Malibu she told her to go see a doctor?

"Great job. Great job," India said, waiting for them to catch their breath.

"Is anyone in any doubt now just how exhausted these kids must be? So ... if you remember the 'terrible twos,' you'll realize that this is simply a version of the same thing. It's a temper tantrum when they can't have what they want instantly."

She gave two sharp hand claps.

"Okay. Now change partners. Get with someone else and tell her how you felt in the middle of your rant. Ask your partner to describe what it was like being yelled at."

She paused to let them move around the room, then gave the signal to begin.

To close, India invited them to lie down, stretch out on mats, and enjoy Tchaikovsky's Valse-scherzo, opus 34. Although her trip with Adam was months away, India had been immersing herself in things Russian. When the piece ended she quickly ejected the Rimsky-Korsakov CD, which she sensed would do nothing to calm Summer, who was lying with her arms outstretched and appeared to be jabbering in tongues.

"Okay, people. Thank you. You've all worked very hard today." "Have a lovely week and remember ... a teenager is just a friend you haven't met!"

≈≈≈≈≈≈≈

"Shit. What time is it?" India grunted, dragging herself out of bed, tripping over a shoe and whacking her head on the nightstand. "Shit ... six thirty," she muttered, hurling the offending footwear across the room.

India now did the school run three mornings a week. This involved getting the girls up and out in time to be on campus by eight o'clock; a tactical operation only marginally less complicated than the Apollo 11 moon landing. Going from the house to the car was about as easy as shoveling cement. Somebody always forgot something, lost something, needed something, or had a crisis over what to wear. (Often, that was India.)

India had observed that, although there was no school uniform for the kids, there did seem to be one for the parents. As dropping off also involved getting out of the car to help unload all the bags, musical instruments, and general sports paraphernalia, she felt it was important to have "the look," especially now that she was something of a celebrity herself and knew so many of the mothers.

She pulled on her Bottega Veneta cashmere sweatpants. "Three hundred and sixty dollars and they still do nothing for my butt." She sighed, glancing in the full-length mirror briefly before running across to the kitchen, where the girls were finishing their breakfast and Maria had their backpacks stacked by the door. India grabbed a quick cup of coffee before steering them out of the house. Luckily today they were ready to leave.

Joining the back of the endless line at the school gates she watched one of the mothers climb down from a Mercedes SUV, her Alexander Wang sweats clinging as tightly to her backside as Saran wrap.

Years of tantric sex and liposuction must have solved the problem for her, India thought. Oh! I give up. I really do.

She dropped her nieces off and looped around Sunset, grateful for the slow-moving morning traffic. It was still a challenge for her to drive on the right side of the road.

"I thought Labor Day was supposed to mean the end of summer," India said when she was finally back, pouring a glass of

Voss and collapsing onto the kitchen couch. "The air isn't even moving and it's not nine o'clock yet."

"It usually stays in the nineties right through September." Annie said, pumping strawberries and soy milk into a blender. "Like those 'false summers' in England. Don't you remember going back to school in the heat in winter uniform; those awful pleated wool dresses?"

"Yes. I do remember. It's called an Indian summer … a late blooming," India said. "But it's so dry and dusty here. My hair's clinging to my head."

"Smoothie?" Annabelle asked, pouring the thick liquid into a tall glass.

"No thanks. I'll get a croissant in a minute when I get some energy back. What've you got on today?"

"I've my trainer at ten."

"In this heat? Annie, you're insane."

India had observed that Annabelle was tackling "not working," with the same intensity and focus she brought to working. Power Pilates three mornings a week, ballet classes on the other two weekdays. Saturday was Tae Kwon Do, and Sunday a drive downtown to a Buddhist meditation center. Her afternoons varied, but usually included a full body massage or solving some general maintenance issue: nails, hair, waxing.

The days were short, because the girls needed to be collected at three. That left several hours during which they had dancing classes or extra tutoring for math. As India was the teacher in the family, she spent part of her evenings helping the girls with homework. And what a ridiculous amount of homework, she thought. When do these kids get to hang out?

She discovered they didn't. Everything was scheduled.

Thérèse

While there was no chill in the air or falling leaves, India did notice the beginning of a "social" season. Annie and Joss went out at least three times a week, sometimes to dinner with friends and often to political fundraisers. Most days Adam was on set at Universal Studios or downtown at the Institute of Modern Russian Culture looking at archives. They rarely went to Malibu now, but there was a whole new scene opening up, with swish private gallery receptions and fashionable art shows. They went to the Huntington Library gardens in Pasadena to see the Rousseau landscapes, the Hammer Museum in Westwood for a book signing, and to a Tibetan installation at LACMA. Adam always took her somewhere wonderful for dinner afterward; Mr. Chow's monochromatic kitchen for crispy skinned Peking duck or the Little Door, India's all-time favorite French restaurant, where they sat on rustic iron chairs in romantic candlelight sharing steamed black mussels and sipping sweet Moroccan tea

"Omygod … Adam, this is terrifying."

Straightening up in the oversize armchair, India uncurled her legs, adjusted the cushion behind her back, and swiveled the computer screen toward him.

Gazing at her over the top of his reading glasses, Adam marked his place in a battered copy of The Brothers Karamazov.

"What is?"

"This Pro-Ana website. The girl's emaciated and she just purged. It's gross; gag reflexes, bingeing. I'd no idea. Look. Look at her rib cage. They actually call it a 'lifestyle choice.' Some lifestyle."

"That's pretty scary." He shuddered. "Why are you on there, anyway?"

"I just found out Farrah's daughter's down to ninety pounds."

"Angel was talking about the exact same thing yesterday." Adam nodded.

India squirmed and looked fixedly at the screen. Yesterday?

"She was saying her Pilates classes are full of anorexics killing themselves to break a sweat."

Well, I hope Angel's not getting her cardio in on you, India thought, noting down the number of a help line. "Okay. I'm done," she said, pushing her laptop across the coffee table then coming over to snuggle up next to him on the couch.

Adam leaned forward and poured a cup of Earl Grey. "I admit it, tea tastes better in a teapot."

"Thought you'd appreciate it; it's an Emma Bridgewater." India smiled, stretching out her legs across his lap and cradling her cream china mug. "So what're you up to tomorrow? I have to leave around eight."

"You don't want to hear. That's the fun bit," he said nodding at the stack of books at his feet and picking up a schedule. "It all starts this week. No carbs, protein drinks, four hours' training a day, and that's not counting the boxing classes."

"That's intense," India said, flicking through the schedule's pages. "Are they sure it has to be such a strict regimen? I mean, you're pretty ripped to begin with…"

"Thank you." He grinned. "But I don't look like I've spent my life hauling bricks up and down the Volga River yet. I don't mind the weight training, but the diet's brutal."

"Well, things could be worse, I suppose. At least you only have to pretend you did it. That was poor Yegor's real life."

"True and that wasn't the worst of it … homeless in London isn't much fun either."

"That must be awful; home's so important. I love your apartment. Actually, in a way it's a bit like my flat in London. I've a ton of books, too, and a baby grand piano. I got to keep our mother's things, and I'm a hoarder. I love flea markets."

"My designer was English," he said, gently massaging her toes. "That's probably why."

"Yes, that dresser could have come straight from Heal's."

"It did." He laughed.

Adam had moved his attention away from her feet and his hand was edging up the inside of her thigh.

"I have another little treat for you," she said, pulling away with an effort. "I think you'll like it even more than the teapot. Be right back ... put on that Shostakovitch CD."

"I'm not going anywhere." Adam grinned, lifting a log and aiming it at the dwindling fire.

India went into the bedroom and pulled out an ankle-length white gypsy skirt from Annabelle's LV overnight bag. She smoothed out the creases and draped a large Hermès scarf over it. I shall wear it handkerchief-style as a top. Très avant-garde. She smiled.

She folded her worksheets into the Fendi tote, dashed into the bathroom and slipped on her Agent Provocateur Fifi slip ($550). She snapped the clasp on her suspender, straightened the seam on her black silk stocking, then gently eased her foot into a six-inch patent leather stiletto.

≈ ≈ ≈ ≈ ≈ ≈ ≈ ≈

Lizzie was not at the house when India arrived. India was disappointed. She was hoping for a quick cup of coffee and a few compliments on her current look. That's a lot of cars. What time is it? Maybe the clocks went back, she thought, running toward the studio and adjusting the Hermès scarf as she went. Damn. It's so slippery. I should have pinned it.

Opening the door with one hand and struggling to adjust her top with the other, she stumbled into the room and looked up. There was a deathly silence the minute she appeared. Every face was turned toward her. She froze. Something was terribly wrong. The women from her Wednesday group were there too.

Why is everyone so quiet? Why are they all looking at me like this? What on Earth has happened? she wondered, looking down and realizing with horror that she should have worn an underskirt. But that was not what this was about, she knew.

India was scared. It was as if she did not recognize these people anymore. Somehow she was the enemy. Summer was the first to speak. There was a tremor in her voice.

"Why…" She paused, adjusting a couple of her bangles. "Why is it better to call yourself a country, India?" she said, her eyes flashing.

"I'm sorry?"

"Than a season? Like why is my name so ridiculous, IN-DI-A?"

Lizzie stood up. "You need to see something that Sophie sent to Joan last night, India. It's on YouTube. When you do, I don't think you'll have any difficulty understanding what Summer means."

She spoke in a very measured tone, and India knew with absolute certainty that this was not a surprise party. Adam was not about to spring out from behind a curtain and propose. Her heart started to pound.

Maybe they've found out I only taught high school. I can explain. This is a terrible mistake,she thought, scrambling through all the wildest possibilities. But she could not find her voice. Her throat had closed up. Then Lizzie turned her iPad round on the table to face her. She looked terribly sad.

It took India a few seconds to make sense of what she was looking at. A line of small screens came up and then she saw the title: "Double Trouble for Annabelle Butler"

Lizzie enlarged the page and pressed play. India was still having great difficulty taking any of this in properly, and then with a terrible shock she saw herself on the screen and realized she looked a complete wreck. Her eye makeup was smudged, her pajamas looked really old fashioned, and what on Earth was going on with her hair? The camera panned shakily back to Annabelle who, India saw, was looking pretty rough too.

"This is not good," she said, half out loud.

Then the awful reality of what she was actually watching closed in on her. She heard her English accent, which sounded somehow peculiar.

Do I really sound like that? she wondered. Then she tuned in to what she was saying.

"Simon talks a load of bollocks… I think he's full of shit… Anyone could come up with some fucking self- help program…," she spat.

India suddenly felt sick. Her legs went wobbly and she leaned against the side of the table. What? When? What is this?

She stared in absolute horror. She began to shake. She sounded so sour. She looked so mean. It was like watching a horror movie where some evil spirit had taken over her body. Now she remembered. It was the week she arrived, the morning she had the hangover from hell after Annie's dinner party.

But how?

She was having something approaching an out-of-body experience now, watching with a weird sense of detachment.

Surely she had not been so nasty. Surely she had never been so horrible about such lovely people. She was horrified at her cheap joke at Summer's expense, at the low punch at Trules. She was mortified. There was no escaping it, she was actually sneering, and then when she thought the worst must be over...

"Adam Brooks ... attention span of a gnat like the rest of them..."

This was wrong. She'd never said that, surely? Why would she? When would she? But clearly she had.

She was seriously panicked now, conscious that her face was burning. She desperately ransacked her brain for an explanation. How could this have been taped? Who could possibly have done this and why would anyone want to put it on YouTube? A zillion thoughts were flying round her head. She felt cornered and ashamed. She needed to explain that the whole thing was out of context.

Oh God! Adam will be so hurt. How can I ever explain this to anyone? Who the hell filmed this? How? How could they? We were by ourselves.

The clip finished with Annie looking appalled and angry, crying, "That's enough!"

With that the screen went black. There was total silence in the room. India was absolutely mortified. Her head was swimming. All eyes were turned on her and still nobody spoke. They were all waiting for an explanation and she had none to give.

≈≈≈≈≈≈≈

It was midmorning when Annabelle heard the car screech into the driveway. One look at her sister's face told her all she needed to know.

Thérèse

"I tried to call you last night to give you a heads-up," Annabelle said, lifting the milk jug, setting the cafetière down on the table and placing a box of tissues next to it. "I saw it last night. Lizzie called me. I tried to get hold of you for hours. Coffee?"

India shook her head. "No, just Advil please. My phone died. Not that it would have made any difference I suppose," she said, slumping onto the kitchen chair. Annabelle sat down opposite and held her hand across the table.

"Annie, I don't know where to begin. I feel terrible. It was the worst moment of my life. On the way back I was thinking how fond I am of Summer and how much I've learned about people these last few months. And my workshops aren't cynical. They're not just some ... what did I say ...'fucking self-help program.'"

"I know, I know," Annabelle soothed.

"It's only now I realize what a bad space I was in the end of last semester. Everyone here seemed to have it all so easy. All your friends were so pulled together and successful and I was eaten up with resentment and didn't even know it."

"Yes," Annabelle murmured. "I remember."

"I can't think what to do. Everyone this morning was so hurt. I couldn't think of anything to say to put it right. I just ran out of the room. I was such a coward."

"You were shocked, that's all," Annabelle said, standing up and coming round the table to put her arm around her shoulder. India began to sob uncontrollably.

"I love those people," she choked. "I love Lizzie. She's been an amazing friend. They all looked so devastated, hurt. Really hurt. Annie, they weren't even angry; they were wounded. Who taped that, Annie? Why? And who hates me enough to put it on YouTube? I'm so sorry, I'm so sorry ... and Adam, what's he going to think?"

"Adam will be fine," Annabelle said, stroking India's hair back from her face.

"How so? I said he was stupid – well, about as much."

"You'd only just met the guy. It won't do him any harm to think you weren't starstruck, and anyway, what about me? I look bloody awful on it."

"Well, yes, it was bad," India agreed, managing a very weak smile and blowing her nose loudly on a tissue. "There's already a pack of photographers out there. I think I'd better warn you," she said, wiping the mascara out of her eyes and leaving a streak across her blotchy face.

"Yes, well, Joss as ever is handling that," Annabelle glanced at the wall clock. "I wasn't planning on going anywhere much today. José-Marie can come and do my hair here. I'll have Tess call him. Why don't you go and take a shower and get changed. Let's talk this through and make a plan. Don't bother charging your phone. Don't call anyone, either. Come back here and let's sit and decide what we're going to do."

India was glad for the direction. She felt completely washed out and helpless. She stood up dutifully and went toward the door, trudged across the garden and went straight into the bathroom. She turned on the faucets in the shower, took off her clothes and went into the stall, where she let the water torrent down her face for a very long time. She dried off, wrapped a towel around herself, and pulled her computer out of her bag.

> To: Ssims@gmail.com
> FROM: Indiabutler@gmail.com
> SUBJECT: All Gone to Shit
>
> Desperately need to talk to you. Too much for
> e-mail. Cell's dead but call the house when

Thérèse

you get in from your shift. I'll be here all day.
Please call. I desperately need to talk to you
about something that just happened.

Indie xxxooooxxx

≈≈≈≈≈≈≈≈

Lizzie had watched the video several times. At one level, she
could see that India had a point; there were a ton of people on
the self-help bandwagon in California. As a lawyer, she was also
trained to look at things with a critical eye. She understood that
there was probably more to it than had been caught on camera.
But it was India's tone of voice that was the hardest to forgive.
It seemed so out of character. After all the betrayals, the disap-
pointments, of the previous months, Lizzie felt like someone had
literally punched her in the stomach. India was a friend. But this
woman on YouTube wasn't the India she knew and loved. This
was someone cynical and bitter, a vicious stranger. She cringed at
the memory of all the confidences that she had shared so easily
with India, how she had opened up to her about everything –
from her lack of sex with Stan to her feelings about his kids. She
felt foolish, vulnerable, and very alone.

When Joan had called the previous evening, Lizzie had been
filling out an application for a part-time position with a legal firm
downtown. This was all part of her plan to reclaim her life. Stan
and she had decided to try to work things out. Through their on-
going sessions with a counselor, they were tentatively discussing
the possibility of living together again.

Stan had been staying at the Beverly Hills Hotel since the
night of their violent row. Lizzie knew it was killing him to spend

the money and was amused when he told her he was bored rigid with the menu. She suspected his motives for agreeing to counseling; he'd probably decided he couldn't afford to pay two sets of alimony and still bask in prestige and sickening ostentation. She also knew he'd recently lost a wagonload in stocks and property portfolios.

But after a few of India's workshops and some sessions with her shrink, Lizzie's resolve had softened, especially when Stan broke down. She'd never seen him cry before and was genuinely moved when he blurted out how he still loved her, how the affair had just been sex. He said he would do anything to save their marriage and the thought of his life without her and the kids was terrifying him.

He was the father of her children. That had to be worth another shot. She determined she would try again, but there would have to be changes. She set out her terms and he agreed to them. She had to get back to work. She needed a life outside the family.

India's about to discover that people in this town will wipe you out faster than you can blink, she thought. She sighed thinking of the friends who'd been ostracized from the social calendar before the ink had dried on their divorce papers. Had that stark reality been part of her own fear when she agreed to try again with Stan? Had it? Could she ever trust her own judgment again?

≈≈≈≈≈≈≈

"Where's the other half of Double Trouble?" Joss said, striding into the kitchen at twice his usual speed, reaching into the chiller and pulling out a can of Stella Artois. "I just got off the phone with Andy Goldberg and he's not happy."

"I'm still trying to work out how serious this is," Annabelle said, almost to herself, as she waited for the video to upload again. "Four hundred thousand downloads in the last twenty-four hours and I look goddamned awful. I'll never work again."

"It's gone viral. That's for sure," Joss said, grabbing a packet of Cheetos off the workstation and sitting down next to her at the kitchen table. "Want one?"

Annabelle shook her head.

"I can remember the fight clearly. India had only been here a few days … it was after we'd all been down to Malibu, the morning after our dinner party, so that would have been just after Memorial Day, yes?"

"Yeah. I remember thinking you two were taking a while to shake down together."

"She'd been having a rough time at school. She's always been prone to rants when she's unhappy or hormonal. Honestly she's like a bloody teenager herself half the time. No wonder she's so good at understanding them."

"Okay," Joss said, leaning back and running his hands through his hair. "Let's work this out. Bella and Cindy were messing round with your iPhone, right?"

"Yes. India had a hangover and she kept telling them to get the damn thing out of her face."

"So that's how this got on camera, same day we went to the Marina. They'd been to some kid's party the night before. You told me to watch they didn't have any more sugar."

Annie nodded. "Yes they were hyper, but they were just mucking around, and one things for sure, there's no way they'd post it, is there?"

"Of course not," Joss said, folding the empty chip packet into neat squares. "So where's your phone? Let's see if we can work out when it was downloaded."

"That's it. I don't have it," Annie said slowly. "I couldn't find it the morning you drove me in for the surgery. I remember because India was joking about me not needing it because I'd be unconscious anyway."

"Any idea when you lost it?"

Annabelle slumped back in the chair and folded her arms.

"I'm not sure…" she said tentatively. "Maybe the afternoon we went to the medical plaza for that first round of tests. I was distracted. There was all that shit going on with India and Max. It's a bit hazy."

Annabelle clasped her hands over her mouth. "Joss, someone must have found it. It could be anyone. It could be anywhere."

"Tess would have canceled it when she ordered your new one, but they may have uploaded stuff onto a computer," he answered steadily. "What else was on it?"

"Well, I don't know … photographs, texts – you know, the usual crap, but it was new, so not all that much, I suppose. Oh, God! I hear what you're saying, Joss. This could come out in installments. We'll have to ask the girls. Please tell me it's the only time they used it. There could be anything on it … anything … at all."

"Annie, we don't know that yet. I'll ask Bella, but it's really important you don't get stressed," he said, squeezing her hand. "This is embarrassing as hell for India, but you handled it like a pro. You didn't fire back. This isn't some Mel Gibson clusterfuck and there won't be anything too awful – we're not the Kardashians."

"I know." She sighed heavily. "You're right. But for India this is one giant cock-up and just when she was starting to get it together. I mean, she must have been distraught when she found out. What happens now, do you think?"

"I'm not sure." Joss hesitated. "How is she?"

"Not good. And it was all going so well for her," Annabelle said into the air.

"I'll get the girls from school. You stay with India," he said, getting to his feet and kissing the top of her head.

"Thanks. I love you." She smiled up at him.

≈≈≈≈≈≈≈≈

India dragged on a pair of Levi's and a tee and climbed on top of the bed. She pulled her knees up to her chin and rolled onto her side. The physical discomfort was overpowering. Her stomach felt leaden, and she had a strange sense of detachment, as if her body belonged to someone else. She buried her head deep into the pillow, craving darkness, a deep dark hole where she would never wake up.

She had felt like this before. She had felt this same sense of humiliation, disgrace, and failure. When? Why? She opened her eyes then closed them again and remembered. The nun was standing over her; cold black eyes peering through her wimple, her face distorted with anger, rows of classmates watching in silence "India Butler, you will never amount to anything. You are contemptible, an aberration in the face of God."

She began to tremble. What had she done? Yes, she had filled a sink with water, yes she had put her face in it, and yes she should have been in the playground... "But sister..." India winced at the memory. Yes. This was how it felt to be disgraced, to feel exposed, and still hear some inner voice screaming, "I didn't mean any harm. I didn't ... I didn't."

She needed to cry, but the pain was lodged so deep inside no tears would come. But now, reliving the morning, she could remember only sadness etched on these women's faces, not fury or contempt. Why was that? What was different? What?

She curled into a tighter ball.

They loved me, she thought. They were hurt. They risked opening themselves up to me. I let them down. I misjudged them all those weeks ago. All I saw was the shiny veneer, the extravagant lifestyles and the privilege. Annie's right. I did have a huge chip on my shoulder. So what changed? What? When?

It was the night at the hospital and those days after, she thought. When I understood how vulnerable they were, when I realized they were just like me. For the first time in my life I felt like I belonged, I could be myself. I felt needed, that I had something to give.

India sat up slowly and climbed off the bed.

But this is not about me. It's about them, she thought. They're the ones who are hurt. I'll find a way to explain to them. I have to. I will, because I was on the right path even though it's all gone to shit. What was it Tony Robbins said? "Step up … be a force for good." Yes, and I WAS a force for good. I was.

She went into the bathroom, splashed her face with cold water, and straightened her hair. She took a long look in the mirror. "Okay… STEP ONE – STEP UP…," she said to her reflection.

India closed the gate tightly behind her before walking slowly across to the main house.

I have to find a way to make this right … but for now, I've made a decision…

≈≈≈≈≈≈≈

Joss and Annie looked up as Clooney yelped and ran cowering to the far corner of the kitchen.

"Even the dog's not speaking to me now," India said, dragging out the chair next to Annabelle, and slumping into it.

"Here, Cloon," Joss shouted, throwing him a well-chewed rubber bone. "Catch."

Coming round the table, he gave India's shoulders a tight squeeze, then sat down next to her.

"Okay, guys. I want to make a speech," India started. "Yes, please," she nodded to Annabelle, who was pouring tea. "Thanks."

She took a deep breath, a very deep breath.

"I can't begin to thank you for all you've done for me, and I can't even begin to tell you how awfully sorry I am for the chaos I've caused."

Annabelle went to say something, but India put her hand up to stop her.

"I think it'd be best if I go back to London. I have no way of earning my living here now, and you guys have been more than generous to me. I'll find a way to pay you back, but really I think after what you've been through you deserve a bit of calm."

Annabelle took her hand. "Darling, I know none of this is your fault. I do know"

"Whose fault is it then?" India asked her, looking her straight in the eye.

"It's nobody's fault," Joss interjected. "Shit happens. I've just spoken to Andy Goldberg again. He's sure there's no damage to Annie. He said if anything it's good PR for her; she comes across as really together. We were worried what else they'd filmed, but Bella's told me that's the only time they messed with Annie's phone."

"Look, darling, there are two issues here. The first one was private lives getting played out in public. I'm a name. People are endlessly fascinated, that's why the thing's gone viral, but it's about as interesting as watching paint dry. They'll hit it, see you ranting on, and maybe they'll try to spin it, but right now the press are more interested in all the red carpet crap."

"What do you mean 'spin it'?" India asked, taking a sip of Earl Grey, her hands trembling slightly.

"Well, there's bound to be some little freelancer trying to sell the 'true story' behind the People magazine piece, but this is LA, and for as long as we've got Lindsay, or Travolta, there's always going to be something juicier for them than that."

"So you're not just saying this?" India said, turning to Joss. "Is Annie right? I've not caused her too much damage? She's not just saying that, right?"

"It's all cool," he said leaning across and grabbing a chocolate cookie. "Annie's not working right now. It'll blow over."

"But the other issue," Annabelle interrupted, "is how this impacts our friends and what we do about that."

"I know," India said, her eyes welling with tears again. "I know, and I will find a way, I'll write an apology to each one of them separately. I will do anything it takes, but Annie, I need to leave. It may be the cowardly thing to do but I can't stay. I can't. I'm too ashamed and it's not fair to you. I need time to think this through, put some distance on what's happened."

She swallowed hard. "I have to make some calls," she said, stifling an almost overpowering urge to cry and lurching to her feet. "Love you...," she mumbled.

And Adam..., she thought, closing the bedroom door behind her. Her stomach muscles tightened like a tourniquet at the thought of speaking to him. Would he have seen it already? She could barely breathe. She picked up the bedside phone and called; he didn't pick up. When she tried to leave a message, she had no words. She hung up.

Thérèse

Moving over to the desk she booked her flight to London online and sent an e-mail to Sarah, who responded on her BlackBerry.

> To: Indiabutler@gmail.com
> From: Ssims@gmail.com
> SUBJECT: Hang on in there girl!
>
> I'll be there to pick you up. (In more ways than one.) Can't wait to see you. Love you. See you Friday. Can't wait.
>
> Hugs. Sarah xxxxxxxxxxxxxxxxxx

≈≈≈≈≈≈≈≈

Robert pulled the car around and lifted India's three heavy suitcases into the trunk. India climbed into the back of the Lincoln quickly. She wanted this part over with fast. She waved to Annie, Joss, and the girls until the car turned into the curve of the driveway and the trees blocked her view. Then she sat back and hid behind her Oliver Peoples sunglasses. She could see the expression of concern on Robert's face as he looked at her through the rearview mirror.

"It's a bad time of day for traffic, Miss Butler, but we'll get you there in plenty of time."

"Thank you, Robert," India mumbled, choking back tears. In time for what? she thought. For the plane that'll take me back … to what? Scrambling around in her purse she found a squeezed up tissue and blew her nose. She felt worn out. Her head was throbbing from lack of sleep and lack of food. Her stomach had been in a tight knot for days now. She felt numb.

This is all so wrong. It wasn't supposed to be like this.

She checked her phone one more time. There was still nothing from Adam. She'd texted to say she was going out of town and still no response. Maybe Angel was easing him into a Downward Dog right this moment.

The security line at LAX seemed endless and unnecessarily intimidating.

Now I come to think of it, they really do treat you like an alien, she thought, edging alongside the conveyor belt while an obese gum-chewing official barked unnecessary instructions. "Shoes off." Okay, I know, give me a second. India struggled to unzip her knee-length Prada boots, then flung them into the plastic tray.

Thank goodness Joss had upgraded her again. She took her wine voucher to the bar in the business-class lounge and traded it for a plastic cupful of lukewarm Chardonnay, two cubes of Day-Glo "American cheese" and a packet of saltines.

A hell of a lot different from the lounge at Heathrow, she thought, remembering how exciting it had been waiting for her flight only two months earlier, tucking into salads and pasta, sipping champagne and stretching out in a cabana. How excited she'd been, how hopeful. After the firewalk, she really had believed that she could create a whole new life if she could focus clearly on what she really, really wanted. And now. Now what? Would she ever be able to believe in herself again? Would she be single forever?

After cramming her carry-on into the overhead locker and handing the attendant her coat, India sat down wearily and fastened her seat belt. She declined the "sparkling water with citrus garnish" and accepted a thimble-size glass of sparkling wine instead. Gripping the sides of her seat, she closed her eyes as the plane tore down the runway. As it tipped sharply sideways she peered out of the window. Catalina Island was shimmering in the distance, outlined against the silvery light of the rippling ocean; stretched out beneath her were the yellow sands of Malibu. Adam might be there right now, she thought. I wonder if I'll ever see him again…

India closed her eyes. She was too exhausted to think. She drifted into a foggy sleep as the captain switched off the seat belt sign and the Boeing 747 headed for London.

≈≈≈≈≈≈≈≈

Turning the corner and trudging past the duty-free store at Heathrow, India could see it was going to be a struggle to balance her cart through the crowd that was cramming the barriers. And then suddenly she was blinded by whirring cameras and flashbulbs firing off in her direction. Putting up her hand to shield her eyes, she turned and immediately recognized the focus of their attention; the strikingly beautiful woman coming up behind her who was holding onto two small children and wearing a baby slung across her famous bosom. For a second, India was not entirely sure whether she was relieved or disappointed.

She tried to spot Sarah. It was almost impossible to plough her way through the crush. Eventually she managed to get to the automatic glass doors and saw the top of Sarah's head bobbing up and down by the exit. Pushing her way through the throng, Sarah eventually reached India and gave her a huge hug.

"You look so LA!" she exclaimed, standing back and admiring India's gray fedora and pink cashmere jacket. "The car's over the road. Here, I'll take one of those for you; the pavement's bumpy. Bloody hell. Have you got a dead body in here?" she said, hauling one of India's Samsonites off the cart.

India followed her out onto the shiny wet street to the crossway. The air was damp and cold and it seemed to take forever to reach the fourth level of the parking lot.

"I'm not sure all of this'll fit inside Mr. Darcy," Sarah said, referring to her ten–year-old Alfa Romeo.

Squashed into the front seat and balancing her feet on Annabelle's hand luggage, India hugged her knees as Sarah's car rattled out of the terminal. Now THIS feels like the wrong side of the road, she thought ruefully.

"India, this is such a balls up," Sarah remarked once they were on the M4 Motorway.

"I've missed you, too," India replied, staring out forlornly at the expanse of gray sky.

"Sorry. How are you holding up?" Sarah asked. "You have to be exhausted. But you look sickeningly amazing, you really do. I've made up the bed in the spare room and you can stay as long as you like," she continued cheerily. "The place is more of a mess than usual – I've been working long shifts."

"Thank you. Don't worry, Sarah, I could sleep on the kitchen floor I'm so worn out."

"You don't have to talk now if you don't want to," Sarah said tentatively.

"There's not a lot more to say," India said wistfully. "I screwed everything up, as I told you."

"Then I suppose this isn't the right time to tell you that your cat just died?"

India looked startled.

"Only joking. Don't worry. The Countess is still alive and dining on fresh tuna daily."

India threw her head back and laughed. "It's so good to see you, Sarah."

"I've got us several nice bottles of Sancerre and a chicken with some garlic up its bum. I have also taken the liberty of purchasing a couple of large bars of Cadbury's Dairy Milk, a DVD of Les Misérables and extra Kleenex," she said, and then added, "I'm off till Tuesday. I'm all yours. Let's get thoroughly wasted."

As they crawled along the Edgware Road, India was struck by how small the buildings seemed to be, how tiny the houses, and how much duller than she remembered. It's so crowded. I feel like I've been away for years. This is how a city's supposed to look; kind of dirty and disorganized. I'm so tired of sunshine. I'm ready for this rain.

They turned off the Uxbridge Road and wended their way to Ealing. It was dark when they parked in the narrow street and dragged the cases up the path of the Victorian terraced house Sarah had inherited from her grandmother. India waited while Sarah rooted in her TK Maxx purse for her keys. It was an odd feeling not to be going back to her own apartment. Nothing I can do about it, she thought. I'll have to rent somewhere, but I can't think about that right now.

"You're in there," Sarah told her, pointing to a small room with a freestanding wardrobe and a dressing table cluttered with books and jewelry boxes. The tiny metal-framed bed had been freshly made up with layers of thick antique quilts. An ancient teddy bear was nestling between the pillows, next to a hot-water bottle and a clean pair of fleecy pajamas. India unpacked her toothbrush, checked her phone yet again, and plugged it into a wall socket to charge.

"Have a bath and a nap," Sarah yelled. "There are clean towels in the hot press on the landing. And there's Jo Malone bubble bath in there somewhere too."

"Thanks so much," India called to her in the kitchen. "Give us a shout later."

"I'll get you up when dinner's ready," Sarah yelled, taking off her red Jigsaw coat and throwing it over a battered armchair.

India gathered up the cat and curled up with her on the bed. She felt utterly exhausted and defeated, and yet there was something so comforting about being back in London. She could hear the background hubbub of English voices on the radio and the clank of pans as Sarah began cooking. Listening to the rain pounding relentlessly on the windowpane, she drifted off.

When she woke up, an hour or so later, India levered herself off the bed, realizing she was feeling hungry for the first time in days.

"Mmm… that smells wonderful," she said, wandering into the tiny kitchen, bleary eyed. Sarah had set out the table with a vintage printed Colefax and Fowler cloth, a couple of bistro glasses, and some candles.

"You packed in a hurry," she said, nodding at the open case on the sitting room floor. "Even customs never make that kind of mess."

"Yes, well, I had things on my mind," India said, climbing over it and taking a glass of Pouilly Fumé from her. "Lovely wine. Thanks."

"I love the new clothes. I had a bit of a rummage. Mind you, the Agent Provocateur would be wasted on me." She laughed, spotting the gilt-edged box. "I spend all my time in my uniform, as you know, and the last guy I went with asked me to wear it to bed, too!"

"From what you were saying that was a while ago."

"Well, no … that would be last week and that would be Signore Antonio…," Sarah hinted.

"Ahh … I think I missed something there," India said, taking a plate of chicken and roast potatoes. "Pass over the gravy and tell me all about it."

≈≈≈≈≈≈≈≈

"I think I must have become unhinged," India confided to Sarah a few nights later when they were sitting in the stained-glass snug at the Cat and Lion pub. "Now that I'm back it seems outrageous that I thought I could reinvent myself just like that," she said, carving into the beer-battered fish.

"How so?" Sarah frowned, turning the bottle of HP Sauce upside down and shaking it.

India sighed. "There was all that opportunity waiting, but I think maybe I went too fast."

"Indie. Stop beating yourself up, will you? You did a lot of things right. You got caught off guard, and yes, you went from Cinderella to the Wicked Witch of the West, but you didn't deliberately set out to hurt anyone. Your classes sounded brilliant."

"Yes. That's the one thing I don't doubt in all this," India agreed.

"So what's next?"

"I'm at the limit on all my credit cards. I need to earn some money."

"Well, I think it was worth whatever you spent. I know it all went pear shaped, but it's been such an adventure, such a ride…" Sarah said, taking a sip of warm Ecco Domani Pino Grigio.

"Yes. Well, it was for a while." India sighed, spearing a couple of chips and picking up her glass. "Sarah, are you sure about this wine? It tastes musty to me."

"I'll admit it tasted better with pasta. I'm not entirely convinced the Signore's Italian," Sarah mused.

"Sarah, it didn't feel like an adventure or a ride, it felt like destiny. If that stupid video had never happened I had a really good chance of earning great money doing what I love. Adam was right; I could have franchised them."

"Yes, it's rotten. But you know you crammed more into the last few months than most people do in a lifetime. You could write a book on the back of this – India's Summer."

"Been there, done that... Well, okay, I didn't write an actual book, but I did write a damn good proposal," India said thoughtfully, putting down her fork. "I need to make a fresh start. I think I'll just stick to what I know. I'm a good teacher at least, I never doubted that."

"Fair enough."

"Sarah, I know I keep saying it and thank you for putting up with me, but it's unfathomable of Adam to just cut me off like that, isn't it? I mean, I'd only met him once and all I said was he probably had the attention span of a gnat. That's hardly enough to hang me."

"True. You don't exactly come across as Mother Teresa on that video, but you're no Atilla the Hun either."

"Right. So shouldn't he want some closure?" India said staring off into the distance.

"You'd think," Sarah said. "You would, but well, in my admittedly limited experience, men are not good at saying what they feel, and although it seems like a lifetime, Indie, it's only been a week, you know."

"True," India said. "But I can't work it out."

"Well, I never met the guy, so I can't help you there, but I do have some good news for you. I've been storing this up for the right moment to give you a lift."

"Go on," India said. What could possibly brighten my miserable existence right now? she thought.

"I spoke to Jane last week just before you came home. She knew all about what's been going on and I asked her how desperate she was to stay in your place and guess what?"

"Go on." India felt a rush of excitement.

"Well," Sarah said, pausing for dramatic effect. "She told me she'd look around for somewhere else and she called today to say she can move out at the end of the week."

"Sarah, you're a star. Thank you. This is fantastic," India said, leaping up from the barstool to hug her. "Fantastic. Thank you." She beamed.

≈≈≈≈≈≈≈≈

If Adam would just call, I could at least explain. India yanked another handful of paperbacks from yet another cardboard storage box and stacked them onto the wall of bookshelves in her sitting room. It's been more than two weeks now.

She kicked the empty container to the far side of the room, where it landed next to a suitcase spilling over with summer clothes. Then she sat down heavily at the cluttered bleached pine table that doubled as her desk. Opening a copy of the Times Educational Supplement she began flicking through the vacancy pages for substitute teaching posts ("supply teaching" she was back to calling it). Babysitting, more like, India thought, idly wondering who might be covering for her own absence. She circled a few ads then pushed the paper away and turned to a sheath of carefully chosen handmade cards she had bought earlier from Harvey Nichols. The women in her classes were worth more than a cut and pasted e-mail.

I'll start with Lizzie, she decided, pulling her long gray cashmere cardigan around her shoulders more for comfort than for warmth. She glanced out of the window into the bleak road below. It was drizzling. The trees looked eerily stark in the dismal streetlights, the pavements were cluttered with wet leaves, the cars crammed up against each other. She watched a woman dragging a shopping trolley laden with trash onto the curb.

It all looked so dreary. India sighed, opening a card and taking the lid off her pen. Two hours later, she finally put it down again. She took a quick bath and set her alarm for seven. I have to get a job and not just for the money. I'll go insane trying to work out why Adam disappeared off the face of the Earth like that, she thought as she climbed into bed.

≈≈≈≈≈≈≈

India had waited until late afternoon to check in with Annabelle. She closed the drapes and curled up on her sofa. She felt cozy in her old granddad sweater and fleecy Cath Kidston pajamas. The room was glowing from the light of a log fire and the two wall sconces either side of her hand-painted mantel mirror.

"God, I miss you, darling," Annabelle said, flopping onto her heavy white linen couch.

"Especially in the mornings, don't tell me," India laughed, imagining Annabelle in her kitchen, the California sunlight pouring through her French windows. "How are you?"

"Good, but really, darling, I am missing you like crazy," Annabelle said, tossing off her gold Manolo thongs and tucking her feet underneath her. "So what's new?"

"Not a lot. I just got some freelance teaching. It's easy if you're not picky. I've four days next week in Tower Hamlets. Believe me, it's a rough catchment; forty percent dropout rate," India said, then hesitating for a second, "Have you talked to Lizzie? I've written to her. I've written to everyone. They won't have got the letters yet, I suppose; I only sent them last week."

"She's been busy with a part-time contract, so I haven't seen much of her. But she's incredibly fond of you, darling. She'll get over it. Leave it with me."

"Give her my love. How's Summer?"

"I've not heard from her for a couple of weeks. Last time we spoke she told me she'd lost confidence in her psychic powers. I can see that, I mean, she was a bit blindsided by what happened."

"How are the girls?" India said, changing the subject quickly.

"They're fine. Bella got her orthodontics sorted yesterday. The braces are pinching but I think she's secretly delighted. She looks really cute."

"Give them my love. Tell them I miss them too."

"I will."

"Are you still looking after yourself?" India asked.

"I'm good. I've had meetings with some people at CAA and we're in the beginning stages of looking at a pilot I might direct. It'll give me a chance to see if I enjoy being on the other side of the camera."

"That sounds like fun. So Annie, I've STILL not heard from Adam. I think he was more offended than you expected him to be."

There was a long pause during which India immediately sensed Annie was holding back.

"Have you spoken to him at all or seen him?" she probed.

"Darling. I thought you knew. I honestly thought you'd seen it by now…"

India went cold. "Seen what?"

"The tabloids … the day you left. I thought you'd have caught it, maybe at the airport. The picture was on the front page of one of the rags…"

"What was on the front page? What?"

"Darling, it's probably a load of bull; you know firsthand how these things aren't true most of the time."

"Annie. I still have no clue what you're talking about," India said, her knuckles getting white clutching the receiver.

"Oh! Well … it was a picture of Adam with someone … I don't really know."

"What kind of a picture? Who?"

"Well… I suppose…"

"Annie, just spit it out!" India snapped.

"Well, it was pretty explicit."

"Okay," India said, attempting to keep her voice steady. "Look Annie, I'll track it down and call you back. My imagination's gone wild here. Bye."

India leapt off the couch and threw the phone onto the cushions. She grabbed her laptop and opened it with trembling hands. Thirty seconds later she found the picture on TMZ. Yes, it was definitely Adam. But who was the hot blonde straddling him, the one with her arms around his neck? And yes … those were Adam's hands … underneath her sheer blouse, on her back. She was certain, because in case she might have missed it (which she hadn't) the tabloid had taken the trouble to enlarge that part of the image and circle it in red.

India felt as if she had been caught around the throat. A wave of nausea flooded over her. She sat rooted to the chair, immobilized with shock.

≈≈≈≈≈≈≈≈

India dashed up the steps of the underground station at Green Park and out into the crowded street and lashing rain, where she made several attempts to put up her umbrella. Deciding it was useless against the biting wind, she shook it down and raced the block to Langan's Restaurant.

"I'm sorry. It's teeming out there," she said, handing her dripping Burberry to the young cloakroom attendant.

"No worries. Do you want me to take those, too?" she asked, looking at India's drenched Scala leather workbag and umbrella.

"Yes, please." India smiled gratefully.

I look like a drowned rat, she thought, catching sight of herself in a large wall mirror. She ran her hands through her hair and followed the manager to a corner table where a dark-haired man in his early forties was waiting. India took in the pinstripe suit, the Thomas Pink shirt, the white contrast collar, and the tightly knotted silk tie.

"I'm Philip," he said, standing up and shaking her hand.

India also noticed his monogrammed gold-plated cufflinks.

God, I hate those cuffs, she thought.

"Sorry I'm late…," she said, smiling. "I had to sit in on detention longer than I was expecting. Honestly, keeping the kids back punishes the teachers and the parents more than the kids – I waited ages for the tube."

"I have been sitting here for almost twelve minutes," Philip said stiffly, gesturing to his fake Rolex watch.

"But I texted you," India said. "I left a message."

"I've never had to wait for an appointment like this before. I'm never late," he said, folding his napkin into sharp creases.

Omygod he's serious, India thought.

"Well, there was nothing I could do about it and I'm terribly sorry. Did you not think to order yourself a drink?" she said. Or maybe some wine for the table?

"I don't drink," he said.

"Yes. Well, anyway, I'm here now," she said cheerily. "Lovely to meet you."

"I think being late is very rude."

"I think you've made your point," India said. "Can we move on now?"

There was an awkward silence. It went on for some time. Philip made no effort to rescue the conversation, and after a few minutes India pushed back her chair.

"You know, Philip," she said, "I'm new at this dating agency game and I'm sure there's a protocol for what I'm about to do. But I'm very sorry you had to wait and that you don't think that I was worth waiting for. Again, I'm sorry. Goodbye."

With that India stood up, collected her things, and walked out onto the street, where she pulled her cell phone out of her purse.

"Sarah, I've just had the blind date from hell. Can you meet me for a drink? Yes... Taj Mahal... Okay, no, that'll be fine. I need the walk. See you in twenty minutes."

"Thank you. I'll have the chicken tikka masala, saffron rice, and a vegetable samosa," India said, handing back the menu and pouring a Kingfisher beer. "Okay that's it, Sarah. I'm not doing that again ever. It was awkward and embarrassing and he was a prick."

"Well, I just thought you needed to get out more. Sorry. That does sound bad," Sarah said, snapping off a corner of pappadam and dipping it into the onion chutney.

"And he wasn't worth ruining my Prada boots for either," she said, looking down at her soaking feet. "I'm just not ready, Sarah. It's only been a few weeks, and anyway, the school is exhausting and it's miles away and frankly I'm still in shock."

"I know. You're right. Give it a bit longer," Sarah agreed.

"I think I was almost braced for Angel to move in pretty quickly after I left, but I had no clue he was seeing that woman. I was so wrapped up in my workshops it never occurred to me to ask who he was training with for the film. If I'd taken the trouble to ask ... if I'd known it was her, then I'd have had my antennae out."

"Well, maybe, I suppose, but you said you did spend a lot of time with him and there weren't any signs."

"No, but he was on the lot at Universal most days. When did this start? I keep trying to work that bit out. I mean, he invited me to Russia. Do you think she was getting her fur coat out of cold storage around the same time?"

"Well, they're all shits. I've reached that conclusion," Sarah said, helping herself to another full glass of Cabernet from her carafe. "I wish we were gay. Life would be so much easier if I fancied you, India.

"The minute India was home, she threw off her clothes and ran an extremely hot, deep Jo Malone bath. She put in a Norah Jones CD and turned her stereo on high before sinking into the sudsy water and idly flicking the bubbles with her toes. She began to sob silently... *"There was a time when I believed that you belonged to me / And now I know your heart is shackled to a memory / Why can't I free your doubtful mind and melt your cold cold heart."*

When the phone rang, she ignored it the first few times, until the calls became too persistent and she eventually grabbed a towel, climbed out and ran into the kitchen.

"Hello, I have a call from Larry Hertz for Miss Butler; please hold."

India hung on, dripping her way into the bedroom, struggling into a pink fleecy dressing gown, and turning off the music.

"Hey, India, is that you? How ya doin'? Good. Good. So here's the thing."

Larry sounded supercharged, as if he were on speed, which he probably is, India thought. What could he possibly want?

"So here's the thing. I've sold your book. Right now I have two publishers waiting to hear back from me by the end of the day, latest. I need to run this by you. We have to make a decision. Warner's offering one seventy-five. I think they're the right ones for this, but…"

India could not take in any more information. He was going far too fast for her. He's sold my book? He's sold my book? He's sold it?

"I want to get this tied down. I need you to tell me if we should go with that figure or if we should hang out and see if we can get them up a bit."

"Larry," India said, "Larry, slow down. I'm not getting this. I just assumed … I didn't know you were … I'm sorry, could you please say all that again?"

India was trembling now. How could he have sold my book? How? Who could possibly want to read it after all that's happened?

"I sold your book and I've sold it for a six figure number. Is that making it clear enough now?" he said, very slowly picking out each word as if India had a learning disorder. He seemed to be enjoying this.

"Yes. Oh my God … this is for real? But how?"

"India, I think I told you. Nothing sells like a profile and you have one hell of a fucking profile."

"But I blew it. I seriously blew it."

"India, the proposal is funny. You're funny. You're up front. You're bitchy and funny – that sells. Look, I'll call you back, just tell me do you want me to keep pitching?"

"How much is the offer, did you say?"

"A hundred and seventy-five. I take ten percent of that. We get a third on manuscript delivery, a third on publication, and a third when we go to paperback."

"This is wonderful. Larry. Thank you. This is incredible. What do you think we should do? I'll leave it with you, whatever you think."

"Okay. I'll make a few calls and get back to you. Don't go away."

The line went dead and India stood frozen to the spot.

"I've sold my book. I'm writing a book," she announced to the Countess, who looked up from her curled position before promptly going back to sleep. "I've actually sold my book!" she shouted. "I've sold my book. I've sold my book…" she repeated, dancing around the room, leaping on and off her sofa, twirling around. "A little shake here and a little shake there! One hundred and seventy-five thousand dollars!" she said several more times. Then she speed-dialed Sarah.

"Sarah, you're not going to believe the news I have," she said.

"India? Are you okay?" Sarah was at a loss to know what could possibly be happening now.

"Sarah, you are speaking to India Butler, AUTHOR. I've sold my book!"

Sarah let out a scream. "Oh my God! Congratulations! Can I be in it?"

As India relayed the conversation with Larry, she began to realize how badly she had wanted to publish her book. How she had pushed it to the back of her mind. She'd been in her element writing the proposal, devising her own programs, and running her classes. Now her ideas would be in print, her very own ideas. She had written the proposal. She had earned this. She was "India Butler, author and teacher."

India put down the phone. This calls for a celebration, she decided, pulling a bottle of Sancerre out of a wooden wine rack and putting it into the tiny freezer compartment of her Frigidaire.

Omygod … I should call Annie, I should quit my job, I should… I should just take a minute to let this sink in. She lifted a crystal wineglass from her French dresser and rooted around in a drawer for a corkscrew.

The phone rang as she was opening the freezer again. She closed it. That might be Larry's assistant…, she thought. I'll be my own assistant…

"Miss Butler's residence," she said haughtily.

But it wasn't a Brooklyn accent this time.

"Hi, India. Is this a good time to talk?"

"Adam…" she started, her knees buckling slightly.

"I didn't know you were going to leave town so quickly," he said, his voice huskier than she remembered it. "I didn't know what to say, how to explain … and then you were gone."

"I left you a couple of messages," she said quietly, "but that was to explain why I was leaving and what had happened to me

… and I only saw the picture of you and … well, it was after I got back to London."

India went into her sitting room. She sank down in an old armchair and pulled a chenille throw around herself. "So why the phone call now?" she said stiffly.

"India. I'm sorry."

"So am I," she said coldly.

"India, we were going so fast, you and I…"

Were? she thought.

"Honestly, there was a moment, and yes, I should have seen it coming. It's not an excuse, but I get scared at a certain point, ever since Chloe left. I've just been … well, scared. I didn't see that coming and I've never worked out how to trust again, I suppose."

"Yes. Well, you didn't look too scared in that picture."

"Look India, I'm doing my best here. I miss you. It's lame to say I'm sorry, but I am. I'm sorry. It's such a cliché – you're on set, there's chemistry, things happen, but you can believe this or not believe it, I wish it hadn't happened. I could lie and say nothing happened, when it did, but it was like an old reflex. I can't explain."

"So are you two playing happy families?" India asked curtly.

"No. India, if the press hadn't got hold of that picture, I probably would have told you at some point … well," he said wryly, "I can't say I would for sure, but I can say it still would have been a one-off. I suppose I didn't realize how much you meant to me until you'd gone. What happened, India?" he asked, confused. "I thought you were franchising your workshops here."

India was conscious that he was using her full name. She had always loved how he had called her "Indie."

"Well…" she said, getting up, going into the kitchen and pulling the wine from the freezer. "Turns out I wasn't the real deal either."

"How do you mean?"

India wrestled off the cork, poured a large glass of wine, and took several swift mouthfuls.

"Well…" she said, "do you want the part where I pretended to have a glamorous job or the part where I bitched about everybody, or the part where I said you were stupid?"

"Max sent me the YouTube link, and I have to say, I saw another side of you, but what do you mean?"

India took a deep breath as she walked back to her armchair, carrying the bottle and her glass. "Okay Adam… I teach twelfth graders, or at least I DID, when I met you. I don't have a glamorous life, I don't have teams of coaches, and, until about five minutes ago, I didn't have my own Stanislavsky-based 'method.' I have no money, no amazing career, and when I was with you I pretended to be something I wasn't."

India could hear the rage in her voice, she could hear the hurt as she was speaking. I have nothing left to lose and I just sold my book. She drained her glass and poured another. So you, your leading lady, and your fabulous lifestyle can all go to hell.

"Adam, I don't know what you want me to say. I'm five thousand miles away. You're a movie star. We live in different worlds. You cheated, and I lied. So we're probably even on some level, and I'd like to talk to you some other time when I'm more prepared for the conversation, if that's okay."

India was stifling tears. And you are not, I mean NOT going to get me crying. Not India Butler – Teacher and Author … not after all these weeks when I was just starting to pull myself together again. And not tonight when I'm feeling I really have achieved something. Tonight is about ME. Nobody is going to spoil this moment for me ... NOBODY, not even YOU.

She poured a third glass of wine.

"Okay. Yes it's unfair of me I suppose," said Adam. "I've been building up to this conversation. Can I call you in a couple of days?" he asked gently.

"S'pose so," she slurred.

"Okay ... Indie?"

"Yes?"

"I really miss you. I'm sorry."

"Goodnight," she mumbled, tears streaming down her cheeks.

India kept the phone in her hand and stared at the wall. She felt oddly calm. She thought back to their very first date in Malibu, how she had been carried away trying to make herself sound intriguing and fascinating. How she had always felt she was never "enough," had tried on so many different personas over the years.

"No more pretending," she said out loud. "No more."

Profound Thoughts Note – I will approach the big 40 with a whole new optimism.

India repeated one of the mantras she planned on using in her book and then appraised herself in the long mirror attached to the back of her wardrobe. "Sophisticated, yet classic," she pronounced, admiring her new YSL black trouser suit and sparkly platform Louboutins. "A look that will take me from day to night." Then she repeated the other mantra also pasted onto the mirror.

I am indeed a woman of supreme courage.

I am indeed a woman of supreme courage.

I am indeed a woman of supreme courage.

As India climbed carefully out of the pantsuit, she thought how quickly the last few weeks had gone by. Contracts had been signed, deadlines agreed on, foreign rights negotiated, copious amounts of champagne drunk. Many new clothes had been bought with her shiny new Amex card. Although she had learned she had only ten months before she would be expected to deliver the manuscript (Omygod) and another six months after that before publication and a book tour, India knew it was time for a whole new image. She had been thinking "French, with a twist."

Unsure what the twist would be, she decided to buy everything in black. Monochrome would be the way to go for this entirely grown-up persona.

One of the many reasons for India's newfound confidence was the emergence of another YouTube video, titled INDIANA Butler, in which she came across as heroic, leading a team of teenagers across thirty feet of burning cinders. She was extremely proud of this, even though it had only been viewed a couple of hundred times and she herself probably accounted for most of the views.

Larry had amazed her by explaining that the YouTube videos were a brilliant hook for a book. They could spin the whole issue of how you build good relationships out of a crisis. That kind of story was inspirational, apparently. It seemed the old adage was true – there was no such thing as bad publicity. It was all about what you made of it.

Pulling on an old pair of jeans and a cashmere cardigan, India went across to the fridge. She took her yogurt to the kitchen table and began sifting through the mounds of paperwork and correspondence. She had taken Sarah's advice about waiting until everything was properly signed before resigning from school, but now she could send that letter to Dr. White, letting him know that she would not be returning in January. She would take great pleasure in explaining that she would be visiting New York instead.

India still had to fulfill the terms of her temporary school contract, but that was fine. She was building up a decent rapport with some of the kids and didn't want to add her name to the long list of supply teachers who just failed to return without warning. Even though she would not be there for long, she knew she was making a difference and felt she owed it to them to be a rare fixed point in their lives. From her new vantage point she was able to see where money and indulgence helped and where it didn't. She decided the common denominator had to be helping kids to discover where their true talents lay, building up their self-esteem, and opening up their worlds. Too little choice was as bad as too many choices, she decided. It was all material for her book.

And there was Adam. He called most days now, and, over the course of the last several weeks, they had become close again. India was unsure where this was going or if she would ever allow herself to trust him again, but there was no denying the intensity of their connection. She licked the last of the Dulce de Latte off the back of her spoon and sighed. Despite being happier and busier than she had been for the longest time, India was still a little miffed that the occasion of her fortieth birthday would now be marked at the Cat and Lion Public House rather than the Beverly Wilshire Hotel.

"I'm still a bit broken up that Annie and I won't get to be together on our birthday after all," she'd told Sarah. "But you've managed to book Thursday off work, haven't you?"

"Of course, my dear. Yes, it's a pity you can't be with her, but isn't it fantastic you have so much to celebrate? We'll call her from the pub."

"You're right," India answered. "After all, yes, there's a lot to celebrate."

That showed maturity, she thought. I mean, who needs a cake and candles and tons of presents and a huge fuss made over them at my age, anyway?

India went to shut down her computer and there it was, the long-awaited e-mail.

Thérèse

To: Indiabutler@gmail.com
From: Lizziel@sbcglobal.net
Subject: Good to hear from you

Hi India,

Thank you for your letter. It was a lovely card. I really appreciated it and the flowers too. Freesia, my favorite, you remembered. I'm sorry that we didn't get a chance to talk things over. Thank you for the check and don't worry, it wasn't that big a deal to return the fees. I spoke to Annie and understand you had her best interests at heart by leaving town quickly. I can also see how the video happened and that everything was taken out of context. We all have our off days and it's a pity yours was made so public. I hope life in London is being kinder to you.

Things at home are improving. I have a new contract (which is why it took me a while to get back to you). I've applied to serve as a judge. It won't happen for another couple of years yet (if it does) and in the meantime I'm easing my way back into the working world.

Stan and I are working things through. It'll take time but I'm strangely hopeful.

Sophie came back from Malibu more together and seems determined to try and focus. Joan remembered your advice about her dancing and signed her up for some arts activities on the understanding she has to keep up her

244

grade point average. Thank you for that. You
did a lot of good while you were here – hang
onto that.

I hope it won't be too long before you decide
to pay us another visit.

Love Lizzie xx

India read the e-mail several times. Was it her imagination?
Did it seem a little cold … distant? It was "cautious" she decided,
cautious, but with any luck the beginnings of a conversation.

She decided to reply immediately, then stopped midsentence
when her phone rang. It was Adam.

"I have a plan," he said. "How does this sound…?"

≈≈≈≈≈≈≈≈

India was up at six the morning before her birthday. The last
day of my thirties, she thought as she brushed her teeth and then
recited the mantra on the Post-it on her bathroom mirror:

I am a powerful and beautiful woman.

I am a powerful and beautiful woman.

I am a powerful and beautiful woman.

She changed the bedding and went into the kitchen, where she
pulled tall-stemmed sunflowers out of a sink full of water and arranged
them in two flea market jugs on either end of the mantelpiece. She
opened her fridge to admire the Sancerre, French cheeses, olives,
and tapenades. She was giddy with excitement. She showered and
clasped on her black La Perla bra with matching lacy pants, her
dark-wash J Brand jeans, a black turtleneck sweater, and a pair
of Comptoir des Cotonniers ankle boots. She threw on her new

black cashmere Max Mara coat and her leopard-print cloche hat, dashed outside to her MINI, and screeched off. Drumming the steering wheel impatiently as she reached the Uxbridge Road, she finally eased onto the motorway and turned up the volume on her sound system.

Non! Rien de rien…
Non! Je ne regrette rien…
Avec mes souvenirs
J'ai allumé le feu,
Mes chagrins, mes plaisirs
Je n'ai plus besoin d'eux!

She made the turn into the short-term car park at Heathrow, slammed the door, and raced across the road to Terminal Three.

Pushing her way through the heaving crowds in the arrivals hall, she joined the crush at the barrier. Holding her breath she watched as one by one the trickle of passengers turned the corner of the carpeted entranceway. It seemed like an age. As the guy in the navy wool peacoat with the collar turned up came toward her she took a deep breath. Suddenly she was in his arms. As he kissed her, she felt the months melt away.

Adam stepped back to look at her properly.

"Indie, you look amazing. You even look great with all those clothes on."

"Thank you." She beamed. "You don't look so bad yourself."

They walked toward the exit slowly, pausing every few minutes to hold onto each other again. Then Adam stopped abruptly. "Wait a minute. I've forgotten something. Stay right here … by this newsstand. I'll only be a minute. Hang onto my trolley."

Before she had a chance to say anything Adam had disappeared into the crowd. India's eye caught a large table of piled books displayed underneath a banner announcing "New Hardbacks."

One day soon, my very own book will be on sale here, she thought. It's going to have a nice red cover just like this one, so people will notice it first.

She lifted up the book and practiced glancing at it casually. She then put it down casually and casually picked it up again.

I shall come back here when it's mine and do exactly this, she decided.

Lost in this little reverie for a few minutes India only gradually became aware of someone standing close by her side. She looked up. There was something familiar about the woman next to her with the black leather cap pulled way down, her face hardly visible under huge dark Chanel sunglasses. It took a second before it registered, before she could even let in the thought, but yes, yes. It was Annabelle. It was Annie. And standing right behind her was Joss.

"Your birthday present!" Adam announced, seeming to appear from nowhere.

India's jaw dropped, her mouth fell wide open, and she gasped. She was completely overwhelmed. She kept staring from one to the other and back to Adam speechless. Then she started to cry and began hugging them.

"Omygod. How? What?" She was still unable to get a complete sentence out. "Adam?"

"Yep. Your birthday present," he said, then turning to Joss he smiled with satisfaction. "Seems to have gone down okay. We did it. Put it there."

"Slam dunk," Joss agreed, high-fiving him. "Great teamwork, yeah. We're staying at Brown's," he said, turning back to India.

"I've a wonderful evening lined up for you girls tomorrow. But we can't hang around here. I'm not in the mood to sign autographs."

India could see a small crowd of women gathering around Joss, who, despite wearing aviator glasses and a parka, was somehow still managing to convey "rock star."

"I don't want to rush this moment," he said, taking Annabelle's hand, "But I should think you two want to be together. Our driver's waiting. We'll see you tomorrow."

"I'll call you later, darling," Annabelle said, giving her yet another hug. "You look fabulous. I'm so happy. Your face was an absolute picture – I wish we'd had a camera."

"You know, I'm kind of relieved you didn't." India laughed.

"We're here for a week; so much to catch up on. I'll call you later," Annie said over her shoulder.

India grabbed Adam's hands.

"Thank you. Thank you. This is so wonderful. How on Earth did you keep this to yourself? I've been going on and on to you all week about how I wished Annie and I could be together for tomorrow. You kept sympathizing. You're good." It's a bit worrying, she thought. What else have you been hiding from me again?

"It's been hard. But Sarah's been great. In fact, I think I've spoken to her more in the last few weeks than I have to you. I bribed her with an introduction to her crush – you know, Michael Mulholland, who hit on you at Fred's party."

"Sarah? She knew? Sarah knew too?"

"She most certainly did." He smiled complacently as they maneuvered their way through the crowds. "And Mr. Smooth will indeed be putting in an appearance at dinner tomorrow night."

"Oh my God, she must be beyond excited," India said gleefully.

"Yes… Well, she doesn't know. We'll keep that our little secret, shall we?"

"I can't wait to see her face. Adam, this is fantastic. It's almost too much to take in all at once. You are amazing." And a bit too good at keeping secrets, she thought.

"Well, it wasn't all just my idea. I was telling Joss that I start shooting in London next week before we go to St. Petersburg and that I was coming out early to see you. We kind of got talking and just hit on the idea you two had to be together for your birthday."

"This is perfect," India said, reaching up and kissing his cheek. "You've all been plotting away and I hadn't a clue."

"Payback, Indie. Let's face it, if you can get away with telling the entire universe I have ADHD, you deserve to be set up."

India blushed. "You promised never to mention that again. You promised."

"You have no idea just how lucky you were you also called me cute!" he answered. "Very lucky indeed."

And you have no idea how lucky you are that I'm giving us a second chance, she thought. Very lucky indeed.

"So are we even now?" she shouted to him as the trunk sprang open.

"I guess," he said, tossing in his two buffalo leather bags. "Though I'd like an opportunity to show you how focused I can be." He grinned.

"There are several parts of me I'd like you to focus on, now I think of it," she said, laughing.

"Let's start here," he said, closing the door. Leaning across to kiss her he slid his hand underneath her sweater.

"Okay, Mr. Brooks, let's get out of here," she said, turning the key in the ignition. "Hang onto that thought. I'll have us home in no time."

Thérèse

"Ta-da!" India said, opening her front door and leading him into her sitting room.

"It's just as I imagined, very cozy, very you," he said, nodding toward the squashy couch, the piles of books, and the open fireplace.

She took off her coat and threw it across the couch.

"Thank you. This way." She smiled as she led him down the hallway into the bedroom. "You can have the full tour later."

"That looks extremely comfortable," he said, nodding toward her bed.

"If a little small." She laughed.

"Where's the shower? Will we both fit in?" he said, pulling his sweater over his head.

My god those abs, she thought. That workout schedule's certainly paying off. Omygod. "It's definitely worth a try," she answered, yanking off her boots. "I'm sure there are parts of you that could do with a little extra soaping after that long flight."

≈≈≈≈≈≈≈

The morning of her fortieth birthday, India woke early. She turned and looked across the pillow at Adam, who was still asleep. 'Well this is better than the Cat and Lion.' She smiled, admiring his five o'clock shadow, the arch of his eyebrow and the strength of his arm across the counterpane. She stuck her head under the sheets and, working her way down, began to kiss his toes. He opened his eyes slowly and then closed them again and rolled onto his back. It was late before they had breakfast at Le Pain Quotidien.

Joss had booked a private dining room at Brown's for their birthday dinner. It had long been his favorite London hotel. He loved its mahogany bars and timeless ambience, the doormen in livery, the gracious service. "English elegance personified," he'd called it.

India, wearing a black DVF wrap dress with her hair piled on top of her head and a pair of gold Jimmy Choo slingback pumps, sat down next to Adam. Next to her at the circular table with its pristine white cloth and white china settings was Annie in a blue velvet Armani sheath, a choker of Mikimoto freshwater pearls around her neck. India didn't take her eyes off the two empty seats opposite them. She watched as Joss steered Sarah into the room and Michael pulled out the chartreuse green chair for her. Sarah sat down in a daze and looked at India. "What the…," she mouthed, her eyes wide with shock, and then her face lit up with a smile of pure delight.

"You look like a girl who likes a vodka martini with an olive," Michael said, in a thick Dublin brogue, pulling out the chair next to her.

Now where have I heard that before? India smiled as a waiter came across and poured Montrachet into Joss's oversize glass. He savored the intense aroma, nodded, and waited until they each had a glass before getting to his feet.

"Happy birthday," he said. "I have a full speech prepared for after dinner, don't worry … and you'd better believe it. But for now … happy birthday. Happy birthday, Annie and Indie."

"Happy birthday, Annie and Indie!" they said in unison, as Joss sat down and gave the signal they were ready to eat. Six waiters came forward and served them beef consommé from silver tureens.

Over the next few days India delighted in showing Adam the city. They went to her favorite wine bars and to see the Clemente exhibition at Tate Modern. They looked down on the Thames from the London Eye while she pointed out the landmarks. One evening they went to the Royal Ballet at Covent Garden, where the performance of Manon moved them both to tears. Afterward they met Joss and Annie at L'Escargot, India's favorite French restaurant this side of the pond, with its golden Grammy-lined walls. India ate her favorite filet mignon in peppered wine sauce.

Annie and Joss stayed for a full week, and there were no tearful goodbyes this time.

"See you in a few weeks," India shouted, waving furiously as the Bentley turned the corner of Albermarle Street, "…in New York!" she yelled.

"I'm going to New York in a couple of weeks," she said to the doorman.

"Lovely, madam."

"I'm going to meet my publisher," she said, cranking up the volume while stepping aside to let a woman in a fox fur coat get into the lobby. "That would be my BOOK publisher…"

"Lovely, madam," he said with a slight bow as he opened the door for her.

Toward the end of the week before Adam started shooting in Ealing and she had to get down to her writing, India drove them out to see the school where she had been teaching for so long.

"This is where I held my *workshops*," she quipped, stopping the car outside the gates.

Adam took in the vast expanse of derelict land surrounding the campus and the boarded-up windows with the scrawled graffiti. Some teenagers were pushing each other around the iron railings, and a couple of girls were leaning against a wall swapping cigarettes.

"You're a heroine, Indie. You know, this is something you should have always been extremely proud of, don't you?"

"Yes," she said. "I do know that now, and if I hadn't slogged away for so long here, I wouldn't be writing my book. I have these kids to thank for that. I was ready to move on; I needed something more for myself. I needed change." She paused for a moment. "But the real heroines are the teachers who stay in places like this and spend their entire lives committed to kids like him," she said, pointing to a boy with a crew cut, wearing jeans and cheap trainers.

She turned to Adam. "It's funny how things work out, isn't it? I sort of grew into the person I was pretending to be. So, in a way, my whole new career wouldn't have happened without you," she said thoughtfully, taking one long last look at the bleak building as she started the engine. She smiled at him. "Thank you."

"You are most welcome," he answered, leaning across and putting his hand on her knee, letting it slide slowly up the inside of her leg. "Let's go back to your apartment. I've just thought of a way you can show your appreciation all over again."

Epilogue

India stepped gingerly out of the Town Car and onto a thin layer of black ice in her four-inch patent leather pumps. This was definitely 320 West 66th Street, but where was the entrance to the studio?

I need to get into the building while I still have some feeling left in my toes, she thought. How can it possibly be colder in New York than it was in Russia?

India stayed rooted to the spot as she scrambled in her purse for a number and called the producer's cell. A few minutes later a large woman wrapped in a plaid padded jacket and snow boots came rushing out to meet her.

"Hi, Miss Butler. Good to meet you. I'm Tracey. Come this way; they've salted the side entrance," she said looking down at India's feet. "Lean on me."

Once mercifully indoors, India was shown through a series of long corridors to a small soundproofed room where a few people were clustered around a coffee table watching a television screen.

"They've come with Tony," Tracey told her. "You can catch the end of the segment."

"Tony?" India asked.

"Tony Robbins."

Omygod! If I'd known, I'd have been here hours earlier. India thought.

"He'll be done in a few minutes, then we'll take you through to makeup and to meet Mike," Tracey explained. "Can I take your things? Would you like some water?"

"No thanks," India said, handing over her coat. "Nothing right now."

India watched as the studio audience in the next room rose to its feet and the women sitting by her began leaping up and down applauding. India jumped up and down with them clapping hard, too. Then Tracey was back at her side.

"This way," she said, steering her over cables and past a couple of cameramen who were blocking the way. "We won't keep you long in makeup, but you don't want a red nose."

India felt a rush of adrenaline as a young man in blue jeans attached tiny microphones to her jacket. Then an arm was steadying her toward a set of plastic doors that swung open in front of her, and Tony Robbins strode through. He gave her a huge grin, almost as if he knew the difference he had made to her life; that he had inspired her to take one step; one step onto burning coals to fight through her fears. She paused for a second to let him go by and to imprint the moment. Then she moved forward and waited for Tracey to give her the signal. Seconds before she was ushered on set, she remembered the voice.

"What's your name?"

"India."

"Are you ready?"

India took a deep breath, a very deep breath. I can do this. She thought. Focus…Focus.

Thérèse

Then she heard another voice. "She's a household name. She's helped millions of overwhelmed parents connect with their teenagers. She's brought harmony into homes. Please welcome New York Times Bestselling author India Butler."

Suddenly, as the studio audience rose to its feet, she was hugging Whoopi Goldberg and the other ladies waiting to greet her. There were whoops from the audience who were still cheering as India took her seat next to Barbara Walters.

"Thank you." She smiled. "Thank you everyone. It is so wonderful to be here."

THE END....or maybe the beginning...

Acknowledgements

What a daunting task. So many people have been wonderful and I have a dread of leaving someone out. If you are that person, then I want you to know I still love you and feel really bad about it. Can I buy you a drink? Okay, dinner.

And so in no particular order but somehow vaguely chronological: sincere thanks to Mimi Peak, mentor, coach and friend, for your wisdom and insight and for helping me to find my voice.

All the friends who read and critiqued the early drafts. As a first-time novelist, I was very vulnerable, and without your encouragement simply would not have written the book; Patti Diane Baker, Tony Barton, Donnell and Mahlon Burch, Anne DePree, Nick Egan, Bronya Galef, Lena Gannon, Lani Hall, Joanna Hamilton, Andrea Hanna, Anne Haugen, Susan Jeffers,Geraldine Leman, Tom Lowe, Bernie McMahon, Avril More, Lynn Pompeii, Ron Pompeii, Christine Ranck, Amy Rappaport, Heidi Roberts, Joel Roberts, John Robinson, Pamela Robinson, Mark Shelmerdine, Michael Rose, Helen Simms, Tom Teicholz.

Ann Dickson, for so much shared for so long and for being the essence of quintessential British style. Jane Arnell for thirty years of creating our own realities together. Beryl Lowe for love, support and excitement for me always. Sheran James, for call way above duty, especially for those focused hours with India on the plane back from Vancouver when the rest of us thought we were going to die. Valorie Armstrong especially for "tea" in the garden with India. Carol King for going above and beyond – a woman of many talents. Bryn Freedman for helping character-build our dream guy and much more. Claudia Barwell and Darina Garland, the London girls, for your enthusiasm and tons of material. Diane McCarter for huge generosity of spirit, making so many introductions and adopting India as if she were family. Sheri Biller for waving a magic wand many times. Jodi Rose for being the world's best assistant, incredible muse and friend.

Barbara Aronica-Buck for a cover that exquisitely captures the story. Jeff Eamer for a photograph that exquisitely captures me (without airbrushing). Jackie Baron Mc Cue for final copy-editing, (and translating Word into Mac). Emily Votruba for understanding English punctuation. Bryan Rabin for calling me an "artist."

Brenda Cullerton, a dream editor, whose humor and tireless energy transformed my writing, and Diana Revson for making that introduction. Lou Aronica for giving me this wonderful opportunity. It is a privilege to work with such a consummate professional.

As always, thank you with all my heart to Ken, my soulmate, whose lifetime work guided me to finding my own "Element." And of course a huge thank you to James and Kate for living with an empty fridge for so long and for cheerleading me every step of the way. I love you more than words can say.

Made in the USA
Lexington, KY
18 January 2012